This novel is
The names, characters a...
are the work of the author's imagination.
Any similarity to real persons, living or dead,
is coincidental and not intended by the author.

Andrew White has asserted his moral right
to be identified as the author of this work

First published in Great Britain by Nova Books

Nova Books
62 Ascot Avenue
Cantley, Doncaster. DN4 6HE

www.novatv.co.uk

This paperback edition 2022 1

ISBN: 9798762496827

Cover design by: Guess Who? Design

To my Mum.
For always believing in me.

I tried to think of
something witty
... but failed.

Chapter 1

Should she do it?

It isn't like she hadn't thought this through over the last couple of days.

It would be a massive change.

But that's what she wants, isn't it? A change to something different; something less intense?

Charlotte Walker leaned against the driver's door of her nearly-new Volvo car, as the rain poured down on a dreadful morning. Her smart pinstripe suit was getting severely drenched - as was the rest of her. She alone should know there's no such thing as bad weather; just bad clothing choices - as a walker. Yes, Walker by name, walker by nature. Only she hadn't thought it would take quite so long to decide to go through with something she'd already decided on.

Of course it was taking so long. The weight of the world was on Charlotte. Or rather, it was inside the envelope she was holding, which was getting wetter as she tapped the corner against her mouth.

Should she do this? Should she?

Somehow the 1960s concrete building that was the Doncaster headquarters of South Yorkshire Police looked fitting in this weather. As if it was designed to always live in awful days like this. Even fans of such architecture could never level the word "beautiful" at it. Opened in 1969, its harsh precast panels and foreboding style served as a deterrent to anyone from committing crime. Perhaps that was what was intended? Yet it had been her home; or rather, place of work for the past year.

Charlotte's mind sidetracked to that often-maligned line in "Four Weddings and a Funeral" where Andie MacDowell says "Is it raining? I hadn't noticed." Often voted one of the worst lines of dialogue in film history, Charlotte was beginning to understand what it actually meant. It turns out you CAN be so wet, you can't get any wetter. She shouldn't have bothered with the time this morning to sort out her regularly wayward long red hair. Perhaps she could do something in the future that wouldn't require the 30 or so minutes of hair preparation time every morning? A writer, maybe? That way, she could stay at home. No hair prep needed then. What could she write about? Crime would be obvious, given she was a Detective Chief Inspector. Was that really three years ago now? And her now only 33; a 'rising star' was the phrase often associated with Charlotte's name.

A sudden flash of lightning and a few seconds later a rumble of thunder brought Charlotte out of this train of thought and back to her predicament.

No romantic movie kiss here on the flash of lightning. Just memories of what happened exactly a year ago today. The event that had brought Charlotte to this very spot, making this very decision contained in this - albeit very wet - envelope.

That's it. She's got to do this.

In one motion, with great speed - partly to get in

from the rain and partly because if she'd paused, she might have decided against it, Charlotte entered the police station.

Inside, this 1960s building wasn't that much better than the outside. Over the years, there had been various attempts to make the interior more welcoming, but most had failed. The current attempt had joined the ranks of the previous; as if the building itself was fighting to make the inside look just like the out.

Charlotte was sitting on a row of seats in a waiting area, with the other three seats taken by other members of the police force; two in uniform and one not. They all, however, were not absolutely drenched, as Charlotte was. They'd probably been sensible and worn some sort of coat, seeing as though the weather forecast was for heavy showers most of the morning, but clearing up nicely later on. But then, they probably didn't have a life-changing decision still to contemplate in the car park - as it turned out - in the rain.

The man on her left, not wearing a uniform, was trying to move as far away from Charlotte and her wet clothes as possible, without falling off his plastic seat. *'It's not acid rain, you know'*, thought Charlotte, and if she would have been in a different mind, she'd have shuffled closer to him, just to see how long it would have taken for him to move.. but that wasn't the Charlotte here today.

Charlotte returned to tapping the now rather damp envelope against her mouth. After she'd done this a few times, she looked at the condition of the corner that was against her mouth, and decided she'd either better stop, or turn the envelope around. In an amazing display of self-control... she turned the envelope around, and returned to tapping this virgin corner against her mouth. The man on the left glared at her. *'What's your problem?'* she thought, having half a mind to say this out loud. But she decided against this course of action.

The two uniformed female officers on her right returned Charlotte's look at them with a smile. "Ma'am." they both said slightly out of sync. One looked to be around her own age; so mid thirties perhaps, but the other; the other looked so fresh faced Charlotte wondered how long had she been out of nappies. She remembered back to a couple of days ago when her Mum said the bank tellers looked like they should still be at school. Charlotte replied with a nod of the head, and wondered what they were doing waiting here.

God, she hated waiting.

Waiting for something normal was a massive waste of time, but waiting when you've just made a monumental decision was even worse. Because you could talk yourself out of it.

After all, it wasn't too late to change her mind...

Just then, Charlotte's phone buzzed. The three other seated individuals looked around as if they'd not heard this particular sound for decades - and that's probably because they hadn't. In this world of iWatches, apps to control your washing machine and self-driving cars, Charlotte Walker's phone was a Nokia 3310. And not the new, updated one either... a good, old-fashioned, completely original blue 3310.

This was a lady who was well and truly old-school; someone who'd the Poni-tails would have sang 'Born

Too Late' about, had they known her and been singing about a person not of her time. Not of her time... that's probably why Charlotte loved 'Ashes To Ashes' so much when she was at uni. Charlotte Walker would probably have fitted very well into the Eighties - the decade she was only just born into.

The female officer that looked like a baby just stared, as Charlotte wrestled this museum piece out of her jacket pocket. The phone displayed "Dad" on the monochrome LCD screen, as Charlotte pressed the middle button to show the text 'Thinking of you today. We're all here for you. Love you x'.

Charlotte perked up - but only for a little while. Perhaps he might not be as supportive if he knew what I was about to do, she mused. After all, her Dad's influence was why she was sitting here now. So he might not be too happy when he learns about this, but he'll understand, Charlotte convinced herself. Her Mum, however, might be a different kettle of fish...

Suddenly, a receptionist's voice pierced the air.

"DCI Walker."

Charlotte awoke from her thoughts, and taking a deep breath, she got up..

* * *

Charlotte sat in a very comfortable chair at a big desk in a spacious office - a sharp contrast to the relative starkness of the waiting area she'd spent the last fifteen or so minutes.

On the wall to the left of the desk hung several photographs featuring line ups of graduate police officers clearly taken at various different times. To the left of those, a bookcase filled with two long shelves of impressive looking leather-bound books, and underneath several trophies, cups and shields.

The office had a decent sized window, although the view out of it didn't perhaps show Doncaster at its best, but the amount of natural light flowing through it did make the office seem a lot warmer.

The desk in front of Charlotte was large, with a big laptop computer open and whirring to Charlotte's right, a few piles of neatly organised papers to the left and a few photo frames of which she could only see the backs of.

Sitting at the other side of the desk looking back at Charlotte was a lady in police uniform; Assistant Chief Constable Sharon Tate. She was a classical beautiful woman with long, blonde hair tied up in a high ponytail, and blue eyes which were at home either showing love or contempt - depending on who needed to be looked at. The uniform suited her tall height - which was clear even when she was sitting down thanks to her perfect posture.

But Charlotte knew Sharon Tate in a different world and in a different scenario. Sharon, as Detective Chief Superintendent, had been Charlotte's mentor through her rise of the ranks at the Met to ultimately become Detective Chief Inspector. But they also knew each other outside of work, as Charlotte's then partner worked with Sharon's husband. They'd regularly have dinner at each other's houses, they played badminton together and even twice went on holiday together. Charlotte had seen exactly what happened when that long blonde hair was let down... Yes, they both knew each other well and they knew how each other ticked.

So when Charlotte returned to her hometown to take up a DCI position last year, following Sharon's move north when she became Assistant Chief Constable, Sharon knew that she'd probably have to deal with this anniversary. Technically, there were two other ranks between them, but Charlotte felt she had a direct line personally to Sharon, and Sharon still felt her mentor - even though she didn't need to be any longer.

After a couple of seconds which felt like hours, with an arm which left a wet trail after it, Charlotte pushed the now-only-slightly-damp envelope across the desk. An inquisitive frown appeared on Sharon's face.

"What's this?"

"I can't do this anymore." Charlotte replied. Sharon still looked a little perplexed. "It's my resignation."

That wasn't what Sharon was expecting. She'd thought Charlotte might have wanted some time off, to go away for the day of the anniversary. She'd even provisionally cleared some time so she could go away as well, if Charlotte had asked her. But the time for leave before the day had come and gone, and so Sharon had wondered whether Charlotte would be ok. Perhaps she'd been able to come to terms with the awful events of that day?

But this envelope on the desk said otherwise. And it was a complete shock to Sharon.

"Look, It was always going to be difficult around this time." Sharon said, as calm as she could muster.

"It's a year - today." Charlotte said emphatically, eyebrows moving to extenuate the point. Just in case Sharon didn't realise the significance of the date.

Sharon drew a long breath. "I know."

Charlotte looked around the room and tried to steady herself with some well chosen breaths. This gave Sharon a welcome moment to think about what she could say. "Why don't you take some time off? Have a holiday? How about Italy?" knowing her love of the country. She instantly regretted that suggestion as it was one of the places the two couples had gone on holiday together.

Fortunately, if the reference to the holiday destination struck a memory with Charlotte, she didn't show it. "What for? I'd be thinking about him all the time. We both know why he's not here anymore. It's this bloody job." The anger started to be palatable.

"By all means take as much time off as you need, but leaving? This is your life."

Charlotte sighed and replied quietly, "That's the point. If it wasn't, he'd still be alive today."

Sharon held onto her bottom lip with her teeth for a moment. "You can't blame yourself for that..."

"Of course I blame myself for that!" Charlotte snapped back, raising an eyebrow from Sharon. "Who else is there to blame?" she followed up, more reserved and looking around the room.

"Well, the ones in the car for a start!" Sharon replied

forcibly.

They exchanged a look, before Charlotte got up to look out of the office window. The rain that had drenched her earlier was still falling, and she suddenly noticed just how wet she was. The more she looked out of the window, the more angry she got. Angry about him being taken from her, about having to live her life without him, and yes, if she's honest, angry with Sharon for not being there for her. She'd already moved up to South Yorkshire by then, and it took a long time before Charlotte lost the feeling she'd been abandoned by her mentor when she needed her the most.

She knew Sharon was trying her best, but she was undeterred. “I've got leave owing. So it's next Tuesday's my last day.” Charlotte continued. It never once crossed Charlotte's mind that really it wasn't for her to decide when she was allowed to leave.

Sharon got up and walked slowly to the window. She wanted to get closer to Charlotte, as a friend, but she still felt she should maintain a degree of professionalism - so she left a window-worth of gap between them. Charlotte turned to look at her for a moment and then looked back to the scene outside.

“Charlotte... I....” Sharon started.

It had gotten too much for Charlotte, and she started to cry. “I've got to, Sharon. I've got to.” was all she managed as the tears began to fall. Sharon tried to move towards her, but Charlotte pushed past her and headed for the door.

Sharon saw the door close behind Charlotte, and the office was in silence.

She slowly headed back to her desk, sat back down behind it, and took the envelope off the desk. Looking at it for a while, she started tapping a corner against her mouth. Now *she* had the weight of the world on her mind.

Suddenly, she opened one of the drawers of her desk, and placed the envelope inside.

* * *

Charlotte closed Sharon's office door firmly behind her, and then turned around to lean back on it, slightly banging her head on the "ACC Sharon Tate" sign as she rested. It was like the door was steadying her emotions.

She took several deep breaths.

There... she'd done it. That's got to be a good thing, right?

Well, it was done now. The end of it.

She wiped away the tears from her eyes, and making a clenched fist brought it to her face. She tapped the fist against her mouth and nose several times, and looked deep in thought.

After a while, she was back in the room. Or rather, the corridor. Another deep breath and suddenly a massive upper body shake - as if she'd just been possessed by the spirit of Detective Chief Inspector, and DCI Charlotte Walker was back, walking down the corridor with as much feist as she could muster right now.

Charlotte's own office was off the Incident Room, where officers were busy going about their business. The air was thick with the sound of hubbub; telephones ringing, telephones being answered, typing on computer keyboards and indistinct chat.

After a stop off at the toilets on the way back from seeing Sharon to see if she could dry off a little more by placing various parts of herself under the hand drier - a trick she used regularly whilst on days walking - Charlotte was ready to attack the day. She entered the Incident Room, exchanging pleasantries with everybody as she walked past, but quickly made her way into her office, closing the door behind her. As much as she seemed outwardly ok, she was still upset at the ramifications of what she'd just done.

The smartly dressed woman in her late twenties who had been waiting outside the office marked 'DCI Walker' for around ten minutes, looked a little lost for words as a figure she recognised power walked past her and entered the office, closing the door with a slam.

'Right. What now?' she thought.

Should she knock on the door? A bit high risk judging by the way the lady was. But she couldn't wait outside the office any longer, could she? She'd already been getting bewildered looks from the officers in the Incident Room wondering what she was doing here.

She took a deep breath and was about to knock on the door of the office when her phone pinged. Surprised, she fished the phone from her inside jacket pocket to see a Facebook Messenger message from her Mum; 'tamara nasib tamne saath aape'. She smiled to herself... *'Mum on Messenger! Hark at her!'* Using the thumbs on both hands, she messaged back 'Thanks Mum. Think I might need more than luck to support me, but I'll try my best. Just awaiting to meet the boss xx'

It was then, Charlotte opened the door, turned to her right and addressed the woman.

"Are you here to see me?"

"Yes Ma'am." came the reply. "I'm DC Stoker, Ma'am. I've just been assigned to your team." in a mix of a Black Country and a London accent.

"Err, right. Yes. I think I got that email. That was when I was able to log in to my computer. Andrea or Alison, wasn't it?" Charlotte headed back into her office, this time propping the door open by seamlessly moving with her foot some sort of door stop DC Stoker couldn't instantly identify, as an invitation for her to follow - which she did tentatively.

Charlotte's office was a much more reserved affair than Sharon Tate's. There was more than enough room to swing the proverbial cat around, put it that way. And there'd be a lot more space if Charlotte's filing system actually involved putting papers in the numerous filing cabinets dotted around the office. Because it didn't, the office was chaotic, fairly messy and generally disorganised. But Charlotte knew where everything was - mostly

The new lady looked around the office. There was a decent sized desk, housing a traditional desktop computer with monitor and mouse over on the left hand side of the keyboard, a couple of files - possibly active cases she thought - over on the right hand side, and a selection of different coloured post-it notes stuck to various parts of the desk which didn't have a job holding something else.

The walls were festooned with photographs of Charlotte and a dog - which looked to be a sheepdog; DC Stoker wasn't hot of breeds of dog - in various epic landscapes. One looked to be on top of the world, with mountains as far the eye could see, a lake on the left and a sort of a sundial thing the pair of them were standing next to. Another must have been in Sweden, as the two were next to a Swedish flag and the dog had a blue and yellow bandana on. The only photograph which wasn't of Charlotte with the dog was of her and a man outside the Colosseum in Rome.

The rest of one wall was virtually taken up with two items; a big Ordnance Survey map of the British Isles, complete with a multitude of multi-coloured metal pins spiked into it; and an open bookcase, which because of the length of the wall had to overlap the map to an extent that the edge of France, Ramsgate, Lowestoft and Great Yarmoth were all partially obscured. The bookcase held a few law-related books, but mainly DC Stoker noticed they were populated by either walking or travel books. She noticed the Cicerone Guide to the Hadrian's Wall Path, 50 Walks in the Yorkshire Dales and AA Guide to Yorkshire, as well as an orange tower of paper OS maps of different ages with some more used than others.

Charlotte looked around the office, as if to be searching around for something in particular. DC Stoker watched her with the eyes of someone trying to work out what she was doing, and promptly gave up on that activity to be just watching her instead. Charlotte moved a few piles of papers, made a kind of sighing sound, and then put the piles of papers back in exactly the same places as she'd picked them up from.

As she continued to look around, Charlotte noticed the weather through the only outside window in the office. The rain storm that was 'set in for most of the day' according to this morning's radio weather lady seemed to be stopping. '*That's about right*', she thought, looking down on how still wet she was.

"Ayesha, Ma'am. Ayesha Stoker." Ayesha finally remembered that Charlotte had asked her a question, and she thought it wise to now offer a response.

"Ayesha it is." Charlotte said, as she walked behind her desk, sat down, and indicated with her hand for Ayesha Stoker to make use of the chair in front of her on the opposite side of the desk. Ayesha looked down at the chair, and almost at the last second realised it was being used as an additional filing area for a pile of papers. In that moment, lifting them up without them all falling over was about as difficult a job as anyone could imagine for Ayesha - as she tried to maintain what she hoped was a good first impression on her new boss. The only issue now they were in her hands was where to put them instead...

She looked around.

Virtually every level, flat surface in the office already had a pile of papers on it. Ayesha looked at Charlotte for some help with her immediate predicament, but Charlotte had started to have an argument with her computer. It made a loud 'ding' sound. Charlotte pressed some keys on the keyboard - and the computer responded with another loud 'ding' sound.

"Why do I have to change my password again? It was only a couple of weeks ago I changed it last!" Charlotte blurted out, arms outstretched in front of her holding her hands out with her palms up in exasperation.

And there she was, thought Ayesha. The Detective Inspector she'd worked with in London. Always one for expressive hand gestures. She wondered whether Charlotte had recognised her, but then she thought again. Why would she? She was only a lowly Constable then, lucky enough to see the great Charlotte Walker in action from the periphery. The joke in the station was they should have given DI Walker the Ripper case, as she'd have solved it no problem. There was perhaps more than a slight element of jealous sexism to these japes, but the thrust was certainly true; Miss Walker was a formidable detective, and now the newly-qualified *Detective* Constable Stoker was going to learn from the best. She had moved her whole world up from London for this opportunity.

Then it came to Ayesha that she was still standing up, alongside the spare chair, with a large pile of papers in her hands that were beginning to feel like they were going to fall. She decided to finally take the initiative and put the Leaning Tower of Papers as neatly on the floor in front of her as she could. She looked up over the desk to see if Charlotte had anything to say about her paper pile placement. She didn't, so Ayesha sat down.

Another unapologetic 'ding' came from Charlotte's

computer.

"Online security is very important Ma'am." Ayesha offered.

Charlotte, realising she perhaps shouldn't be quite so frivolous with someone she'd just met replied "Yes. Yes. Quite right. I just wish I could remember one that I'd set up long enough before having to set up another one." Charlotte bashed the side of the monitor.

Ayesha let out a smile.

"If you are going to be working with me, DC Stoker, you need to know I have an arms-length relationship with technology." Charlotte said.

Ayesha's attention is slightly distracted by an increase in chattering outside the office in the Incident Room. Ok Ma'am. Noted." she replied, and then, having shifted her attention back to Charlotte asked in a slightly playful way "Anything else I should know?"

Charlotte noted the tone. "I'm sure I'll think of things as we go. You may need to take notes, Detective Constable..."

Ayesha smiled. She started to wonder why she was so nervous about today. After all, she knew her stuff. And she knew Charlotte Walker was certainly no ogre. She had seen her cut fellow officers down to size back in London - but thinking about it, they'd pretty much all been male officers and they all asked for it. No, this was going to be good.

But, try as she might, Ayesha can't seem to ignore the noise coming from the Incident Room. Turning around, she sees a number of officers gathering around

Charlotte's office window. "What *is* going on?" she asked frustratingly.

"Oh, they've probably heard the news I've just quit." Charlotte remarked casually.

"What?!"

"Don't worry, DC Stoker, I'm sure they'll find someone equally as brilliant as I to replace me."

This news doesn't cheer Ayesha up at all. She looked truly devastated - much more than she should be.

"Anyway, I'm sure we'll have a quiet week to end on..."

Just then, a tall, blond haired man pushed his way through the collection of people outside the office, knocked on the open door and waited for a reply.

"Yes?" asked Charlotte inquisitively, but sharply.

"A woman has been reported missing, Gov." he replied, stony faced, flicking a look to Ayesha and then immediately returned to the incident room.

Charlotte looked across at Ayesha, her face breaking out into a slight smile with a rise of her eyebrows, "...or maybe not!"

Chapter 2

Ayesha followed Charlotte down the steps of the police station, across College Road and into the car park. As they stopped at what must be Charlotte's car, she asked "Where's this address?"

Quickly flicking through her notebook, Ayesha replied "Norton, Ma'am." she replied quizzically, as she had no idea whether that was a hamlet, village, town or city.

"Over the bridge then," said Charlotte, as she got into the driver's seat of her car. Ayesha opened the passenger door, only to be confronted by a range of documents on the passenger seat. "Come on DC Stoker!"

It was like a repeat of Charlotte's office - only this time, Ayesha acted more swiftly, grabbing the papers and moving them to the back seat as Charlotte started the car. She only just had a chance to close her door before Charlotte reversed out of the parking space, and they were on their way.

Charlotte's initial haste was hampered by the inevitable queue of traffic on Trafford Way to pass the railway station. As they sat in the line of vehicles, Charlotte turned to Ayesha. "So with that accent, you're not from 'round here then..."

Ayesha had managed to lift herself a little from the mood she left the office in and broke away from trying to form her mental map of this part of the town. "No Ma'am. Wolverhampton, via Camden."

"Camden?" Charlotte said with interest. "Oh wow. I was there from 2014. I became a DI there in 2016."

"I know, Ma'am."

The reply took Charlotte a little by surprise. "Should I be a bit worried? Are you my secret stalker, DC Stoker?

"If I was Ma'am, I wouldn't be about to tell you, would I?" That's a fair point, Charlotte thought. They exchanged a look. "I know because I served under you at Holborn."

As they'd just pulled up at the red light displayed on traffic lights just before the underpass beneath the Frenchgate Centre, Charlotte took the opportunity to study Ayesha more closely.

And then she remembered.

"Of course! You were uniform…"

A big smile grew on Ayesha's face. She was very pleased Charlotte remembered her. "Yes. I was. Actually, Ma'am, it was you that inspired me to go for being a DC."

"Really?"

"God, yes. You were amazing at Holborn. Ran rings around even the DCIs!"

A smidgen of a smile developed on Charlotte's face. "Ah! Well, yes. I was pretty damn good." The red light had changed to green, so she was only allowed a moment to reflect, as the traffic in front started to move into the mildly-illuminated semi darkness of the underpass. After mulling over Ayesha's time with her as a DI, she said "I always thought you'd be good out of uniform."

With a glint in her eye, Ayesha pretended to be shocked by this comment. “Ma'am?!” she exclaimed.

“I meant as a detective!” Charlotte quickly clarified, but then realised Ayesha was playing her when she saw her mischievous smile..

Indicating and turning left, the car travelled over the North Bridge. Ayesha looked out of the side window past Charlotte. “Two bridges?” said queried, spotting another in the near distance.

“Yes, this is the original over the railway and and river but it couldn’t take all the traffic, so they built that one, I don’t know, in the early 2000s, something like that.”

“Looks quite high”

“Yeah, it is an incline actually.” Charlotte replied, only just giving the fact contained in the statement a thought.

“So , tell me a bit about yourself, DC Stoker.”

The question was like being tossed a hand grenade with the pin out. “What kind of things, Ma’am?”

“You know, where you're from, your family..... Stuff like that.”

“Right, eh, ok...” and so Ayesha entered into a brief autobiographical summary; of her life growing up in the Park Village area of Wolverhampton; about her sister and brother; how she studied Criminology and Criminal Justice at the University of Wolverhampton; became a neighbourhood police officer in 2014 and served under the recently-promoted Detective Inspector Charlotte Walker.

"That's pretty much it in a nutshell, Ma'am."

"I feel properly informed now." said Charlotte, with one of her winning smiles.

By now, they had travelled through Bentley and Toll Bar, out onto the A19, where Doncaster's rural side finally showed itself.

"And you ended up here in Yorkshire rather than Camden?" Charlotte said.

Ayesha bit her tongue for a moment. What should she say? On the one hand, she wanted to say she'd come here to work with Charlotte, but on the other, she didn't want to upset the start she'd made so far. She decided the truth was the only way. "Well, when I became a DC I saw there was an opening here, and when I heard you'd moved here, well, the chance to work with you was too good to miss."

'Ah!' Charlotte thought, and so she decided to tackle the elephant in the car directly. "And now I'm leaving."

"Yeah."

Charlotte nodded in appreciation. It was more than a little awkward to discover your new Detective Constable had moved 200 or so miles for the chance to work with you, only to find on their first day you were leaving. That probably explained why she was so taken aback in my office, Charlotte mused.

There was silence in the car as the Doncaster countryside moved by. What was needed here was one of Charlotte's famous/infamous conversation handbrake turns. Anyone who got to know her quickly became used to her conversation handbrake turns -

as she changed the subject to something completely different with apparent ease. It was a technique she used to devastating effect on suspects.

“Do you like The Seekers?” she asked.

The question seemed so completely out of kilter to the previous conversation that it took Ayesha aback. “I beg your pardon?”

“The Seekers. The group from the 60s?”

“No, can't say I've ever heard of them.

“Really? Come on! The most perfect tales of love won, love lost; the whole of human emotion in a sub-3 minute song!?”

Ayesha looked as though Charlotte was talking in a different language. “I'm more a garage music fan myself.” she said, shaking her head.

“Here.. listen to this one; you'll love it…” she said, as her eyes darted between the touchscreen display and the road. Pressing some buttons, Charlotte only managed to get radio static to blurt out of the car speakers. “Bugger! Hang on.” she said, pressing more of the virtual buttons on the touchscreen. “What I'd do for a CD player in this car.”

“CD Player? Who uses them these days?!!” Ayesha replied, assuming Charlotte was joking.

“I DO! Or at least I would... “ she shouted up into the sky to the mythical Volvo gods, “...if they bloody fitted cars with one!”

“CDs... god I can't remember the last time I used a CD.” said Ayesha in wonderment.

"Technology, DC Stoker; technology." said Charlotte, reminding her of their office chat. Eventually Charlotte makes it and 'I'll Never Find Another You' by The Seekers plays from the car's speakers - although she had no idea how she made that happen.

There's a new world somewhere

They call the promised land...

It wasn't long before Charlotte had found the house and had pulled up on the main road in Norton and parked behind a police car.

The new team got out of the car and walked along the shoulder-height dry stone wall to the recessed black wrought iron gates of the driveway, which squealed as they were opened. The house was a detached, stone-built building, probably built in the 1980s Charlotte mused, with a front door in a porch in the centre and bay windows either side. The flashings looked like they'd recently been replaced and there was a single store extension on the left hand side, which probably had been added after the white uPVC windows were fitted to the rest of the house - as the one in the extension was brown.

Charlotte stopped for a moment, and watched as Ayesha simply walked up to the front door. Every so often she had to remind herself that not everyone looked at the world as she did; *really* looked at the world.

She shook her head and followed Ayesha inside the house.

* * *

Jason Knight was beside himself with worry. Sitting in one of the two individual chairs from the dark brown leather three-piece suite in the living room, he'd been almost paralysed with worry for several hours. So much so, his Mum had come around on the bus to look after his son.

It wasn't like his wife Sarah not to get in contact after so long. Hours without any sign of her. That's why he knew he needed to phone the police. And the time between phoning and the two lady detectives arriving and sitting across from him on the sofa seemed an eternity. But now, at last, they were here.

The living room of the Knight's house was neat, ordered and very tidy. The walls were painted a warm shade of cream and were punctuated by many photo in frames of the family trio in recognisable locations around the world; one taken from below of the three of them wirth the Empire State Building in New York behind them; another of them on the Spanish Steps in Rome; another hanging of one of the famous trams in San Francisco. A large flat screen television with associated set-top boxes was fixed in the middle of the longest wall, connected to three different games consoles. A large bookcase was to the left of the television, holding mainly biographies with the odd romantic fiction paperback.

Charlotte looked across at Jason. His legs couldn't stay still, and Charlotte couldn't decide whether it was from the worry and stress of the situation, or from something more long-termly medical. He was late middle-aged, tall, pale-skinned with a gentle face and his grey-green eyes provided a contrast to his dark brown hair. He was probably clean shaven normally, Charlotte thought, but missing that was understandable today.

She smiled her most reassuring smile and asked, “Mr Knight, I realise this is difficult and you've already told us a lot when you reported your wife missing but can you go through it again for us please?”

Ayesha opened her notebook and patted her pockets for a pen. Damn, she was sure she had one somewhere. Where the hell was it? As she looked up from staring inside her bag, there was her pen... being held aloft in front of her face in the outstretched left hand of Charlotte, as she was still focused on Jason. “Thank you , Ma’am.” Not the best of starts, Ayesha couldn’t help but wonder.

With Ayesha now pen equipped, Jason started to speak. ““Err, well, she never came back from work yesterday. No phone calls or anything. If she's working late, she always calls; but nothing. Something has happened to her, Inspector. She wouldn't just go on her own.”

“Where does Sarah work?” Charlotte asked.

“Err, she's chief developer and lead programmer at Tempto Digital.”

“The software company?”

“Yes. But she didn’t have an office there. Since we had our son, she’s worked mainly from home upstairs. She just went into the office when she needed to, for meetings and the like.”

"Did she ever talk about her work at all?"

Jason looked as if he was racking his brain for the information. "She did say at the start of the week that she was working on some sort of investigation project for the company, but I don't know what it was, sorry."

Ayeshav duly wrote lines in her notepad. "Can you think of anyone who might want to harm Sarah; someone she'd fallen out with perhaps?" Charlotte asked.

"Well, yesterday morning she was supposed to be meeting with her immediate manager - Kelvin - to share her initial findings. I've not heard from her since then." He suddenly realised the implications of what he'd just said.

Parking that for a while, Charlotte was keen to know whether Jason knew more about what Sarah was investigating, and whether she'd found out anything.

"I'm sorry, I don't know. She was very closed off about her work; she rarely discussed anything about it. In fact, now I think about it, it was strange she mentioned about this meeting."

"Do you think she'd already discovered something?"

"I guess so. She didn't really bring her work home with her. Well, except in her office upstairs, but she didn't talk about it much."

Charlotte pondered for a while, and Ayesha stepped in. "We'd need details of places Sarah often visits, please, such as friends, relatives; places she might go to get away from things?"

Jason became quite defensive. "Of course, yes. But

she wasn't getting away from anything. There wasn't anything going on here..."

Charlotte noted Jason's defensive tone, and her years of experience told her to roll back a little from the quite clinical words of Ayesha - no matter how correct she was... "No-one is saying she was, Mr Knight, but we've got to look at everything; no stone unturned."

Suddenly, a young boy pushed open the living room door, and rushed past the two detectives to cuddle Jason's legs. An elderly lady hovers at the door. "I'm sorry, Jason, he just wanted you."

"It's ok, Mum."

Jason looked down at his son. "Hey, hey. it's ok. It'll be ok. These ladies are police detectives."

The boy turned around to look at Charlotte and Ayesha, whilst still clinging onto his Dad. His whole world had been turned upside down, so he wasn't going to let go of one of the few remaining constants.

Seeing how worried and upset the boy was, Charlotte got off the sofa and dropped to her knees to get down to his level. "Hi there. My name's Lottie. What's yours?"

"Daniel." the boy said. Never, thought Charlotte, had a word spoken said so, so much. The fear; the upset; the questions; the need.

"That's a lovely name." Charlotte put on her best, warmest smile. "Hello Daniel. Are you missing your mummy?"

Daniel slowly and almost imperceptibly nodded. His Dad squeezed him lovingly on his shoulders, to say

'I'm still here'.

"Well, that's why we are here, because we're from the 'finding mummies' part of the police. And we're going to do all we can to find your mummy and bring her back so you can have a mummy cuddle. Is that ok?" asked Charlotte.

There was a more confident nod this time.

"Now, can you do something for me please? Until we find you mummy, I think your Daddy is going to need a lot more cuddles to keep him going. I think he'll need special Daniel cuddles. Could you do that for me?"

Daniel nods a lot more vociferously this time.

"Lovely" said Charlotte.

A slight smile appeared on Daniel's face, as his Dad squeezed him again on his shoulders."Daniel, can you go back with Nanna now please?" Daniel was a lot happier now, and went out of the living room to find his Nanna.

Jason smiled at Charlotte, who was still on her knees from talking to Daniel. "Thank you Inspector. He's taking it very hard."

"Of course he is. Mr Knight, if you could give Ayesha here as much to go on as you can, please. I'll just have a look upstairs if I may? See if anything seems important in your wife's office."

"Of course. It's on the right."

"Thank you." acknowledged Charlotte with a smile, as she got up off her knees and left the room.

She climbed the stairs, noting more photographs

of the family of three on the wall of the hallway, and turned right on the landing. Gently pushing the slightly ajar door open, she looked inside. Unlike the rest of the house, which seemed light and airy, Sarah's office was dark and moody, with the blinds on the one window to the world outside firmly down and closed. Only a tiny shaft of light coming from a gap in the fitting at the top of the blind illuminated the room.

Charlotte looked around for the light switch; first on the left side of the door and found it on the right. Flicking the switch gave rise to a blue, almost neon light, instead of the traditional white Charlotte expected. Looking up at the three bulbs in the light, she figured they were probably those wifi-colour-changing-app-controlled ones David has throughout his house.

The blue coloured light seemed to provide less illumination than pure white, but as one herself who preferred a more dark aspect in her house, she understood the desire for some mood whilst working. It did, however, provide enough light to see the contents of the room. It was busy, with lots of technology items dotted around - hard drives, various mobile devices, tablets - many of which she had no clue on - but it did look ordered and neat.

The wall the desk ran along was awash with post-in notes of different colours, each full of very neat but small writing. 'A lady after my own heart.' she thought, clocking the post-in notes. Except even Charlotte would admit her own handwriting was about as far removed from Sarah's succinct script. On studying them further, there didn't seem to be anything that stood out as important.

Looking at the desk, Charlotte noticed a gap on the desk for a laptop. The USB cables which attached it to the very large monitor and the very clean keyboard were all still there, but the space where the computer regularly sat was clear from the papers, the notebook and the pens arranged around it. *'So has that been taken then?'* was Charlotte's thought.

With the very fetching white gloves on her hands she opened a couple of the drawers. Scouting through them they were seemingly relating to the various apps and software Sarah was working on.

The next drawer was the same.

But the one after was locked. Charlotte's face developed her famous frown. She tried the drawer a little harder, just on the off chance she could force it open, but to no avail. *'Maybe if Sarah did find something out, the evidence of it could be in there?'* Charlotte thought. The key... could be around here somewhere perhaps... She looked around the office; imagining all the places she'd hide a key in this room - but that too proved fruitless.

After one last sweep around the room with her eyes - in case she'd missed anything obvious - Charlotte returned downstairs.

Re-entering the living room, she was just in time to see Ayesha finishing off writing down the information from Jason. Ayesha flicked her a nod, to say she was done, and Charlotte threw a small nod back.

Charlotte turned to Jason. "Mr Knight, there's a drawer locked in Sarah's office. Do you know what's in there? Or whether there's another key anywhere?"

Jason looked perplexed. "I'm sorry, no. I don't go into her office, so I've no idea what is in there or whether there's another key. I would have thought there would be somewhere."

"No problem. We'll need a recent photograph of Sarah for..."

"I've already got Mr Knight to send me one, Ma'am. He's bluetoothed it to my phone."

"Oh, right. Excellent" said Charlotte, her frown revealing a slight agitation Ayesha had done something under her own initiative. She recovered and asked, "And just in case, do you have a set of spare keys for Sarah's car? For when we find it. Jason nodded and gave Charlotte the spare set of keys from a drawer. "And possibly a piece of her clothing in case we need to use our dog unit to help with the search?" Charlotte continued.

Jason wore the same perplexed face at the sound of this request, but said, "Yes, of course." He went over to pick up a green top of Sarah's which was on the top of a pile of washing in a basket, but Charlotte stopped him.

"That's ok, I'll get that." she said, and in one motion she used regularly to remove dog poo from the floor, she placed it in an evidence bag without touching it, and then sealed it up. Watching Charlotte, Jason sat back down with a sigh. "Ok, thank you. We'll be in touch if we have any developments." she said to him.

"Thank you both." he said, lifting himself up to be the polite host.

"Don't worry, we'll show ourselves out." Charlotte said quickly, with a wave of her hand. As they left,

Charlotte checked the spare keys for anything small enough to be a drawer key... but there was only the chucky key for a car and a house-style Yale key.

* * *

Outside, Charlotte allowed Ayesha through the front door she'd just opened, and then closed it behind her, checking it was properly closed before walking to catch up with Ayesha, who was waiting at Charlotte's car on the main road.

"It's not usual practice to collect a piece of clothing for the dog unit, is it Ma'am?" asked Ayesha. It was something she'd been wondering since Charlotte had made her somewhat surprising request inside.

"No, no it's not," replied Charlotte, "but I'm just thinking ahead. This is a missing person investigation, and one of the jobs the dog unit is very good at is tracking missing persons... providing they have their scent..."

"Ma'am." Ayesha took that on board.

"Get that list to uniform and get them to follow up on all those places."

"Ma'am."

Charlotte's eyes narrowed. "Although my money's on the place of work being the most interesting... Let's have a look at her photo."

Ayesha woke up her phone with her thumbprint and offered the screen towards Charlotte; the photo was still open from earlier. It looked to be taken on the same holiday as one of the photographs in a frame in the living room. Sarah was wearing the same clothes and her hair was the same length, Charlotte noted. She studied the image on the screen. Sarah was smiling; that's the first thing she saw. A happy lady on holiday, somewhere warm judging by the casual shorts and t-shirt, in the middle of her life and very content with her lot. If was difficult to get a handle on her height from that photograph, as there wasn't too much to judge it by in the street were she was standing, but Charlotte guessed she'd be between her and Ayesha - average height, warm complexion, mousse coloured long hair that looked even longer than hers... but it was those eyes that stood out. Charlotte pinched the screen to zoom in, and focused on Sarah's radiant brown eyes.

Happy, she thought, as she zoomed out to the original size of the photo with her figures and handed the phone back to Ayesha. A wistful look crossed Charlotte's face with a determination to return this lady to her family.

Waiting for three cars to go around her parked vehicle and the police car in front, she walked into the road to get inside. Again, Ayesha had only just settled into her seat before Charlotte set off around the police car at speed.

Turning the ignition on allowed The Seekers to continue their musical journey on the stereo, with Charlotte miming the lyrics channelling her inner Judith Durham. That was until a grey Audi pulled out in front of them from the side road of Manor Garth without looking, causing Charlotte to brake sharply and exclaim "What the flip!!!"

The jolt - and the lack of an expletive - caused Ayesha to look up from her phone to see what the problem was. "Thinks the Highway Code doesn't apply to him." explained Charlotte, gesticulating towards the Audi as it speeded away doing more than the limit.

Ayesha returned to her phone with a smile. "Done." she said, receiving a puzzled look in return. "Uniform have the list."

Charlotte raised an eyebrow in acknowledgment and then looked in deep thought as they traversed the level crossing. Ayesha mused that she'd be busy cracking the case already... so the comment, "I love cheese; but mainly the British non-mouldy stuff." came as a big surprise.

"Ma'am??"

"A good mature Cheddar. Extra mature, even better." Ayesha looked at her bizarrely as if to say *'what?'*.

"Things you need to know about me."

"Right!" she said. "Cheese preferences. Ok!" her eyes looked up.

If Charlotte was sharing, then there was something Ayesha wanted to ask. "Have you got kids Ma'am?" Charlotte turned the stereo down, with a look of a parent having their favourite song interrupted by their kid. It was alright for her to talk over her music choices, but she wasn't accustomed to others doing it.

"Good lord no!" Charlotte wondered where this particular line of questioning had come from, and then it clicked. "Oh, you mean cos of back there?" Ayesha nodded. "My sister Nessa - Vanessa - has two girls and a boy."

"Sister. Ok, added to the list." said Ayesha; her eyes looking up once again as she said it as if accessing the file in her head named 'Things I should know about DCI Charlotte Walker'.

The junction on to the A19 gave Charlotte a brief opportunity to look across to her. "Two sisters, actually. And a brother. And a dog." Turning right, Charlotte looked back and saw Ayesha with her eyes closed for a moment. *'That must be the file writing process'*, she thought.

When Charlotte was content the interruptions from Ayesha had stopped, she returned the volume to the previous level...

Until my life is through

But I know I'll never find another you.

Actually, thought Charlotte, as much as I love this song, it might be a little too close to home right now. She switched the stereo over to Radio 3. There. At least with classical music there's no chance of words to bite her today.

She was right. Georgia Mann was just introducing Nicola Benedetti and the orchestra of the Academy of St. Martin in the Fields with Mendelssohn's Violin Concerto in E Minor - the last movement. Ah, that's probably safer, Charlotte thought. No chance of the lyrical violin of Nicola being anything other than joyous.

But the feelings of the moment didn't want to be left unsaid. "No, never happened for me."

Ayesha by this time had moved on from that conversation and was looking out of the window at the countryside of Doncaster passing by. "Ma'am?" she asked, turning back towards Charlotte.

"Ran out of time." Charlotte saw Ayesha's puzzled look. "Kids." she established.

More of the Doncaster countryside sped by.

"I mean, we might have done. Given a few more years. Who knows?" Charlotte continued.

Ayesha might only have been a Detective Constable for several weeks but she could detect an exchange that she didn't fancy being a part of, and just nodded her head, acknowledgingly.

There needed to be a conversational hand-brake turn, Charlotte realised. "So where are you staying?"

"Just in a B&B in town for now. Until I get myself sorted with a house share or something. Then maybe look for a house and get the rest of my stuff sent up from London."

"How much stuff could a twenty-something have?" Charlotte wondered. But she seemed to have said it out loud.

"Promise you won't laugh, Ma'am..."

"Of course not."

Ayesha plucks up the courage. "Well, I'm..." she pauses. *'Perhaps I shouldn't say'*, she thought.

Charlotte pulled up behind three cars waiting at the closed level crossing barriers. The car directly in front a fairly familiar grey Audi. Putting the hand brake on, she turned to look at Ayesha. "Nothing that you say now could be any worse that what's going around my head now!"

"Ok." Here it comes. "I'm into comic books." she said, with all the emotion of an alcoholic admitting their drink problem.

"Is that it?" asked Charlotte, relieved.

"Well, I've got a lot."

"How many?"

"Over five thousand." Charlotte raised an eyebrow. "Five thousand, two hundred and seventy, actually."

Charlotte blew a whistle, to say 'wowzers'. At this point Charlotte's attention is taken by the sound of a locomotive passing in front of them. "Light engine. A class 66." she said, albeit to an audience to whom the words meant nothing - so she decided to keep that knowledge to herself for now. The barriers were up, and the line of traffic steadily moved off towards the town of Askern.

"So where are they now?" asked Charlotte.

"In storage in London. But I want to get them up here as soon as I get my own place."

"Y'see? You sit there looking all prim and proper and actually you're a secret superhero." Charlotte teased. Ayesha appreciated her tone.

"So, if you know of anyone with a spare room..."

Charlotte wasn't quite sure whether this was a request for information about people who might have a spare room, or a fishing expedition to see whether *she* had a spare room. She decided to treat it as the former, and said "I'll keep my ears open." She wasn't ready to be sharing her house with anyone right now, let alone a work colleague who wouldn't be a work colleague very soon.

"So, you must be good with smartphones, Ayesha..." Charlotte asked.

"Errr, I can figure most things out, Ma'am. Why?"

"I need to get some more frozen dog food, and apparently there's a new store this side of town, so I thought I'd pop in now. But this car is one of those that needs a smartphone to use as its sat nav..."

"And yours isn't up to the job?" Ayesha ventured.

Charlotte smiled slightly. The revelation of the Nokia 3310 could wait for another time. "You could say that."

"Have you got a cable?"

"There should be one in the glovebox."

Ayesha found the cable, and plugged her phone into the car's USB socket. She then pressed some virtual buttons on the car's touchscreen unit, then did the same on her phone, and within a few moments had paired the phone via Bluetooth. The car recognised the phone, and suddenly the touchscreen showed the cut-down version of Ayesha's phone.

Ayesha looked across to Charlotte for some kind of recognition; but Charlotte was lost in thought. She looked back down at the touchscreen. Google Maps - click.

"What was the shops' name, Ma'am?"

"Taylors Pet Supplies. Only opened a few months ago I think."

Ayesha typed 'Taylors Pet Supplies' into Google Maps - and got nothing. "Hmmm, it's not coming up with anything Ma'am." she said.

Strange, thought Charlotte. She knew that was the name, as her brother David emailed her to let her know about their opening offers when he saw it in his newspaper. Charlotte had intended on checking it out - with her dog, of course, but work at that time had been relentless and so she missed it. But with her forgetting to order the dog food online in time, she needed to buy some today.

"It was definitely Taylors. Try doing a normal Google search."

Ayesha obliged and eyes widened. "Odd. It's here. They've a website, social media and stuff. But they aren't on the map."

"Where is it then?"

"At the junction, turn left." the almost human voice of Google Maps bellowed out of the car's speakers. Charlotte looked at Ayesha.

"What she said, Ma'am!"

* * *

Fifteen minutes later and thanks to the power of satellite navigation, Charlotte and Ayesha had found the new pet store and were chatting as they walked in.

“..it wasn’t difficult to find when you knew the address.” Ayesha finished off.

“But even easier if you could have found it on Google Maps.” replied Charlotte, grabbing a green mesh-style shopping basket from the pile to the left of the door.

The man behind the counter next to the door, who Charlotte assumed was the owner, tentatively asked “Sorry, I couldn’t help overhear... are we still off the map apps?”

Charlotte approached the counter and said “Er, yes, it does look that way.”

The man - a small, quiet-spoken individual - rested his head in both his hands and said “This could kill us.” And with that, he shook his head, walked out from behind the counter and straightened some bags of dog food on a side display, in a clear attempt just to do something.

Charlotte turned to look at Ayesha, turned her bottom lip down and frowned for a moment - before walking away from the counter to find the frozen food section.

A wall of the industrial unit, which had been converted into the shop, was taken up with freezers, and Charlotte walked slowed down along them, peering into each through the frost-covered glass lids.

Occasionally, she lifted one up, and a faint cloud of frost escaped. Grabbing a few bags of dog food and putting them in her basket, Charlotte moved to the next freezer.

Ayesha looked as much like a fish out of water as it was possible to be. She wasn't a pet person as her parents didn't have pets when she was growing up, and the desire to have a pet when she'd have been able to, had never arisen. She looked around at the many and various products on offer for the discerning pet owner and concluded that the manufacturers could obviously see the pet owners' coming.

The owner returned behind the counter, and looked with great relief at the haul Charlotte was intending to buy. He wasn't big on small talk with his customers, Charlotte thought, as she watched him meticulously grab an item from the basket on her left, flip it over and around several times to find the barcode, zap it with his scanner thing and put it into a box on her right. Perhaps it might be because he hasn't had enough customers to perfect his patter yet, she thought, looking behind her to reacquaint herself with the distinct lack of customers.

Maybe she should say something; break the ice? "So, how long have you been open?"

"Two months." came the reply.

More silence; save for the 'beep' every time he managed to find a barcode on an item.

Charlotte nodded.

"And.... you say you knew you weren't on the mapping apps?"

The man stopped suddenly and looked at her; the scanner thing in one hand and tub of Lamb Tagine in the other. “It's going to kill us.” he said, with a sombre face. And then he carried on scanning.

Charlotte nodded.

“Have you contacted anybody about it? Google Maps? Apple Maps?” She could see he possibly wasn't giving her a lot of attention, as he tapped on his computer keyboard with all of the items scanned. “Banana Maps?”

“£123.57 please.” came the reply.

Charlotte frowned. Partly at the cost of what she'd bought in dog food, and partly because of the man's distinct lack of enthusiasm for entering into small talk. But mainly about the cost.

She showed the man her payment card, and he pointed to the machine. “Please type in your PIN number.”

'It's either just PIN or it's PI Number. It's not PIN number, because that would make it Personal Identification Number Number.' she could help herself thinking, but she managed to hold that one back. “Thank you.” she said, as she lifted the heavy box of dog goodies, and walked through the doors being held open by Ayesha.

“Didn't that strike you as odd, Ma'am?” asked Ayesha, as they walked back to the car.

“Yes. It's clearly *not* PIN Number. I mean, why would anyone say that?” Charlotte wrestled with trying to get her keys out of her trouser pocket.

"I mean them not being on the mapping apps!"

Charlotte had decided that putting the box of dog goodies on the roof of her car would be easier than trying to hold onto it whilst retrieving her keys. A click of the key fob, and she opened the boot, lifting the box inside.

She shrugged her shoulders and reminded Ayesha, "Arm's length relationship with technology..." Ayesha playfully nodded her head. But looking at Charlotte, she noticed that it probably had piqued her curiosity somewhat.

Chapter 3

Walking from the large car park, the lavish headquarters of Tempto Digital seemed more than a little out of step with the drive to it. It was built on land reclaimed from one of Doncaster's many coal mines closed in the 1990s. The impressive building - which was described by one of Charlotte's nieces as 'like a pyramid without the pointy top bit' when they drove past it once - seemed to be constructed from mainly massive sheets of glass held together by as thin sections of metal as possible, giving it an almost transparent quality. That said, many of the glass sections at floor level were tinted black, but into the rest you could see straight inside.

The entrance to this world of technology was on one of the corners of the flattened pyramid via a wide selection of automatic doors. Once inside, Charlotte and Ayesha walked into a large, open-plan atrium-style reception area. For a moment, they looked around. On the right, behind the reception desk, was a break-out-style area, full of carpet and big multi-coloured scatter cushions, where several groups looked to be having brainstorming sessions - complete with hi-tec whiteboards. Charlotte swore she heard 'core competencies' and ''everage best practice' wafting over from them. She'd been in enough management meetings to spot a waste of time when she saw one.

On the left side was the canteen, and from a brief look at the menu Charlotte was glad she didn't work here. 'Infusion of braised sea bass laced with pan-fried mung beans' wasn't a food option she particularly found appetising.

Whilst they were standing there, several employees walked passed in and out of the headquarters, and there was some sort of security gate straight ahead of them with turnstiles the workers were passing through in order to access the more critical areas of the building. Charlotte watched as the employees were signing themselves in and out with wireless key cards, rather like the Oyster cards in London, through the turnstiles.

Ayesha left Charlotte's side and walked up to the reception desk. The blond-haired receptionist switched on the same smile she used hundreds of times a day to visitors. "We're from South Yorkshire Police, we're here to see Kelvin Thomas. He's expecting us." The receptionist acknowledged the request and phoned to let upstairs know. Ayesha walked back to Charlotte, who was still looking around the building. "It's impressive." she said, watching her looking.

"Yes. To think this all used to be a coal mine..."

"Really?"

"Mmmm. The designer won some sort of award for it, as far as I remember." This time, when Charlotte looked around again, she did so with different eyes. In an almost robot fashion, her analytical eyes soaked up everything; from the location of emergency exits to the position and number of each of the CCTV cameras. And there were quite a few; nine in this atrium area alone.

After a short while, a man in his mid 50s entered the reception area. Wearing black plastic glasses and looking rather dishevelled with badly chosen clothing options, Charlotte surmised that Kelvin Thomas - as she learned through his slightly battered lanyard - probably prefered computers to humans.

"Detectives?" queried Kelvin.

As the superior officer, Charlotte set about introducing the two of them. "Yes, I'm DC..."

"This way please..." Kelvin interrupted with a viger Charlotte couldn't at first quite put her finger on the reason for. Then, as he was ushering them out of the reception area, he was all the while looking up and around at the same CCTV cameras Charlotte had just clocked. He was so eager to get them out of the reception area, he took off his own lanyard - which doubled as a key card - to get Charlotte and Ayesha through the security turnstiles, instead of signing them in at reception as his guests and getting temporary visitor key cards for them.

Charlotte had enough of a collection of visitor key cards and lanyards that receptionists had failed to take back from the numerous times she'd visited companies, so she was glad they didn't have some more for this trip - but it did cross her mind to investigate the security of this building.

Kelvin took them to the first floor in the lift. Charlotte's natural instinct was to always use the stairs - after all, it was only two flights of steps - but both Kelvin and Ayesha headed straight for the lift.

Turning right once on the first floor, Kelvin ushered Charlotte and Ayesha down a corridor, whilst all the time looking up and around the edges of this thoroughfare. Various potted plants dotted the corridor, which Charlotte couldn't help but think were rather a health and safety hazard. They passed several offices on the left, then a room where the pine-coloured door was labelled 'Meeting Room', and then Kelvin stopped outside the door to the next office, marked 'Kelvin Thomas - Room 104'.

Kelvin was obviously a very disorganised man, as he simply couldn't find the keycard he needed to open his office door. Charlotte needed a little more time to look around, and so after spotting there weren't any CCTV cameras in this corridor and a pictogram sign indicating the toilets were further down the corridor past Kelvin's office, she reminded him the lanyard was still around his neck.

Kelvin unlocked the door to his office, and opened it, standing back to maximise the gap in the doorway for the detectives to walk through. "It's better if we talk in here." he said, rather quietly.

Charlotte looked at Ayesha, but she didn't notice a) her look and b) the fact Charlotte thought this was a bit too 'cloak and dagger' to be normal. But then Ayesha was already inside the office, so Charlotte followed.

Kelvin's office was like stepping into a teenage boy's bedroom. It was dark, with partially closed horizontal blinds letting the briefest of light through the windows into the corridor, and the roller blind on the outside window looked to have seized in the closed position sometime ago. An 'L' shaped desk sat in the corner opposite the door, running one side along under the window to the outside. The desk was packed with computers; several desktop PCs, laptops,

Macs of various flavours and - something that caught Charlotte's eye - an original rubber-keyed Sinclair Spectrum.

There were various posters of characters from computer games peppering the walls, with more than a few of Lara Croft. Not the Angelina Jolie version from the live-action films, but the actual character as seen in the video games of the same name.

It was geekdom turned up to 11 - and Charlotte loved it.

Kelvin quickly moved a pile of old computer magazines off the only other seat in the office, and gingerly offered it to the detectives. If he had realised he'd shown two detectives one seat, he didn't show it. Ayesha looked at Charlotte, following the clear single seat etiquette of offering the opportunity to sit down to your superior officer, but saw she was too busy closely inspecting all the posters, framed works of art and photographs on the walls of the office - so she sat down instead.

He sat down on his seat, and Charlotte caught him checking out the corners of the room and smiling. Following his gaze, she noticed a lack of CCTV cameras - is that what Kelvin was happy about?

"Mr Thomas, we're here investigating the disappearance of Mrs Sarah Knight."

"Yes, quite. Awful business." he said nervously.

With Charlotte looking around the room, Ayesha took over. "Can you tell us what your job is here, please sir?"

"Well, I'm the Senior Project Manager here at Tempto Digital, so I manage all the projects we are doing, hence the title Project Manager." He was clearly nervous, but Ayesha couldn't decide whether that was from having to talk to people or because he was hiding something.

Charlotte studied a framed screenshot on the wall. It was from a game, and Charlotte knew it looked familiar. "War Craft III?" she asked Kelvin.

"Yes, I know the designer." replied Kelvin.

Charlotte nodded in approval, before asking, ."So what is it Tempto Digital does?"

"Errr, we're a web services company, Inspector. We handle the back end of many websites and apps on our multitude of servers." Kelvin continued to talk as his head followed Charlotte's walk around the office. "And we run our business service software applications too."

As walks go, it wasn't Charlotte's longest, but the trek around the office did start to elicit some interesting background - especially Kelvin's wall of photographs. Looking closely, her focus was drawn to one particular photograph of three men, probably in their mid 30s; one was clearly Kelvin and the other two were twins. Kelvin saw which photograph Charlotte was looking at. "Carl and Scott Remington," he said, "they started Tempto Digital in 1985 writing games for the Commodore 64."

Charlotte looked away from the wall for a second and noted Ayesha's puzzled frown. "The best selling single home computer of all time, I believe." she said, before returning to the wall to notice another photograph; this one was of Kelvin, one of the twins and a lady at a posh event - the name of which was presumably out of the picture but the last line of it was at the top of the frame… 'Awards 2016'.

A quick scan of the caption underneath revealed the twin to be Scott, and the lady… a certain Sarah Knight. The caption read 'Sarah Timms', but it was certainly Sarah Knight before she was married. It was the brown eyes Charlotte was drawn to.

Interesting.

"Impressive knowledge, Inspector" came Kelvin's reply, which broke Charlotte back to the here and now. "My Dad's still got one somewhere. And the five and a quarter inch floppy disk drive too."

"Ahhh the 1541!" reminisced Kelvin. "So you're a gamer, Inspector?"

"Oh god you betcha. Nothing better than a good game. I particularly like…" but at that point she spotted Ayesha - whose face was wearing a 'Ma'am, we should be sticking to the job at hand' look. Chastised, Charlotte returned to the questioning. "So you were involved right from the start?"

"Yes, I ported the games over to the Spectrum. I always used to joke that I had the harder because you had to design the games around the attribute clash issue of not being able to select the desired colour of a specific pixel…"

"What is Sarah Knight's job here?" Ayesha abruptly interjected, before he could go into any more technical waffle that she didn't understand.

A little put out, he replied "Sarah is one of our

most experienced programmers. She's single-handedly developed most of our most successful software and she's an expert debugger."

Charlotte needed more clarity on that. "Debugger?" she quizzed?

"Yes. Finding problems in a piece of code; getting to the bottom of things that have gone wrong. Much the same as yourself, Inspector."

Charlotte nodded,looking at some framed front covers of Sinclair User magazine. "What software has she developed?"

"Her fingerprints are on virtually everything since we moved out of gaming. She developed the accounting software that changed our fortunes pretty much overnight back in the 2000s; she developed our first mobile app 'TimeSMS' in 2017 - where you could schedule text messages to be sent out at an allotted time..." Kelvin pointed to a photograph on the wall, which Charlotte walked over to investigate.

"What has Mrs Knight been working on most recently Mr Thomas?" asked Ayesha.

"Err, the mapping apps. We handle the back end work of virtually all the major mapping and sat nav apps out there." he replied.

"All of them?" Charlotte asked, rather surprised.

"Pretty much. They virtually all secretly use our back end." His back straightened from pride. "No matter what name is on the app or what it looks like, they all use *our* back end." If he had left a pause for the two ladies to be impressed, then the pause didn't need to have happened. *Tough crowd,* he thought, and continued; slightly ducking his head as and moving closer to the sitting Ayesha as if to stop anyone else nearby from overhearing. “We'd had reports of several locations suddenly going missing off the base map…”

Kelvin looked up at Charlotte, and even he with his notable lack of people skills could read the look from Charlotte. She needed a greater explanation on this...

“Err, the master map from which all the apps draw their data from. If something isn't on that master map, it can't be seen on any of the apps.”

“Right.” replied Charlotte.

It was then Ayesha had a realisation. “Ma’am? That could be what happened to the pet store.”

Charlotte turned to her compatriot and said “Could be.”

“You know of somewhere that isn’t on the map?” Kelvin asked.

“Yeah, a pet store not too far away. Opened a couple of months back. They added all their info online; was on the map for a bit, and then *poof*… disappeared one day.”

Kelvin suddenly became very agitated. “Yes, YES! All of them were like that! On the maps, then *poof*.” he said, in the same manner as Charlotte. Kelvin pushed down with his left leg and wheeled his chair across the office to move closer to Ayesha. He waited for Charlotte to join them, and when she didn’t within his timescale, he waved at her to come over with an almost child-like vigour.

Charlotte frowned, but complied, kneeling down

next to Ayesha. Kelvin moved even closer to the lady detectives, as if to tell them a secret. “Well, I'd assigned Sarah to it; as our most experienced, she seemed to be the perfect choice... despite Amber's objections.” he said quietly.

“Amber?” enquired Charlotte, in the same low hushed manner..

“Yes, errr, Amber Remington, CEO and majority owner of the company.” he replied.

“She didn't want Mrs Knight on the project?”

“She said her attitude wasn't right for such a delicate project.”

“And you disagreed?”

To this, Kelvin suddenly became agitated and loud. “Yes. I over-ruled her!” he shouted, loud and proud of his actions. The two detectives moved quickly back from their previous positions close to Kelvin and shook their heads as if to shake his shout from their ears. “One of the few times I have. And I feel the scars now from that.” Kelvin continued, his tone more thoughtful.

Charlotte wondered what ‘scars’ could be? Social, mental, or physical even. She pressed on with her line of questioning. “Did Sarah Knight have a meeting with you yesterday morning?”

The man stopped and narrowed his eyes somewhat. “Eeerrr, yes, yes she did. It was a project progress report on the progress she had made on the project.” He pushed himself back across the room to his desk.

Charlotte ignored the awkwardness of the reply. “And what progress had she made on the project?”

Again, Kelvin stopped before answering. "Well, none up to that point."

With Kelvin's attention firmly on Charlotte as she was asking the questions, he didn't see a visible gasp from Ayesha. Charlotte knew what she was thinking; that didn't marry up with what Jason said. Charlotte flashed a glare at Ayesha, as if to say 'shhh', and by the time Kelvin had turned to look at her, Ayesha's expression was back to a flat smile.

When his gaze had returned to Charlotte, she stood up quickly from her kneeling position. "Ok, I think that will be all for now, Mr Thomas." Charlotte said, as they started to leave Kelvin's office.

At the door, Charlotte said ""Just one more thing... who would we need to talk to about the CCTV in the building please?"

"That would be our Head of Security, Frank Drashler. I can page him for you, if you like?"

'Page'? Even Charlotte knew that went out with the arc... "Yes please." she replied, with a smile.

* * *

Perhaps Kelvin's office was so dark because it was compensating for the illumination show of Frank Drashler's place of work. Every light conceivable was here and switched on. So much so, both Charlotte and Ayesha blinked more than a couple of times when they first walked in, to get their eyes to adjust to the intensity.

After Kelvin had paged him, the Head of Security had come up to his office and brought the two detectives personally down to his office on the ground floor. In the lift, much to Charlotte's ire. *'Why don't people use the stairs when they can?'* she thought.

That was several minutes ago, and now Ayesha was sitting on a chair facing on the opposite wall a large desk with a selection of monitors cycling through the various CCTV cameras in the building. Behind her, a smaller desk with a standard work computer and monitor. Charlotte was standing, even though there was another chair next to Ayesha. That seemed to be her style. She was looking around the office, which was covered with photographs and memorabilia, rather like Kelvin's. Except this chaps' passion was snooker.

Frank Drashler was also standing up. He was a tall, stocky individual with muscles bulging everywhere they should be underneath his well-fitting light grey designer suit, with matching waistcoat - very snooker. He would be in his late fifties and had a face which had definitely seen the world. It worked perfectly with the very short light grey hair over his head, and the similar-coloured goatee-style beard which dominated around his mouth.

The man was blinged up to ten, with countless rings on his fingers, two bracelets on his right arm and the hint of a gold chain around his neck just visible with the open two buttons of his royal blue shirt. No tie, Charlotte thought, as she caught a glimpse of a very fancy watch on his left wrist. The ring in his right ear completed the picture, and he had an air about him which made you never quite sure whether he'll laugh with you or shoot you. That's probably why he was perfect for his job.

Charlotte was surprised to find herself rather attracted to him. He had the look of Bruce Willis about him, and she found herself smiling at him - to which he smiled back.

'God sake Charlotte!' she thought, having to seriously reprimand herself. *'Be professional. And today of all days.'*

She toned the smile to a more business-like version and explained to Frank why they were here, and how they needed his help.

Frank listened, and replied, "CCTV and key logs? I can't do that, I'm afraid - Data Protection."

"May I remind you under the provisions of the Data Protection Act 1998, you can release information to the police." Ayesha's matter-of-fact attitude was all very correct - but it wasn't winning Frank over.

Charlotte saw she needed to step in. Turning from looking at the various signed photographs of him with famous snooker players in the parade on the wall, she said, "Mr Drashler, we're dealing with a missing person here, and the information we think you have could seriously help us. Our investigation would be harmed if you don't provide this information." This, and adding a smile afterwards, seemed to do the trick.

Frank's prickly demeanour changed, and he said, "What is it you want?" smiling at Charlotte.

"We're interested in Sarah Knight's movements

inside the building yesterday and when she arrived and left the building. So any CCTV or key card logs would be most useful."

"Well, it will take me a while to sort out the CCTV for you, but I can get the key card logs for Mrs Knight now."

Charlotte recognised the accent and thought Frank could almost be the typical East End barrow boy - but every so often he seemed to slip into a different accent that she couldn't place.

"Thank you ever so much."

He walked from the middle of the room, past the sitting detective taking notes, to his desk. Ayesha turned to look back, and Charlotte gave her a wink. They were getting what they wanted. Grabbing the mouse, Frank woke up the monitor, typed a password in and then brought the requested information on the screen. As he did so, he was a little too close for comfort for Ayesha, so she pushed her wheely chair away slightly - on the pretence of giving him more space, and then her attention switched to the monitor.

When he'd finished, Frank turned back to Charlotte, still bent over in front of her at the level of the computer. She found herself caught admiring his bum, and so moved her eyes away quickly and down to the floor, as if to be continuing a previous eye trajectory. When she turned back to Frank, she wasn't sure whether he'd noticed her original point of focus - but if he had, he didn't indicate it.

"There you are." he said, as he straightened up. Charlotte walked towards the desk.

"Thank you. Are we ok to look over this..." Charlotte continued the question with her hands, in a gesture which said *'for us to look alone?'*.

Frank took the hint. "Err, yes, no problem. I'll just be over there." He pointed generally over to the large desk of CCTV monitors on the other side of the room.

"Thank you." Charlotte was all sweetness and smiles until Frank walked away, and then her face switched into work-mode as she squatted down next to Ayesha.

The two of them studied the data on the screen, working out what it told them.

"So.. arrived at 8:30; lunch at 1pm until quarter to 3." Charlotte started, her chin almost resting on the deck.

"10:55am to 'Room 105'?" Ayesha queried.

"That's the room next to Kelvin Thomas' office.", Charlotte remarked, casually.

Ayesha looked down at Charlotte without her noticing. She's done it again, she thought, that amazing eye for detail. Charlotte, oblivious to her wonderment, said, "That must be their meeting Jason mentioned."

Ayesha nodded. She ran her finger down the monitor. "Left at 6pm."

"Fairly long lunch..." Charlotte noted.

Ayesha spotted what Charlotte had seen. "Mmmmm? Can we go for lunches that long?"

That raised a smile, as Charlotte looked over her shoulder casually to see if Frank was paying them much attention. As it happened, he was sitting at the other desk deeply engrossed in the monitors showing CCTV images from around the building.

"While we are here, pull up Kelvin Thomas..." she said, quietly.

"Ma'am?"

Charlotte's expressive eyebrows and forehead seem to extend beyond her head, as she nods forward, indicating for Ayesha to take the opportunity of the information at her fingertips. *'Clearly expected to know my way around a piece of software I'd never seen before now, eh?'*, Ayesha thought. But Charlotte's confidence was rewarded, because within a couple of mouse moves and button clicks, up popped Kelvin Thomas' activity.

Studying this new data, Ayesha looked puzzled. "So Kelvin wasn't in the meeting with Sarah? His key card doesn't show it."

"It won't do - Sarah went to the room first and used her card to open the door."

What Ayesha had noticed already was Charlotte never held back showing and sharing her skills in deduction and reasoning - but never at any time was it done in a showy or condescending way. Just merely like a sneeze, she couldn't hold them in. Now Charlotte had said it, it seemed so logical and clear. If Sarah went to the room first and unlocked the door with her key card, then of course Kelvin's wouldn't show him opening it... it was already unlocked. She wondered whether Charlotte would think less of her for making what she thought were basic errors... but Charlotte had already forgotten about it and was deep studying the record on the screen.

Ayesha thought maybe there's something here Charlotte hadn't spotted - but then she gave that up as almost impossible. "He went home early... 4pm." was all she could come up with. Feeling more than a little angry at herself, she turned back to see what Frank was doing, only to see him on his way back over to them. With adept speed, Ayesha got back to Sarah's record on the computer screen. Charlotte instantly knew the cause for this, and switched back into sweetness and smiles mode ready to talk to Frank.

"Many thanks Mr Drashler." Standing back up to her normal height, Charlotte's eyes are taken again by the sheer amount of snooker paraphernalia around Frank's office. "Do you play?"

"I have been known."

"I haven't had a game in ages. Not since I came back up here"

"You'll have to get your name down quickly to play me... there's a queue."

Charlotte smiled at the snooker-related pun. And then it hit her. *'Wait a minute'*, she thought, *'is he flirting with me?'*

It had been a long time since she'd remotely considered even something as harmless as flirting - let alone doing anything like going on a date. She felt somehow it would be wrong, so soon after her partner's death. And yet that was a year ago, and she'd found herself almost avoiding any such thoughts even now. It wasn't like she didn't socialise - Charlotte was often the life and soul of the party - but taking anything that might happen further hadn't been on her radar.

And, to be honest, she missed it. She was a natural flirt - and she enjoyed it. So why had she closed off a part of her personality? God, it was times like this she'd prefer not to be a deep thinker. She decided she needed to have further thoughts on the matter - but possibly not in the middle of the working day. Must be professional.

"If you can supply us with the CCTV footage as soon as possible please? That would be most helpful."

Charlotte passed Frank her business card - which he looked at in intense detail, before looking back at her and with a slight doff of the head replied "Of course."

Charlotte smiled sweetly to Frank.

* * *

Ayesha didn't really understand why Charlotte was leaving the Tempto Digital building at a pace only slightly below running, but she assumed it was because they needed to "pop back home to get that frozen dog food in m'freezer." as she said upon leaving Frank's office.

Doubling her steps, she caught up Charlotte, who clocked her in the corner of her eye. "So we're no closer to establishing when Sarah went missing." Charlotte said, avoiding eye contact in case Ayesha saw she was blushing.

"We know her key card swiped her out at 6pm,

Ma'am..."

"Yes, but that only proves her card left the building."

"You think someone took her card and swiped her out?" Ayesha asked quizzically.

Charlotte stopped abruptly, causing Ayesha to almost walk past her before she too stopped. "Well, we got in and out of that building without a visitor's card. Security clearly isn't *that* tight. And without anyone having positively seen her, it's a possibility."

Realising she still felt a little flushed, Charlotte avoided looking at Ayesha again, and power walked to her car.

"Perhaps their CCTV will come up with something?" Ayesha half-shouted as she tried to keep up.

"Perhaps."

Charlotte had already reached the car and unlocked by the time Ayesha caught up. Charlotte hadn't got in immediately, but instead, she stood next to the driver's door in a pondering mood. Ayesha adopted a similar stance on her side. She looked at Charlotte across the roof of the Volvo - which for a lady of her petite height was just about possible in her heeled shoes.

After what seemed like minutes, Charlotte finally spoke. "I want you to check ANPR for the area around here, and all possible routes between here and Sarah's house. At the moment, we've no idea when she went missing. Might give us something to work on."

"Ma'am."

"And get the Tech Team to record or screenshot or

whatever a sample area of one of these mapping app. See if any locations go missing in the next couple of days, and if so, whether there's any pattern to them."

"Ma'am."

Charlotte nodded to this. Ayesha wasn't sure whether this was to acknowledge her own affirmation of the requests, or whether it was to recognise Charlotte's own cleverness. She decided it was probably a bit of both, and climbed into the car at the same time as her boss.

* * *

The thought of seeing where Charlotte lived interested Ayesha. She had a mental image that a small cottage in the middle of the countryside would be a great fit for her - especially one with lots of land for the dog she now knew she had to roam free.

But from what she'd seen of Doncaster so far, that image didn't look to fit with the landscapes available. To be fair, she'd been pleasantly surprised with the parts of the town she'd seen as far. She corrected herself - the parts of the *borough*. Charlotte had just pointed out Doncaster was both the name of the town; the town centre bit, AND the name of the wider borough - and that she lived in Sprotbrough - which was a village to the north west of the town centre.

Sprotbrough. Right. Although Charlotte didn't pronounce it like that; as it was written. Charlotte's version was more like 'Spro'ber' - and Ayesha found herself saying Charlotte's way over and over in her head. After all, she'd need to get used to the local ways in order to feel a part of the community.

The closer the car got towards her house, the more Charlotte felt more like herself. She'd been locked in her own thoughts ever since they left Tempto Digital's building. Sure, she'd been chatting to Ayesha along the way - explaining something about Doncaster's structure - but not even she was paying any attention to herself. She'd been far more preoccupied trying to work out what happened in Frank Drashler's office. The problem was, the more she thought about it, the more upset she got. Why did it happen today - of all days? The feelings of guilt threatened to overwhelm her.

"That looks a nice pub." Ayesha said - possibly trying a conversational handbrake turn.

Charlotte took the bait. "My local. Named after the book, you know."

"The Ivanhoe? Never heard of it."

Charlotte shook her head. "By Sir Walter Scott? It was partly set all around here."

"Oh." was the only reply to come back.

Charlotte stopped, and indicated to turn right into a driveway of a house that Ayesha not unwisely assumed must be hers, hidden away from view by a tall dark green hedgerow growing from behind a shoulder-high rather ornate brick wall. She had to hold back slightly to allow a fair amount of traffic from the other direction to pass, which was made more difficult by a large burnt orange coloured minibus-style taxi parked as if it was picking someone up from Charlotte's house.

Eventually the traffic subsided, allowing Charlotte to turn onto the driveway. The herringbone patterned block paving driveway went right up to the house, then continued right in front of it too, in a flipped over 'L' shape. Charlotte was in a hurry and so simply drove straight on and parked; the car looking straight at a bay window.

"Not be long." Charlotte said, as she grabbed the bag-for-life she'd put all the dog food into, unlocked the red front door and went inside.

This gave Ayesha a moment to look at her house from the window of the car. At first, she was a little surprised because it was big; for some reason she'd thought living on her own, Charlotte would have a small house, but this one was detached with a two-storey extension too. This made what would have been the protruding end section of the original house into a middle feature - together with the full height bay windows - with the newer extended section to the left.

And then it hit her. Perhaps she *didn't* live on her own? All Ayesha knew was she wasn't married - no rings and she had the same last name as she did in Camden - but she could well be living with someone.

It was at that precise moment that she saw through the bay window Charlotte walk into a room... and then another figure rose into view; standing up after being sitting down on a sofa, she presumed. She'd expected the figure to be a man, but it was clear it was a female; not as tall as Charlotte - possibly the same height as herself - and slightly on the larger side, not that Ayesha was judging. The two ladies stood opposite each other for a while, and watching Charlotte's expressive hand gestures showed she was doing most of the talking. Then the other lady talked for a short while.

And then they hugged. At first it looked like a hug of support, but as it continued past the point Ayesha had expected it should, she thought it had actually started to turn into something different. When the embrace ended, the two moved away from each other, but still holding each other's hand. Then Charlotte leaned in to give the lady a long kiss on her forehead - which was easy given Charlotte's height. But when the kiss ended, Charlotte rested her head on the lady's head and gave her another hug.

From the car, there was only one possible explanation.

'Oh my word!' Ayesha thought. "They're a couple!"

Chapter 4

The car's satnav - powered by Ayesha's phone - told them to turn off the road very shortly. A row of semi-detached houses lined the right hand side, with decent-sized front gardens pushing them back from the road. On the left, a wall built of stone rose from the ground to around shoulder height, with ornate black wrought iron fencing on the top. Behind that, a succession of tall conifers far exceeding the height of the fencing ensured the privacy of anyone living inside.

'Turn left now' prompted the satnav, and Charlotte duly manoeuvred through a gated entrance down a long tree-lined driveway, maintained to a higher standard than more public roads these days. It wasn't the longest in Europe - that honour belonged to the limetree driveway of Clumber Park, just down the A1 from here - but it certainly would be up there on the list. Past the trees, either side was grassed and looked pristine. Charlotte thought if it was a National Trust place, they'd be a 'Please do not walk on the grass' sign.

The driveway eventually swept around in front of the house to join back onto itself, to allow horse-drawn carriages in days gone by to drop off their passengers without having to turn around. Charlotte followed in the hoof-prints of those travellers and parked right in front of the house.

Charlotte got out, and looked at the various original outbuildings and stables to the left hand side as she walked around the back of her car to lean on the passenger side. The large triple garage on the right was unmistakably not original, but had been built sympathetically to blend in with the rest of the buildings.

The house itself was an imposing Victorian double fronted detached home built in the mid 1860's. The bright limestone finish had been recently cleaned and looked stunning in the afternoon sunshine. The centrally positioned front door, which was protected from the elements by a stone porchway held up by gothic-style columns, had four large sash windows on either side.

The house, the stables, the garage, all had a grandiose feel to them, and the smell of opulence pervaded the air. As did the faint smell of horses coming from the stables.

Ayesha finished off on her phone, climbed out, and lent on the car next to Charlotte.

“We’re in the wrong business.” Charlotte said. “I didn't realise there was so much money in maps!”

A lady emerged from the stables on the left and walked across towards the visitors. “Not maps... *Apps*. *Apps* and *data*. That's where the real money is these days.” she chipped in, winking as she finished off the sentence. Charlotte and Ayesha turned to see the lady talking.

She was in her late fifties, tall, with shoulder-length brown hair, which complimented the drippingly expensive light blue three-piece pantsuit. Carrying a black riding helmet, she was clearly confident; her walk suggested to Charlotte she was bordering on arrogance, and there was an air she knew what she wanted and probably wouldn't let anyone stand in her way of getting it.

“You see this place? Built on fortunes of coal. Now, in the 21st century, I'm mining data, and it's reaping rich rewards.” The mention of ‘rewards’ made the lady very animated indeed; raising her eyebrows and dilating her pupils to extenuate the point.. She saw the two in front of her were on the back foot, and she liked that. She liked often keeping people on the back foot. Charlotte and Ayesha waited for an introduction. And they waited a little more. A wry smile appeared on the lady’s face. The back foot.

Charm personified, the lady eventually offered “Amber Remington. Pleased to meet you.” The tone of her words made Charlotte wonder if she understood the same definition as her of the word ‘pleased’. Her mouth moving just as much as her make-up would allow.

Charlotte smiled, giving the lady the benefit of the doubt. “DCI Charlotte Walker; DC Ayesha Stoker.” She offered a hand to shake.

“You're here to investigate the disappearance of Sarah Knight?” Amber asked, rhetorically. She looked at Charlotte’s hand, hanging in the air, and deliberately ignored it. That was all a bit beneath Amber. She turned on her high heels, making a scraping sound in the gravel, and headed into the house in a trot. “Please come on in.”

Charlotte slowly withdrew her hand and looked across at Ayesha, pulling a face to say ‘that was a bit rude.’ Ayesha looked back in agreement. Charlotte then gestured with her hand to Ayesha as if to say 'after you'. Ayesha doffed her head in acknowledgment, and they headed inside in single file. A pretty nice working relationship was developing.

Once inside, the two detectives were instantly lost. Amber had trotted off so quickly that she was nowhere to be seen. Charlotte looked into the room on the left; it was a living room - a large living room, without anyone in it. Ayesha looked in the room to the right; no-one.

It took them six rooms to eventually find Amber - in a room which was clearly her office. "Oh you found me at last!" she proclaimed, with a wry smile on her face. She was sitting behind a large oak desk at the far side of the room. Charlotte entered first, her eyes soaking up the scene.

The one word you'd probably use to describe Amber's office was large. Everything about it was large; from the desk to the monitor of the computer; from the two chandeliers to the Egyptian rug on the floor. Lots of wooden panelling and paintings make the décor in keeping with the country house this place one was. The only thing which really stood out were the numerous Latin quotes peppered on the walls of the room.

"Please, detectives, have a seat." said Amber, pointing towards a large brown leather sofa that seemed to be both too far away from Amber's desk and too low down. Ayesha sat down first, and sank further down than she expected. Charlotte thought she saw another wry smile appear on Amber's lips, as if she enjoyed the spectacle of her guests being a lot lower down than her. Charlotte was determined not to do the same, and lowered herself on the sofa with intense precision. She didn't get to see Amber's reaction to this, as the lady of the house turned away suddenly, her attention moved to her well-stocked drinks cabinet.

"Can I offer either of you a drink?"

"Thank you. No, we're on duty." replied Charlotte.

"Are you sure? It's a ten year old Glengoyne Whisky..." she said, to which Charlotte thought probably sounded very impressive if you knew anything about whiskeys.

When she was certain there were no more takers, Amber returned to the seat at her mahogany desk, and slowly sat back down.

Charlotte opened her questioning. "Mrs Remington..."

"It's *Ms*, actually." Amber interjected. "Since the death of my husband I prefer 'Ms'."

Charlotte took this on board. "*Ms* Remington, what can you tell us about Mrs Knight?"

Amber held up the hand not holding the glass and said "I can't help you much there, I'm afraid, Inspector. She was one of our brightest programmers. Been with the company for a long time I understand. But I hardly knew her." She took a rather long sip of her drink, and looked at the two of them over it.

"Did you ever have any close dealings with Mrs Knight?"

"No, as I said, Inspector, I hardly knew her."

Charlotte was beginning to be less than impressed by this stonewall. "But you knew her enough to not want her looking into the issues with the base map, I take it?"

Amber placed the glass fastidiously on a coaster, and allowed her fingers to linger around the rim, playing with it and playing for time. Amber hoped it would deflect their attention from the look of slight surprise she had in knowing they already were aware of the base map. It half worked; It might have caught Ayesha's attention, but Charlotte caught the look..

"Well, that was nothing personal…" Amber replied, in a low, almost growl.

"Oh? Seems to me it was completely personal. If it wasn't, why else wouldn't you want your best person on that project? A person who is renowned for finding stuff out?" Charlotte's eyes gleamed at her good point.

Amber glared at Charlotte, and was determined not to give anything away. "She just wasn't the right person for that role."

Charlotte nodded her head slightly in acknowledgement of the reply. Watching Amber take another long sip of her drink, Charlotte indicated for Ayesha to have a go with a question.

Ayesha composed herself and asked, "Do you know of anyone who might want to hurt Mrs Knight? Business rivals perhaps?"

"We don't have rivals, Inspector." came the reply, laced with arrogance and Condescension. Charlotte noticed the deflated look on Ayesha's face as Amber cut a strip off her, and suddenly became all protective. "And as I've said, I…" Amber continued - only to have her predictable response of "hardly knew her." said at the same by Charlotte. *'Take that!'* Charlotte thought.

Amber glared at Charlotte, as the detective decided to have a walk around the room. The numerous Latin quotes around the room caught Charlotte's eye, and she decided to change tack. Without turning away from one of them, she asked, "Are you a bit of a scholar Ms Remington?"

"Mmmm? Oh the quotes?" she tried to sound nonchalant. "I studied Latin at Oxford."

Ayesha raised an eyebrow, which didn't go unnoticed by Amber. Charlotte, however, wasn't as impressed as Amber had hoped by that revelation. "Ahh..." came the response.

Amber tried to brush off her disappointment at not getting the surprised reaction she'd hoped for from the senior detective. "Motivational. Helps me focus on the prize."

She looked around the room, and pointed to one quote above the old fireplace.

Audentes fortuna iuvat

"'Fortune favours the bold.'" she translated. Then, she pointed at the one Charlotte had been studying all this time.

Faber est suae quisque fortunae

"That one is my motto - 'Every man is the artisan of his own fortune.' Or, in my case, every *woman*, of course."

Ayesha decided she would pick one. "And that one?"

she asked, pointing in the direction.

Draco Dormiens Nunquam Titillandus

Amber smiled deliciously. "'Never tickle a sleeping dragon'"

“Ehhh?”

Charlotte walked behind the sofa Ayesha was steadily sinking into and whispered to her ear. “Harry Potter.” to which Ayesha’s face had to look of someone who had been duped. Turning to Amber, Charlotte enquired “‘The Sorcerer's Stone’?”

Amber raised her eyebrows. Understanding Latin AND knows Harry Potter. “Very good Inspector.” Charlotte took the compliment.

As a fully-paid up member of technological revolution - the one Charlotte had tried desperately to avoid - Ayesha had suddenly realised her phone had been remarkably quiet of late; no messages, no Twitter notifications, nothing. She pulled her phone out of her suit pocket as discreetly as she could... but not much got past Amber. “There's no reception in this room, young lady. Old building; stops the signal. Only the rooms on the left side of the house upstairs get a mobile signal.” Ayesha took note, and put her phone away.

Charlotte wanted to get back on track. “Are you originally from around here, Ms Remington?”

“I suppose you could say that. My father was in the RAF and was posted to RAF Finningley when I was born. But we moved around a lot when I was growing up, eventually settling at Brize Norton as he got higher up the force.”

Charlotte walked slowly around the room, looking more closely at the various Latin quotes. She indicated to the quote *'In absentia lucis, Tenebrae vincunt.'* "So are you the light shining through the darkness, Ms Remington?"

A wry smile crossed Amber's face. "I like to think so, Inspector."

"Would everybody agree? Would Mrs Knight?"

"I'm sure Mrs Knight appreciated the opportunities I brought her way. She certainly appreciated the salary." replied Amber, rather abruptly. This was met by a steely smile from Charlotte.

Ayesha definitely felt a little out of the loop with her extremely limited knowledge of any Latin. She leaned back as Charlotte walked behind the sofa again and whispered "What does that mean?"

"In the absence of light, darkness prevails." Charlotte whispered back.

"Ah."

Charlotte's attention returned to Amber. "So given how you hardly knew Mrs Knight, you wouldn't have met her in the last week or two, I guess?"

The question stopped Amber for a moment, and she found herself struggling to maintain the act that she intended to pause right there and then. "No, no, I hardly get involved in the day-to-day workings of the company. I leave that to others."

"Not even for something as crucial as missing data on the all-important base map?"

"No, again, Inspector, that's the responsibility of Kelvin Thomas, I believe."

If you knew Charlotte, you'd have known the smile she gave Amber was her *'I know you are telling porkies'* smile. Amber didn't know Charlotte, but the smile started to unnerve her a bit. Amber decided that her best course of action would be to call time on this interview. "Is that all, Inspector? It's just I've a lot to do, and I did give you my time at a moment's notice..."

"Yes. Yes, that's all, for now Ms Remington. And thank you for your precious time. We can show ourselves out." Charlotte said as Ayesha struggled to lift herself out from the clutches of the sofa.

As the duo made their way out of Amber's office, Charlotte turned back around the door and asked, "Do you know what my motto would be, Ms Remington?" Amber looked interested. "*De omnibus dubitandum.*" came the answer.

Charlotte waited a while to see if Amber could translate... After all, for someone who studied Latin at Oxford, it shouldn't be that much of a challenge. In fact, the clues were there for non-Latin speakers; omni, as in many, all, everything; dubitandum, from where the English doubt is derived from.

But Amber's face is blank with her usual bland smile; just waiting for Charlotte to provide the English translation, which she did with a cheery smile. "'Be suspicious of everything.'"

The point Charlotte was making suddenly became clear, and Amber managed a look of disdainfulness, whilst still maintaining her fixed smile, as Charlotte left.

* * *

Charlotte walked down the stone steps of Amber's country house and onto the gravel drive towards Charlotte's car, where Ayesha was standing waiting. "What do you think Ma'am?"

Charlotte was pensive. "She's definitely not telling us the whole tale there..." she replied, and received agreement from Ayesha..

The DCI screwed her face up in deep thought, as if she was in the running for first place in the annual gurning contest, and then said "I want to know everything possible about *Ms* Amber Remington and Tempto Digital. And what happened to her husband - could be relevant."

"Ma'am." Ayesha acknowledged.

They reached Charlotte's car and again ended up talking across the roof. "So did you study Latin then, Ma'am?" asked Ayesha.

Charlotte was rubbing her forehead, trying to get the various pieces of this jigsaw into some kind of order. It took a few seconds for Ayesha's question to filter through. "Good god no! I had a boyfriend at Uni who was studying it."

"I bet that was fun!" replied Ayesha with more than a splattering of irony, and slight disappointment at hearing 'boyfriend'.

“Hey! You haven't lived until you've received dirty texts in Latin!” Charlotte exclaimed, and climbed into the car, leaving Ayesha smiling and raising an eyebrow in surprise; she didn't expect that!

Just at that moment, Ayesha’s phone buzzed, and she checked what it was.

“Come on…” Charlotte said impatiently.

“Ma'am? Uniform have found Sarah's car.”

“Outstanding!” beamed Charlotte.

Chapter 5

Charlotte had been gone for around five minutes in the Jet garage, and Ayesha had started to wonder whether she'd need a search party to look for her. She'd only gone in to pay for the petrol and to get a sandwich, as she said she was hungry. Charlotte had asked her whether she wanted anything, but she politely said no. But as she was sitting waiting, she rather regretted that politeness.

The windows of the shop were mainly covered with writing, graphics and logos, so it wasn't easy to see if she was even in the queue to pay yet. Ayesha decided to check her phone for information about where they needed to go. She knew they needed to be in Thorne, which was where apparently they were on the outskirts of now - but she needed to know where exactly the industrial estate was.

Suddenly, Charlotte barged into the car, carrying not just a sandwich, but a range of chocolate bars, several packets of different crisp flavours and a few bottles of drink. As she sat on her seat, the collection of goodies fell out of her folded arms into Ayesha's lap.

"Sorry about that. Forget to take a bag in. Listen, I know you said you didn't want anything, but I figured you haven't had 'owt today, so take your pick."

"Thank you, Ma'am" Ayesha said, slightly touched and gathering everything together tightly as she knew the inevitable speedy departure was imminent.

Turning out onto the road called Fieldside, Charlotte asked “Who's on the scene?”

“Uniform, DI Sheldon and DS Price.” she replied, with a slight inflection on the names of the detectives as if to question who they were.

“Ahh, well, time to meet some of your fellow officers then. You’ll need all the info you can get once I’ve gone.”

“Ma’am.”

“DI Sheldon - top bloke; will work his socks off for you; good detective.”

Ayesha duly noted all this. She’d already begun to realise that she trusted Charlotte’s opinion on things; if Charlotte thought well of DI Sheldon, then that’s a good start, she thought.

“DS Price.” continued Charlotte. “Well, my Mum always said if you can't think of anything nice to say, don't say anything... so....” and then Charlotte shut up.

They passed underneath a railway bridge and Ayesha waited for Charlotte to continue. She thought that Charlotte was perhaps pausing for comedic effect and any second now would continue her views on DS Price. But she didn’t. She actually *had* stopped talking.

“And…” prompted Ayesha.

“I've nothing nice to say, so I've shut up!”, and with that, she stopped talking again. By now, Ayesha was so full of anticipation for the information she looked like she would burst. “Ok.” Charlotte relented. “All I will say is I think he's got a problem with confident women; you have to check over everything he does; and he smells of very bad B O... “

Right. Ayesha felt informed now.

Then Charlotte offered a follow up. “Actually, I think he thinks that all women are lesbians. Perhaps that’s what his psyche has constructed to explain why he’s never had a long term relationship…” Charlotte surmised, ever the psychologist.

Ayesha smiled at this. After what she’d just discover watching outside Charlotte’s house, he’s probably not all that wrong, she thought.

They pulled up at the traffic lights in the middle of Thorne. Waiting at the red light ready to turn left, Charlotte looked around her car and scowled. “I've been thinking... I'm going to have to get another car.” she said, almost speaking out aloud.

“Ma'am?”

“Leaving the force. I need a different car. One that reflects who I am. This one is a bit too corporate and too much tech for my liking…”

Ayesha smiled, despite not wanting to think about Charlotte leaving. Playfully she continued, “…and has no CD player..?”

Charlotte picked up the playful tone and shouted back, “CD player! Exactly!” She felt now Ayesha understood. The lights changed to green, and Charlotte turned left down Field Road.

She pondered the dilemma of another vehicle some more. “Perhaps I need something completely different. I mean, if I'm going to be changing my life, I need to start with this. Something individual; something that says who I am. And... something... “

Charlotte looked across to Ayesha. "...with a CD player!" they exclaimed at the same time, looking across at each other. They both relish the moment before Charlotte added, "Besides, these are all ten-a-penny now..."

"Oh I don't know about that Ma'am..." Ayesha replied, as they turned into the industrial estate.

Charlotte drove past the various units, home to the standard selection of independent garages, tyre fitters and body repairers, and went to the far end, pulling in her car to park on the right next to two identical Volvo cars. One, the metallic Osmium Grey coloured machine, belonged to DI Sheldon; the other clearly belonged to South Yorkshire Police, as it was a marked battenberg-style police car with "South Yorkshire Police" all over it. Charlotte and Ayesha got out of Charlotte's Volvo, and immediately Charlotte indicated with an outstretched hand and upright palm over the top of her car to the other Volvos. "See?" she said, playfully victorious to Ayesha, who acknowledged the fact with a wry smile.

Ayesha recognised one of the detectives as the blond haired chap who knocked on Charlotte's office door this morning. He looked up from finishing something on his iPad and acknowledged Charlotte's arrival with his customary "Gov.".

Charlotte introduced the newest member of the team to the lads. "Ayesha, this is DI Dean Sheldon..."

DI Dean Sheldon was tall, smart, well-spoken and respectful. She could see all the attributes Charlotte mentioned in the car fitting him perfectly. What Charlotte didn't mention was he was extremely attractive. She looked at him and saw the most wondrous green eyes, which, with his elegant bearing made for a pretty good package. If she was that way inclined, she could have been very interested. She wondered why Charlotte hadn't mentioned his looks - after all, some people just *are* attractive; that's a fact. But then she remembered the lady Charlotte embraced at her house and realised that was probably why.

"...and DS Vincent Price." Charlotte continued, trying to hide a smile.

DC Price equally tried to hide his annoyance. *'She'd only gone and done it again'*, he thought. "It's *Vernon*, Ma'am!"

Charlotte replied, with just enough sincerity for it not to creep into sarcasm, "Oh yes, You know, you'd think I'd remember after all these years..." Knowing full well it had been less than a year she'd been back in South Yorkshire.

DS Vernon Price was, in many ways, the antithesis of Dean Sheldon. He was in his late fifties, overweight, clearly very old school, and although he tried to make an effort to be tidy, he never quite achieved it - the tweed suit not helping him in that regard. The scowl he wore seemed to permanently etched onto his heavy-jowled face. And Charlotte was right; the way he looked Ayesha up and down before returning to his partly-read Daily Mail certainly suggested he would rather women not be in the police.

Ayesha shook both their hands, whilst managing to throw a knowing smile at Charlotte. "Ayesha." she said to the two men, filling in her first name, which

Charlotte didn't say in her introduction.

"So who found it?" asked Charlotte.

"These two." DI Stoker said, head bowed toward the two uniformed officers.

"Excellent work, ladies. How did you find out about it?"

The fair haired officer spoke up. "My partner works at one of the industrial units here, " she said, pointing to the right one with her right hand. "He thought he looked suspicious and phoned me up."

"That's what I call links with the community!" Charlotte replied, and then leaning into the officer asked with a straight face, "Do you get discounts on your servicing?"

The officer noticed the glint in Charlotte's eye, and blushed. Not wishing to embarrass her, she said "Good job." and then turned back to the car.

DS Vernon Price walked over to the bonnet of Sarah's car. Touching it with an open hand, he proclaimed confidently, "Completely cold. Must have been here a long time."

Almost without thinking, and certainly without due reverence to her superior, Ayesha blurted out "Err, it's an electric car, Sir..."

Vernon's confident look melted away. He looked down at the registration plate and noticed the green shape on the left hand side. Bloody hell... of course it was. How had he missed that? Horror on Vernon's face turned to a glare at Ayesha, as he tried to work out whether the young whippersnapper had any malice in that statement, no matter how correct it was. He decided after a while she hadn't.

Charlotte, however, tried almost half-heartedly to hide her laughter, and had to move away from the car for a short while in order to gather herself to be more professional, and DI Dean Sheldon only just managed to suppress his giggle. *'It wouldn't have been half as funny if DS Price wasn't always so straight-laced and up his own arse'*, thought Charlotte.

The cause of this hullabaloo had walked around the side of Sarah's car to duck down near a tyre. "With an electric car, you have to check the tires..." as she puts a hand on one of them. As it happened, they were cold, and Vernon regained a little bit of face after that discovery.

Composed and professional again, Charlotte took the lead. "Right, let's see if anything in here sheds some light on this whole thing..." She retrieves from her trouser pocket the key fob to Sarah's car Jason gave her earlier and presses the unlock button. The sleeping car jolted suddenly into life with lights and the doors unlocked.

The detectives, now all wearing gloves, went about their search in a particular area of the car. Vernon opened the door on the passenger side, whilst Dean focused on the driver side. Charlotte was studying for any footprints she could see heading away from the car, but the area was a busy place with tyre marks everywhere from vehicles turning around, making it difficult to see anything clearly. Ayesha opened the boot and immediately struck gold.

“Ma'am?” she exclaimed, holding up a laptop in her hands.

Charlotte looked around the open boot door, and replied, “Excellent!”

She was about to go and have a look when Dean shouted.

“Gov?” Dean said, holding up a mobile phone to an onlooking Charlotte. She raised an eyebrow as he checked it out. His face full of disappointment told the full picture. “Dead.”

“Right, that'll give the Tech Team something to do over the weekend. We'll take these back now...” Charlotte said. “Finish off here and get it recovered.” she continued, talking about Sarah’s car and aimed at Dean.

“Gov.” came the reply.

Ayesha brought the laptop and took the mobile phone from Dean over to the now open boot of Charlotte’s car.

“Just a second” said Charlotte, and still with a gloved right hand opened the laptop up and pressed the power button. The power light flashed... as it would do when there’s not enough power in the battery to turn on the computer. “Drained.” she said, thinking out loud.

“Ma’am?”

“Perhaps someone has used this recently who hasn’t had the correct charger to run it on mains?”

“And hasn’t had the correct charger to charge it afterwards.” Ayesha followed up.

Chapter 6

The way back to the station from Thorne was simple, according to the route on the satnav Ayesha had just plotted - back to the traffic lights in the middle of the town, then left on to the M18 and off onto White Rose Way. Except Charlotte had decided not to go that way and instead had opted for 'the scenic route', and took Ayesha though several of the more rural villages in the north of the borough. Through Fishlake, with its historic church dedicated to St Cuthbert; then Braithwaite, Trumfleet and Thorpe in Balne. Eventually they arrived at the urban areas of Arksey, where Charlotte was disappointed the level crossed wasn't down as it usually is, and through Bentley - which she recognised from earlier. Ayesha's mental map of Donny was building, at least on the north side.

Charlotte was deep in thought. Ayesha couldn't tell whether it was case-related, something about her, or something entirely different. But there was an uneasy quiet for the first time since Ayesha had met Charlotte. Good God, was that really only four hours ago, Ayesha thought. Seemed a lot longer; in a good way though. She thought she'd better say something, just in case it was the middle one of her possible reasons that was troubling Charlotte. "I'm sorry if I overstepped the mark back there."

"Eh? What?" Charlotte replied. Her tone wasn't as kurt as the words implied, brought seemingly out of some sort of mind trance - whilst still driving the car, of course.

"When I said that to DS Price"

"No, not at all. He's a pompous arse and deserves to be taken down a peg or two."

Ayesha was reassured, and thought she'd ask a supplementary. "Ma'am, why does DI Sheldon call you Gov?"

"It's his idea of humour. It's because he thinks I'm more of a bloke than the blokes are, so he calls me 'Gov'. It started up as a wind-up, but it's kinda stuck now."

Ayesha smiled.

They'd stopped at the Bentley Road traffic lights just before St Mary's Roundabout, which led on the left to St. George's Bridge and which led in turn to Doncaster town centre. Charlotte was rapping her fingers on the top of the steering wheel in thought.

"Something's not quite right here."

"What's that Ma'am?"

Charlotte frowned. "I don't know... the laptop; the phone... all a bit convenient and easy perhaps? As if we were supposed to find them?"

The traffic lights changed to green, and they headed under the little grey iron railway bridge which straddled through the middle of the roundabout - and which Charlotte noticed needed a lick of paint. Keeping in the left hand lane, marked 'A19 Town Centre' they turned onto the two-laned approach for St George's Bridge and started to climb up. *'Actually, it is rather high'* thought Charlotte, scrolling back to the previous conversation that morning.

The traffic seemed busier than usual, and instead of driving across the bridge at a decent speed, all the vehicles were fairly bunched together and moving steadily. Charlotte's focus was on the traffic, but Ayesha, not having this burden, was starting to notice something happening on the other carriageway.

Like the side of the bridge they were on, the other carriageway - the one heading away from Doncaster town centre - was a two-laned affair with a narrow pavement on the left of their left-hand lane. It was narrow because it didn't need to be wide as pedestrians were not allowed to use the bridge for safety reasons. Ayesha knew this as she'd seen the 'Pedestrians Prohibited' circle road sign a few hundred metres back.

So why, she thought, is there a person walking on that narrow pavement on the other side of the bridge?

By now, they were getting near to be level with the figure, and as Ayesha had a better sight through the traffic, she could see it to be a man. She could see he'd stopped on purpose at a certain point on the bridge, and was looking out away from the traffic - then he looked below.

Warning bells sounded inside Ayesha.

"Ma'am…" she said, urgently.

"Hmm?" Charlotte responded, still focused on the stop-start traffic on their side of the bridge.

Ayesha pointed to the man, just as he started to climb onto the raised concrete side of the bridge at the highest point over the East Coast Main Line.

"Bloody hell!" came Charlotte's reply, as they just passed the man. Charlotte took a brief glance in her rear view mirror and saw the car behind was a good distance away - and so she slammed her brakes on.

The car behind only just realised in time, and the sound of screeching filled the air.

Putting her hazard warning lights on, Charlotte looked over her left shoulder, and then in her driver's door mirror on the right to see if there was a break in the traffic to safely get out. The traffic in the right-hand lane was stopping and starting, just the same as their lane.

Beep Beep Beeeep

Looking back again, she saw the driver of the car behind aggressively sounding his horn, and then gave her some unfavourable hand signals. The beeping soon became a chorus, as the drivers behind all started to vent their frustration at stopping completely.

"Radio it in." Charlotte said urgently to Ayesha. "St George's Bridge." she added, realising her new partner wouldn't know the names of where they were.

There still wasn't a break in the traffic on the lane to the right - especially now as some of the vehicles Charlotte had held up in her lane had started to pull out to go past her.

Charlotte just readied herself to get out of the car, and she'd take it from there.

"Ma'am, shouldn't we wait for trained officers?" asked Ayesha, sensibly.

Charlotte leaned into Ayesha, and said quietly but firmly, "He might be gone by then."

Without hesitation, Charlotte opened her door just enough for her to squeeze out of. She slammed the door shut and rested on the side of the car for a moment to evaluate when there'd be that suitable gap in the traffic coming towards her that she needed to cross over to the middle of the bridge. Charlotte kept looking between the traffic coming towards her and the man on the other side of the bridge - who was still balancing rather precariously on the concrete side edge.

Suddenly, a break in the traffic, and Charlotte ran across her carriageway to the centre concrete reservation. Vaulting that with ease, she waited for a gap in the traffic going out of Doncaster. Here, there were still two lines of traffic in a constant stream heading northwards. Some drivers in the left lane who had noticed the man tried to move across into the right lane, but none had attempted to stop.

The traffic lights on the roundabout to Charlotte's left abruptly halted all the vehicles coming over the bridge, and Charlotte took her opportunity to sprint across the carriageway to reach the small, narrow pavement next to the bridge's edge.

The man was so taken by his own thoughts, he wasn't aware of Charlotte being so close by. Why would he be? Pedestrians aren't allowed on this bridge... it says so with the red circle road sign.

Charlotte knew that to surprise the man at this time could possibly be disastrous. As she walked very steadily towards him, she wondered how she should open. Her concentration was slightly taken by a train passing beneath them. With the speed it was going, it had obviously just stopped at Doncaster station, and was speeding up on its way to York. Ok, it might not have been going 125mph, but she wouldn't like to have been in front of it on the tracks at the speed it *was* doing.

This was what was at stake.

In the car meanwhile, Ayesha had done as she was instructed and called it in. But there's no way she was waiting in the car to do nothing to help. But what could she do? Noticing that traffic had started again to speed past the two people on the bridge, she decided that at the very least she could swing this car around to the other direction and block that left lane.

She climbed over the gear stick and the central console of the car, switched on the ignition - Charlotte had left the keys - and started to drive forwards in the lane the car was blocking. To avoid Charlotte's car, all the traffic going into Doncaster was going into the right hand lane - the lane Ayesha needed to be in to be able to U-turn around the roundabout and come up the other carriageway on the bridge towards Charlotte. Ayesha looked in the rear-view mirror - a constant stream of traffic. She indicated right. No-one was letting her in, and she was almost out of bridge. So, she almost closed her eyes and hoped, as she swerved violently into the right hand. Frantic horns blurted out... but Ayesha was still in one piece.

Charlotte held her position, around twenty metres or so away from the man, who still hadn't spotted her. Then suddenly, she noticed the traffic was missing from the lane to her right. She wasn't complaining at all; it was bloody dangerous walking on a bridge with traffic not designed to be walked on. All the traffic seemed to be in the right hand lane. Turning around she saw her car parked blocking the left lane, with Ayesha standing in front of the car looking very concerned.

It's probably her first jumper, Charlotte thought. Mind you, it wasn't like Charlotte was an old hand in these situations either.

Whilst Charlotte had been preoccupied with the activities on the surroundings, the man had climbed carefully onto the concrete side of the bridge and had swung his legs over the side to sit on the ledge.

He'd got this far.

He looked down. He wasn't afraid of heights, so the ten metre high bridge didn't pose him any problems; and now he was right above the East Coast Main Line. That was his plan.

Charlotte was watching the man carefully, and as he slightly leaned over the edge to check his position was correct over the railway line, she mirrored his gaze, looking to her left and down. Now the man might not have been affected by the ten metre height, but Charlotte definitely was.

A wave of panic suddenly splashed over her and she held out her left hand onto the concrete side to steady herself. She suddenly had flashbacks to the times she'd been in heavy debates about how the irrational fear of heights wasn't vertigo but actually *acrophobia.* Actually, all those occasions seemed to be with men - exercising their god-given right to mansplain little old meek Charlotte. Well, at this moment it was *definitely* acrophobia and it *definitely* didn't seem irrational.

'Actually, there's no issue with keeping my left hand on

this side of the bridge,' she thought, *'I mean, if I don't hold it on, it might fall off... dodgy build this, clearly'* not really adequately justifying to herself her need for a little reassurance as she made her way closer to the man.

Close enough to say, "Hello."

The last thing the man expected was a voice saying 'Hello' to him. He looked around to see the person the voice came from.

"I'm DCI Charlotte Walker, South Yorkshire Police. But my friends call me Lottie. I'm here to listen to you. What's your name?"

"Don't come any closer." the man warned.

Charlotte stopped where she was. "Ok. I'm staying here. What's your name?"

"Alistair Cowal." said the man, his voice full of desperation.

Charlotte took a deep breath. "Hello Alistair. Turned out rather nice now." she said, looking to the sky and contrasting the weather now to when she was standing outside this morning in the horrible rain.

Alistair was slightly taken aback by this, and, "Yes. I suppose." was all he could muster.

'So far so good', thought Charlotte. Need to find out more. "Why are you here Alistair?"

"I can't go on with it anymore."

"Go on with what?"

"Everything."

"Ok."

Charlotte knew she needed to make connections with him. She needed all her observational skills right now. Anything. Something as a clue to help her. Then, she saw Alistair was clutching something tight. She squinted. This is not the time to realise you might need those glasses you never got, she thought. There was something dangling out of his hand. It glinted in the sunlight as he moved his hands, cascading and swaying. It was a chain. Perhaps it was a necklace? Necklace… that's it.

"Alistair... have you just lost someone? Someone very dear?" Charlotte was confident there would be a positive reply.

Alistair looked at Charlotte. My god, how did she know? Perhaps I could talk to her, he thought. "Yes. My wife."

Progress, thought Charlotte. Married. A connection. "I'm really sorry to hear that Alistair. Had you been married long?"

"Two years."

"But you'd been together for a lot longer, right?"

"Yes. Since school." Alistair replied, genuinely surprised at both Charlotte's insight and that at last someone was listening; really listening to him.

"Did you know you were going to lose her?"

"Yes. Cancer."

"I'm sorry."

Alistair sneered at Charlotte. How many times has he heard that? "Yeah, everyone is."

“That's probably because they are.”

Alistair didn’t want to reply. Charlotte took the opportunity for a deep breath. There was silence.

Actually, thought Charlotte, it seemed *too* quiet. She now realised the constant drone of traffic going past them had stopped a while ago. She looked over her right shoulder, and she could just make out the entrance to the bridge at the roundabout had been blocked off by police cars. Then she noticed the traffic had disappeared from the other side, and surmised a similar roadblock had been put in place there too.

Ayesha was still standing by Charlotte’s car, which by now was the only vehicle on the bridge. She looked apprehensive back towards Charlotte.

Another deep breath.

“Well, I've decided I don't want to be here.” Alistair said with quiet conviction. He looked at his watch.

It was nearly time.

A swell of realisation swept over Charlotte. Time. He’d planned it with the railway timetable.

He wasn’t just going to jump, he was going to jump in front of a train.

Jesus, he’s getting ready, thought Charlotte. She turned to her left and looked down towards the station. Squinting, she couldn’t see past the blue span of North Bridge to get a clear view. But a train had just gone northwards a few minutes ago. She knew enough about railways to know there had to be a gap between one service and the next. And there hadn’t been enough for the next train to be coming...

So that meant it was a service heading south - coming on the other line. She turned quickly to look the other way; to see if she could see a train coming towards them - but the concrete edging on the other side of the bridge was too high.

Her mind was racing now. It probably made more sense to use a southbound train. You wouldn't have to decide to go seeing it coming towards you, she concluded.

Charlotte knew she had to get him down safely and fast.

She had to connect to him somehow.

"Alistair, have you got any children?"

"No. All that has been taken away. Not going to happen now. All those plans. The future. Now nothing."

'Bugger, that was a dead end. Think quick.' Charlotte told herself.

Alistair looked at his watch again.

It was time.

With sincerity he said "Thank you for trying DCI Charlotte Walker..." as he carefully started to get to his feet and began to stand up on the narrow concrete side, the six railway lines into Doncaster station beneath him.

In the distance to the right, they both heard a train horn sound. Alistair took a deep breath. Charlotte needed to think. How long had she got left? She closed her eyes for a moment to visualise the area. She'd been walking around here only a few months ago, and walked over the railway on a crossing coming from Bentley Ings. If there's a crossing, there would be a 'W' sign to the driver to sound their horn as a warning for people on the crossing. So the train must be between the Arksey level crossing and Fowler Bridge Road.

'Jeez. Can't be much more than a minute away.'

She opened her eyes and looked across at Alistair. Now he was standing up fully on the concrete ledge.

Right at that moment, Charlotte doubted herself. *'What the bloody hell am I doing,'* she thought. *'I'm not trained for this. What on earth made me think I could do this?'*

Her heart pounded heavy in her chest and she could hear the blood pumping in ears. Her breathing had become fast and panicked.

Why hadn't she waited for backup?

The rumble of the oncoming express train started to become noticeable.

All of a sudden, the tension was pierced by a monotone ringing.

It was Charlotte's phone. But it wasn't a phone call; it was an alarm.

14:20.

It was the alarm to remind Charlotte her boyfriend died exactly a year ago… at 14:20.

An astonishing amount of emotion unexpectedly bombarded Charlotte, and within an instant threatened to overwhelm her.

But it was the jolt Charlotte needed. Of course she could do this. Especially on this day.

No-one is dying on *this* day; at *this* time.

Right. Connections. If he doesn't have kids, go the other way. Perhaps he's still got parents. Yes, that's it. Parents.

"Alistair... what about your parents? What about your Mum and Dad? What about them?" Charlotte yelled.

The train was getting nearer and nearer.

Alistair paused for a moment. "Mum and Dad?"

A flicker. Some hope. *'Carry on Charlotte,'* she thought, *'you might have it here.'*

"YES. What about them when you are not here? They've just lost a daughter-in-law. Don't make them have to lose a son too." she shouted as the train went under the bridge. She closed her eyes tight; if he was going, she didn't want to see it.

The mention of his Mum and Dad and the thought of how they'd be afterwards stopped Alistair. As the train sped underneath him, he started to cry.

Charlotte had heard the sound of an express train fading into the distance many times, but not under these circumstances and not with her eyes closed. She wondered whether she'd done enough to stop Alistair.

There was only one way to find out. She slowly opened her eyes.

He was still standing on the concrete edge of the bridge.

The relief she felt was so palpable, she could touch it in front of her.

She calmed her breathing and started to think straight again. Because it wasn't over yet... he was still standing on the concrete edge.

"How about sitting down again, Alistair? Take the weight off your feet." Charlotte said lightly.

He turned to look at her, agreed and carefully sat back down again on the cold concrete.

For a moment, there was an uneasy stand-off; neither Alistair nor Charlotte moved. Not one inch.

Then Alistair spoke. "Why would they want me? I've just let everyone down."

"Who have you let down?"

"I let her down." he cried, turning to look at Charlotte. "I wasn't there with her when she went. I couldn't cope. The hospital phoned to say she was going, and I didn't go. She died and I wasn't there." Alistair turned from Charlotte to look down at the ground.

Charlotte paused. Her breathing was getting shorter now. It was all getting a little close to home for her now. "I know what you mean." she said slowly and quietly.

Alistair turned. This was one pacifying statement too many. "YOU DON'T! YOU DON'T KNOW HOW THAT FEELS!" he screamed at Charlotte, angrily.

For a moment, Charlotte was frozen. Unable to say or do anything as she took in what had been said to her. She stared at him with a steely gaze which had him transfixed, as she told herself to take slow, deliberate breaths. Trying not to shout back, she replied "Oh I do."

Her tone was one of calm - well, trying to keep calm - but also of determination to make the point. Something about her manner led Alistair to realise he might have gone a bit far. His body softened as he looked down on the floor for a while to hide from Charlotte's piercing gaze. Perhaps it was his turn to listen.

Charlotte gathered her thoughts and emotions.

"I lost my boyfriend a year ago today."

"I'm sorry."

"Yeah." Charlotte replied tersely, with the follow on line 'it's what they all say' in her head.

Alistair realised it was his line thrown back at him. It was a fair point. "What happened?"

Jeez. This wasn't supposed to happen, thought Charlotte. Today of all days. But here it comes....

Charlotte took a deep breath and started. "There was a ram-raid on an ATM and I caught two of the men but the other two got away. They went to shoot some passers-by and stood in the way; I got shot." She pointed to her left shoulder. She said it all in a very matter-of-fact, calm way. She couldn't let the emotions of the memories get the better of her now.

Bloody hell... this wasn't what Alistair had been expecting. After a moment to let this sink in, he turned more to the left, to look at Charlotte, shifting his body away from the edge of the ledge.

Professional Charlotte probably noticed this, but emotional Charlotte was in charge now, and this subtle move mostly was missed.

"So I was awarded the George Cross." she said, incredulous at the mere notion. "Got an invite to Buckingham Palace. My boyfriend and I took a few days off our work and we went - met her Maj - lovely day."

Alistair smiled at the mental picture.

Taking another deep breath, she continued. "We were supposed to have the day after off too; celebrate and all that. But there was a blag going off and I'm a copper; I couldn't miss it." Tears started to stream down Charlotte's face. "That's when someone ram-raided our house. Took out the whole front; collapsed. Car was in the living room. And so was Richard. Massive injuries. Died minutes later before I could get there. At 14:20."

The significance of the time just struck Alistair like a lightning bolt. Charlotte couldn't hold back her tears any more. "So.. If I hadn't gone to work that day, we'd have been out celebrating and he'd still be alive. So it's my fault he's dead."

"You can't blame yourself Lottie."

"I can and I do." Charlotte said firmly. "Every hour of every day."

Alistair nodded. He understood. He understood the feeling of helplessness; of thinking you should have been there to do something, no matter that there was nothing you could have done; of self-loathing.

Charlotte's gaze was fixed on something, but she couldn't make out what she was even looking at. It wasn't in focus. She was breathing slowly on purpose again. She swallowed as her body became motionless. Deep lines of thought had appeared on her forehead, and she squinted, as if she was having difficulty seeing.

Something had snapped in Charlotte.

Eventually, she moved. "You know what? You might have the best answer here."

"What do you mean?" came Alistair's reply, a wonderment creeping into his voice.

"The answer to the pain; the guilt." Charlotte said, cold and calculated.

"What?"

Charlotte slowly turned to Alistair. "How about we do it together?"

She walked towards him, and before he knew what was happening, Charlotte had climbed on the ledge and was sitting next to him, legs dangling off the side of the high bridge. Somehow she was fighting every fibre of her being screaming out at her.

"What are you doing?" Alistair exclaimed.

"I see this is the best way."

Alistair's mind was in a spin. He'd come here to end his own life; he was prepared for that. Then he decided not to. Then someone he'd only just met decided *they* were going to do it as well. This was too much.

"No. NO! You can't."

"Why not?"

Talking someone down from doing the very thing

he was going to do wasn't on Alistair's 'to do' list for today. "What about all the people who love you?"

"Probably won't be bothered I'm gone. Like the people that love you. Eh? None of them will care."

"No... no.. They will. You'll be missed. I can tell you will be."

"Does it matter?" Charlotte said coldly.

"I don't want to hurt anyone." Alistair replied emphatically.

Ignoring him, she asked, "Are we doing this?"

Alistair took a moment to respond, and said, "No. no. My wife wouldn't have wanted this."

With that, he slowly swung his legs around onto the bridge side, and stepped gingerly onto the pavement. Charlotte had made a difference.

But Charlotte didn't move.

"Lottie?" Alistair said, with an uncertain tone in his voice.

Charlotte didn't hear him. She was fixed on the edge of the ledge. All of a sudden, her very rational fear of heights started to slowly reappear, taking her back from whatever had gripped her before. Looking down for one last time, she realised how bloody high it was, and she too swung her legs around to put her feet firmly and finally on the bridge.

Alistair and Charlotte exchange a look only two people who had experienced something intense together could - and then hugged each other.

It was over.

The support network that has been keeping its distance up to now, suddenly moved in. Two female officers took Alistair away, Ayesha rushed up to Charlotte, with Sharon following in at a more measured, senior-officer pace.

“Are you ok Ma'am?” Ayesha shouted as the emotions of the situation became too much and she gave a surprised Charlotte a hug.

“Mmm.” came the reply, from deep inside the hug.

Ayesha realised she might have overstepped the mark, and released Charlotte from her grip. She looked with trepidation to see Charlotte’s reaction, but if she had minded, she didn’t show it. Instead she had a fixed, glazed expression on her face.

“That was incredible. I didn't know you had training.”

“Err, Psychology at uni. Good to know I still know some of it.”

“And they way you got up with him to win his trust.”

“Yes...” Charlotte replied, trying to convince herself as much as agreeing with Ayesha. She looked across to Sharon, who clearly understood more about what almost happened than Ayesha did, and she threw back a look of worry with a mix of disapproval.

Eventually, Sharon walked over to Charlotte and Ayesha. “You should have waited. That's the protocol.” she said sternly to Charlotte, whilst also throwing a glance over at Ayesha.

"He'd be gone by now." Charlotte fired back, moving in front of Ayesha as if to protect her. "And thank you, I'm ok, you know."

Sharon looked around Charlotte to address the person behind her. "Ayesha - take DCI Walker home." Leaning into Charlotte's left ear, she whispered "We'll talk on Monday."

* * *

There was an uneasy quiet in the car on the way back to Charlotte's house. Part of it was the responsibility of Ayesha, who was desperately concentrating on driving the Volvo back in one piece when she wasn't familiar with it at all; and part of it was the responsibility of Charlotte.

The admonished detective was staring out of the passenger window, rather like a petulant child.

Every so often, Ayesha looked across at her passenger when it was safe to do so, and considered starting a conversation, but she wasn't sure the conversation would be welcome. She looked in the rear view mirror and wasn't surprised to see the marked patrol car still following them.

The silence in the car was only broken by the robotic voice of Google Maps informing Ayesha on the route back to Charlotte's house. She was good with directions and remembered most journeys, but the way then had come earlier was different to this.

Eventually, Ayesha thought she had to break this

silence. “Ma'am?” Charlotte turned to listen. “I didn’t know about today. I only heard a bit of it on the bridge.” she ventured.

Charlotte took a deep breath. “My partner died a year ago today. And yes. *That's* why I'm leaving.”

“I understand.”

Charlotte half smiled at Ayesha - and then returned to the petulant child looking out of the passenger window.

* * *

As they got closer to Charlotte’s house, Ayesha recognised the area, and turned off the unforgiving voice of Google Maps - who had done nothing to help the atmosphere inside the car. Turning into Charlotte’s driveway, she noticed the large minibus was still parked on the road outside the house. *‘Charlotte’s partner must still be here.’* she thought. That was good - at least there’d be someone who loves Charlotte looking after her.

The patrol car parked across the entrance to Charlotte's driveway on the road and behind the minibus. The two uniformed officers emerged from their car and walked down the drive to meet Ayesha, who was standing waiting for Charlotte to get out of her car.

Inside the house, the lady entered their line of sight through the bay window, and once she’d clocked the scene outside disappeared to unlock the front door and emerged from the house.

Charlotte had only just managed to open the car door, when Ayesha turned to meet the gaze of the lady. She was right; she was about her height, in her late fifties and wore a loose fitting baby pink outdoor t-shirt and black walking trousers - both of which were perfectly chosen around her larger frame and ample bosom. She had one of those faces which looked like its natural state was smiling; the lines on her eyes and cheekbones showed that. But right now, her face was full of shock and worry as she realised Charlotte was in the passenger seat of her own car, and looked like she couldn't get out.

"Lottie?!! What's a matter? What's happened?" the lady shouted.

Climbing slowly out of the car, Charlotte tried to offer reassurance. "It's ok Tones, I'm fine." Charlotte said, despite clearly not being at all. The lady looked to any of the other three for some sort of explanation. The uniformed officers seemed to bat away her looks, and so it's left to Ayesha to explain.

"DCI Walker talked down a man from St George's Bridge. It was a little too close to home today." Ayesha's voice trailed off towards the end. Maybe she should say more, but really, she doesn't know this lady from Adam. She figured Charlotte must know her fairly well; she *was* her partner for heaven's sake, but it wasn't Ayesha's place to tell her stuff Charlotte might not have wanted her to know.

In the end, this was another example of Ayesha overthinking everything. The lady suddenly realised about the date. Her face dropped. “Oh Christ, no. That's awful? Is he alright?”

By now, Charlotte had got out of the car, but was looking decidedly shaken. The two uniformed officers went over to her to make sure she was alright.

“Yes, thanks to DCI Walker. I'm her new partner, by the way, Ayesha Stoker.”

“Oh, I'm Toni Madden; Charlotte's friend and dog sitter.”

“Dog sitter? I thought...”

Toni raised her eyebrows, and replied “...thought what? I was her Mum?”

“No! I thought; I... saw...” Ayesha was saved the embarrassment of continuing the reply.

Then it clicked with Toni - she'd spotted the embrace earlier because she was in the car! She smiled and let out a giggle. “We’re friends. Good friends.” Toni clarified, and then moved closer to Ayesha, as if to tell her a secret. “And between you and me, Charlotte is already married.”

“She is?”

“To that job of hers!” Toni smiled.

“Ahhh, yes.” Ayesha half-smiled back. Probably true.

“BRONTE, COME!” came the very loud shout from Charlotte, who by now had collected herself enough to join the other two ladies.

A young Border Collie dog bounded out of the house and leapt up to Charlotte’s open arms. It’s a sight Toni had seen many times before, but to Ayesha it was a big surprise. The collie had very traditional black and white markings - exactly like the archetypal sheepdog - and with one of the most waggy tails ever. The dog was clearly pleased to see Charlotte, putting a paw on each shoulder and giving her lots of doggy kisses.

"Hey boy! Nice to see you too!"

It seemed like the cue for Ayesha to go. "Are you going to be alright, Ma'am?"

"Yes, I'll be fine now." she replied, when she could catch her breath between the licks and kisses from the dog in her arms. Realising Ayesha was going, she put Bronte on the floor and shooed him inside the house. Ayesha acknowledged Charlotte, turned and started to walk down the drive, when Charlotte shouted, "Ayesha!?"

Ayesha stopped. That's the first time Charlotte's used her name today! She turned around to see a genuinely grateful Charlotte.

"Thank you." Charlotte said sincerely.

"You're welcome, Ma'am." Ayesha looked both a little touched and embarrassed. After a short while to take in the moment, she turned back and walked up the drive to get in the back seat of the patrol car. Engine running and the uniformed officers already waiting, Ayesha was whisked away.

Toni returned from closing the front door, and entered the living room to find Charlotte sunk into the sofa. The frown on her face topping an otherwise blank expression showed she was clearly troubled by the events of the day. Only Charlotte knew she was worried about more than bridge and the significance of the date.

Slowly Toni perched herself on the edge of the sofa. It wasn't often Toni Madden was lost for words - but this seemed to be one of those occasions. She looked thoughtful across at the friend who'd done so much for her since she came into her life.

"Bad day for it, huh?" she asked eventually, cautiously but caringly.

"Yeah. Not the best of timings."

Just then, Toni's mobile phone buzzed in her trouser pocket. Retrieving it, she looked at the notification and winced slightly. "Yeah. As is this - got a booking."

"Ok."

"Sorry. It's from Bawtry to Leeds Bradford. I'd better go now."

"Ok." came the same reply.

"Listen, are you sure you'll be alright? You could come with me?" It was possible, but Toni wasn't sure in that instant how the client who just booked her would feel about a 'plus one'.

Fortunately for Toni, Charlotte didn't entertain that option, although she did appreciate it. "We'll probably go for a walk; clear my head a bit."

"Ok. I'll see you tomorrow for mantrailing. Half past One?" she reminded Charlotte, knowing time-keeping wasn't one of her strong points. She reached across to pick up the keys to her minibus from the large coffee table next to Charlotte.

"Yeah, thanks Tone." she replied, almost trace-like.

Toni looked again at the young lady sitting in front

of her. She certainly wasn't happy about leaving her in this state, but a booking is a booking, and she knew Charlotte understood that. She walked over to Charlotte and kissed her on her forehead, gave Bronte a goodbye fuss and then left.

The closing of the door left an eerie silence.

It only took a few moments for Charlotte to know she couldn’t sit inside, and so went into the back garden.

‘Keep busy’ she told herself, so she toured the garden picking up the various dog toys Bronte had been playing with, and put them away in the box. That done, she sat down at the patio table, having changed her mind about keeping busy. Because it was such a lovely day, her plan now was to try to zone everything out and enter a mindful trance.

It might have worked, if it hadn’t been for the constant drip of the leaking outdoor tap.

It had been leaking for several months now, and was one of the jobs she’d always meant to get around to doing. Actually, there was no reason why she couldn’t have gotten a plumper into doing it for her - she could afford it, after all, but something had been holding her back.

Richard.

It was Richard who always did those kinds of things. The DIY, electrics, decorating were all Richard’s domain. And to attempt to fix the leaking tap was almost like stepping on his toes.

So it had never been fixed.

For the first few months, it hadn't been too much of a problem... but now, the once occasional drip had increased to pretty much a constant flow. Charlotte had to put a bucket underneath it to collect the water to stop it from seeping into the ground. What normally happened, though, was she forgot to empty the bucket regularly enough, so once filled, the water splashed on the wall - discolouring the bricks - and into the ground.

"God, I miss him." she said aloud.

Trying to fight back tears, she closed her eyes tight shut and dropped her head into her hand.

She needed to get out...

"Bronte! Come on boy!"

* * *

One of the reasons Charlotte bought the house in Sprotbrough was its closeness to the River Don, the Sheffield and South Yorkshire Navigation Canal and the Trans Pennine Trail. The latter was a 215 mile trail stretching from Southport on the west coast of England, right through to Hornsea on the east.

She had heard about the trail on one of the editions of the TV series Walks Around Britain, where the presenter Leah Hather walked on a tiny part of it on a route around Sprotbrough and the nearby village of Cusworth. Ironically, that very walk was now one of Charlotte and Bronte's standard walks since they moved back.

The pair took their familiar route down to the 'Trail - shortcut through New Lane Playground, out on Cadeby Road, turn right after the school, along the public footpath and down the steps to reach Nursery Lane - right on the banks of the canal. As they descended the steps, Charlotte smiled at the 'Public Footpath' finger sign, which still had the South Yorkshire County Council logo on it, despite being over thirty six years since the council had been abolished.

Crossing the road, she looked around. It was always busy here, it being a favourite place for many, but at least with it being a Friday afternoon, it wasn't up to weekend busy-ness. An elderly chap with three tiny dogs on leads passed in front of them, heading back to his car up on the left. "Afternoon." he said cheerily. Charlotte replied and Bronte responded with a wag of his tail. Watching the four of them walk at a similar pace together filled Charlotte with a warm glow.

Life goes on.

She suddenly realised she probably looked rather odd; a smart suit with walking boots and a dog. This raised a smile.

They crossed over the narrow road, and headed past The Boat Inn to join the Trans Pennine Trail. The sound of water cascading over a weir filled the air, except the water in front of them was flatly calm, as this was the canal cut designed for safe passage of vessels. The original River Don section was a little in the distance, and that was the location of the weir, known to all as Sprotbrough Falls.

The hard path below their feet was a well-maintained one, popular with cyclists as well as walkers - which was why on this section through trees, Charlotte kept Bronte on his lead. Bikes could just appear at speed, and even if they were paying due attention, they didn't need a loose dog just around a corner to contend with.

After crossing under the railway bridge though, the landscape opened out, and she knew it was safe to let Bronte off his lead. Although he'd been very happy and walking to heel, Bronte responded to his impending freedom to roam with a few excited barks - and didn't stop to look back at Charlotte once his lead was off. Wagging his tail and darting into every nook and cranny of the landscape, he was the picture of contentment and excitement.

Charlotte watched his adventure along the trail with increasing joy. She wondered whether he could realise just how much she needed him; how much pleasure he brought her; how much she loved him. Just then, she was snapped out of her reverie by Bronte running back to her and checking in.

"Good boy!" she praised, and gave him some of his favourite treats - homemade liver cake. He took some time to eat them and then ran off again.

The unmistakable sound of the Nokia 3310's ringtone emanated from one of Charlotte's pockets. Putting Bronte's dog lead around her neck, she fished the phone out and looked at the screen. It was her sister Vanessa.

"Hi Nessa." Charlotte answered, as cheerily as she could.

"Hi Lottie. Just thought I'd phone; see how you are today..."

For a moment, 'today' had no meaning, and then it returned to Charlotte. "Yeah, alright. I guess."

"Good. Good. Look, it's bound to be hard today, you know? Don't be too hard on yourself if it's all gets too much. I know how you are."

"Yeah, I'll bear that in mind."

"Are you out on a case?"

"No... I'm..." she paused to decide whether she should say what she's actually doing, but then Bronte looked rather interested in two geese swimming in the middle of the river, and so she shouted him away. "...I'm out walking Bronte. Lovely day and all that."

"Good. Good. Well it was a good idea to have had the day off today. Last thing you need today is something, you know, happening you have to deal with."

'Yes,' Charlotte thought. *'Why didn't she think of that earlier?'* She replied with a non committal grunt.

"And I'm glad you got some good weather down there - it's been raining all day here in Leeds. Anyway, got to go, the twins are both off school with chicken pox and I've got tea to sort. Love you."

"Love you too. Thanks." The phone went dead. Charlotte looked at it for a while and imagined Vanessa's life; a husband, three kids, one dog in suburban Leeds. Was she jealous? Or envious? Not really. As much as she loved her nieces and nephew, she'd never really imagined herself having kids. She'd talked about it with Richard, of course, and she'd liked to have the option, sure, but she couldn't get over the idea that perhaps having children didn't really fit with being a Detective Chief Inspector. No disrespect to anyone who is and does, but to Charlotte, it felt a step too far.

She was snapped out of her reverie once again by Bronte running back to her and checking in. "Good boy! Good boy! Listen, we're nearly at the viaduct, and you know what you did on the viaduct, so it's lead time, ok?"

Clicking on the lead to his harness, Bronte relaxed, and returned to his obedient lead walking persona, as they climbed the path to a junction, and turned left.

The viaduct Charlotte was talking about was the Conisbrough Viaduct; an impressive structure spanning across the Dearne Valley, over the River Don and the still operating railway below. Opened in 1909 as a link between the Great Northern and Great Eastern Railways and the Hull & Barnsley Railway, it was vast, to say the least.

They'd been walking with it in sight along the Trans Pennine Trail for a while now, and Charlotte never failed to be in awe of the twenty-one arches and the lattice iron girder span over the river. It closed as a railway in 1965, and in 2010, it began its new life as corridor in the sky for walkers and cyclists, and there was hardly a week went by that Charlotte and Bronte didn't walk across it - usually twice.

The first time they walked across was three days after they'd moved back. Charlotte had seen the viaduct on television, and wanted to walk across it. She had Bronte off the lead before going across, and didn't realise how quickly the land around the bridge suddenly dropped away. Without warning, Bronte ran and jumped up on the brick sides to the bridge, just managing to stop himself at the last moment from falling off. So, every time since, Bronte was on the lead going across the viaduct.

Charlotte stopped half way across, and climbed up on one of the brick raised sections on the right for a better view. The River Don meandered around to the right, and above it, the romantic tower of Conisbrough Castle. She just soaked in the outdoors for what seemed like hours. At that point, she wanted to be nowhere else but here.

Chapter 7

Richard Meadows died and was buried in London - which was fitting for a Londoner. The whole of Richard's family were Londoners too, but as they had all moved to Scotland, Charlotte was the only person tending to his grave. When Charlotte started to look at moving back 'up north', she didn't want Richard to be left alone, so she moved him to Doncaster. The decision to do this was easy to make... sorting it out wasn't. It turns out you *can* move a dead body 200 miles, but it was something Charlotte wasn't going to be in a hurry to do again soon. Not that she wanted there to be a need to do this anyway.

The outcome of several weeks of forms, phone calls and a very long round trip in a hearse, was the headstone Charlotte was standing in front of now. It wasn't the headstone he'd had in London; that got smashed during the moving debacle, so Charlotte had another made in Doncaster replicating the original exactly save for one, small addition. Charlotte and Richard's mother never quite saw eye-to-eye; it wasn't that Charlotte disliked her, or vice versa, but they just clashed. Frequently. And often. Actually, truth be told, they'd probably go so far as to say they *did* dislike each other. Charlotte felt his mother seriously needed to let him go, and Richard's mother felt Charlotte was a bad influence on her perfect son.

This explains why, when Richard's parents had the original headstone made, there was no mention of "a wonderful partner", or "boyfriend", or "lover", or of "missed by partner Charlotte". So this was the small addition Charlotte had asked to be included in the replica. She knew Richard's mother wouldn't have approved it, but then she never agreed to Charlotte moving Richard's body in the first place. Despite several attempts at talking to her about the issue, Charlotte was always snubbed before she could get anywhere; so she went ahead with it regardless.

To be honest, it probably wasn't completely legal without his mother's permission, and Charlotte had to pull in a couple of favours to sweeten the paperwork, but it was all in a good cause. His parents hadn't been to visit the grave since the burial, so at least this way if they ever did want to, they'd be getting off the train at Doncaster, not London, and therefore she'd cut two hours off their journey. They could thank her later... Besides, even the insufferable mother would have to agree it was better to have Richard's grave near the only person who had been attending to it, she thought, as she walked into the cemetery.

It wasn't far from the viaduct that Charlotte loved so much, so it was often a weekend's trek to Richard's grave via the Trans Pennine Trail and the viaduct. Although she hadn't planned it that way today - it just kind of happened.

In a way, Charlotte had always secretly liked cemeteries. True, they weren't everyone's favourite places by a long shot - and many saw them as dark, awful places - but to Charlotte, they were full of memories; full of celebrations of lives lived; all neatly lined up in rows and rows of headstones. Even as possibly the least religious person around, Charlotte felt a measure of spirituality in these places. Sure, it wouldn't be the first place she'd come, but now she had a reason to visit regularly, she often felt better after coming.

The place this evening was respectfully quiet, with a few people around taking the opportunity to see their loved ones, and rekindle memories. Charlotte walked through the cemetery to where Richard was buried, with Bronte following - occasionally stopping and stretching his lead to check out some interesting smells every so often.

After ambling down the various paths, Charlotte stopped a distance away from Richard's grave. A family were gathered around the grave next to Richard's, and Charlotte decided to wait awhile and let them have their time without her next to them. She watched as an elderly lady shuffled gingerly towards the headstone, placing a bunch of flowers in the special hole on the mount. Charlotte suddenly thought 'bugger, flowers... I've not bought flowers.' She made a mental note she needed to come back sooner than normal with flowers.

The elderly lady made her way back to her daughter, who gave her a hug. After a moment, the daughter lifted her Mum's chin up, and wiped the tears away with a tissue from one of those plastic packs - and then cuddled her again. The daughter then turned to look down at her twins in the pushchair by her side. Charlotte could just see from where she was standing one was asleep, while the other had a soft toy they were playing with. And Charlotte thought, the cycle will probably continue. Mum, daughter, grand-daughter...

such is life.

Charlotte started to feel a little self-conscious watching them, and decided to look around at the nearest graves to where she was standing. Most were fairly standard - apart from one. Scanning around the immediate area, this particular one seemed the most ornate around; it was double the size of any nearby, and made from a bright white marble. The large gold lettering said 'Jules O'Connor. Loving Wife and Mother'.

The four of them slowly passed Charlotte and Bronte, with Charlotte throwing them a consolatory slight smile when she caught their eyes. As they passed, the child playing with the soft toy dropped it. She turned around, looking backwards as her prized toy apparently moved away from her. Her left hand made a grabbing motion, as if to wish it back to her. Charlotte noticed and indicated to Bronte to pick up the toy and take it to her. The dog faithfully and carefully picked up the toy in his mouth and made his way to the girl - his lead dragging on the path behind him, as Charlotte had already let go of it in anticipation.

The daughter, initially perturbed about a seemingly rogue dog by the side of them, looked on with amazement as it deposited a toy ever so carefully into the lap of the child who had lost it. The lady looked around and after spotting Charlotte shouted "Thank you! I didn't know she'd dropped it!" After receiving some praise, Bronte headed back to Charlotte, his tail up and with a confident strut, feeling very pleased with himself.

"Good boy" said Charlotte, giving him a handful of dog treats from her coat pocket. Picking up the lead from the floor, they headed towards Richard's grave, and around to the left side to the headstone. Charlotte cleaned a couple of splats of bird poo off the double curved top with the cloth she had for just such purposes, and then promptly sat down, with her legs folded underneath her, by the side of the dark grey stone.

The headstone was cold to her touch, as she ran her right hand over the words "Richard Meadows". Feeling the words triggered feelings Charlotte had tried hard to forget. No, actually, not forget - tried hard to cope with. After all, it hadn't been what you might call a 'standard' death. Perhaps she could have coped with that better.

Bronte laid down next to Charlotte. He'd been here enough times to know what was expected of him. And being here always meant there had already been a good walk, or one was just about to happen.

Charlotte took a deep breath and started. "Well, who'd have thought it, eh? A year. I'm still here; I said I would be." At that moment Bronte barked, and Charlotte leaned over to give him a fuss. "Bronte's says he's still here too! He's my best friend now, you know. Goes everywhere with me - well, almost. Haven't got him into work with me yet, but trying!"

The mention of work stopped Charlotte in her tracks. It broke her rule. The rule of not talking about work when she visited Richard - because in Charlotte's view, that's what made this awful situation happen.

A few moments earlier, a man in a wheelchair arrived in the cemetery. He'd clearly been before, as he knew exactly the way to get to where he wanted to be.

And that somewhere was a hundred or so metres away from Charlotte, Bronte and Richard's grave.

He was a tall, attractive man, with chiselled good looks extenuated by what in the 80s would have been called designer stubble and a dazzling smile. His short brown hair was already twinging towards light grey, despite him being in his mid 30s. Wearing a fairly expensive light grey suit, the man moved to behind a tree to watch Charlotte and Bronte, which for someone with nefarious intentions would be a pretty rubbish hiding place. But the man was behind the tree to keep a respectful distance - much the same as Charlotte had moments before.

Obvious to being watched, Charlotte was trying to hold back the tears, with only a modicum of success. *'Sod it'*, she thought. If the 'work' rule had been broken, then she might as well tell him. "I thought you should know... I'm leaving the police. I can't do it anymore." she told Richard.

She paused, as if to listen to his response. And then she replied "I know. Me leaving the force... 'over my dead body' I always used to say..."

Charlotte looked down at the grave... 'over your dead body' was left unsaid.

The tears she'd done so well to fight back suddenly breached the dam. She patted her walking jacket to locate which of the many pockets contained a pack of tissues like the one the family had. Before she found it, her hand squashed a packet of dog treats, which instantly made Bronte's head turn and look hopingly.

She dried her eyes with a tissue, and then used it to

blow her nose. Bronte layed back down.

“If only I'd have done that before, eh? “ she continued to Richard.

But at that moment, was there a fairly major realisation? A realisation being a police officer was perhaps a part of who she was?

“If only I'd have stopped being me.”

The man in the wheelchair saw this as an appropriate time to move forward from behind his tree hiding place.

“I'm so sorry.” Charlotte said to the headstone, before stopping as she was very close to losing it completely.

With Charlotte still focused on Richard’s headstone, it was Bronte who noticed the man first. The dog looked at the man first with suspicion. If this was someone who is coming to threaten his human, then they’d soon know about it. But as the man got closer, Bronte’s tail started to wag and he broke his patient stay to go across to give him a big fuss, tail wagging enough to generate electricity.

“Hello Bronte!” said the man.

Charlotte’s attention was wrenched away from her reverie. She went to wipe the new flood of tears away with the tissue in her hand, and then realised just in time she’d used it to blow her nose. Having used a new tissue from the pack, she turned to look at who Bronte had gone to see.

“Hi sis.” the man smiled.

"David! What are you doing here?"

"Looking for you. You weren't answering your phone."

Charlotte turned her body more towards David. "I... I... I think it's dead, or I've left it somewhere..."

"Yeah, I figured that." David smiled at Charlotte's stock answer for not bothering with her mobile phone.

"Anyway, how did you know I'd be here?" Charlotte asked, with a large quizzical frown.

"You weren't at home, so where else were you going to be today?"

Charlotte looked across at her brother. He knew her so well. "Yeah, I just needed to talk to him."

"Yeah." David said understandingly.

Charlotte looked back to the headstone. She was relieved David was here as he might help lift her mood. And, in a way, it was kind of apt, as David and Richard got on so well together, with them both loving football - and in particular Chelsea. When David came down to see Charlotte in London, he always managed to time it when Chelsea were playing at home, so the boys could go to Stamford Bridge for the match. Come to think of it, thought Charlotte, he never did come down when Chelsea *weren't* playing at home! Apart from the funeral, of course.

"Did you hear much?" Charlotte asked, when she realised what she'd said to Richard.

"I heard you said you were leaving the police."

Ah. Charlotte looked a bit sheepish and winced. Oh

well. It's out there now, she thought. "Yeah. I think it is time."

She waited for David's response - and when it came after seemingly minutes of him just fussing Bronte, it was with typical David brevity. "It's a big move."

Charlotte thought she had to bluster this through. "Well... I've tried this year to go on. And it hasn't got any easier."

"Are you sure? Looks to me like you've got quite settled into a new life..." Charlotte chewed on her tongue. He was sort of right, but it wasn't what she wanted to hear.

Conversational handbrake turn.

"Mum hasn't messaged." Charlotte said, hoping the change of subject wasn't too noticeable. If David had spotted it, he didn't comment.

"You know what Mum's like. She'll be thinking of you though."

"Yeah. She won't be happy with me quitting."

"It's your life, little sis, not hers."

True. Charlotte smiled at him. Although they both knew their Mum would at the very least have an opinion on the situation.

"Aren't you going to tell me how I'd be mad to throw away everything I've worked for?"

"Would it make any difference if I did?"

True again. Charlotte scrunched her nose up at him, and then decided it was time to move on. She stood up, leaning on Richard's headstone as she did, and walked over to the side of David. The ever-faithfully collie moved to the side of Charlotte, and she picked up his trailing lead from the floor.

"I heard about the bridge." David said as they started to move away to the car park.

Charlotte looked at him astonished. "Bloody hell! News travels fast! How did you find out?"

"Hey, I'm a journalist, remember? You can't close off the main way out of Doncaster on a Friday afternoon and expect it not to be noticed!"

Fair point, Charlotte thought. Possibly because she refused to own any kind of smartphone, she always seemed astounded by the speed communications operate these days. And social media was a whole different ball game. Charlotte was on Facebook, but because of the risks associated with her job, she used her middle name and Richard's last name - Georgy Meadows. And because she eschewed a smartphone, she only ever went on Facebook on her laptop... which seriously reduced the amount of time she ever spent on it. Oh, the numbers of birthday notifications that she missed between log-ins...

"Are you ok?" David asked.

"Yeah. Just trickier today. Of all days."

Charlotte continued to look straight ahead. Occasionally she looked down at the path... but at this moment she couldn't look at David. If she did, he might have seen that she wasn't ok. But David knew. He looked at her as they walked, with love and care. These two, possibly more than any other combination of the four Walker siblings, had gone through so much together in their lives. They knew more about each other than possibly anyone else.

With Charlotte still looking into the far distance, the conversation had come to a fairly abrupt stop. David decided to 'do a Charlotte' and changed the subject. As the policewoman was never far away from the surface of his sister, the journalist in David was pretty much always present. And there was a big story his sister might have some inside scoop on.

"So... ", David said with his typical bravado and lack of tact, "are you on this missing woman?"

Charlotte glared at him playfully; both for the double entendre and the impertinence of the question. "I can't tell you that..."

David was never one for letting a dismissal go without a challenge; that's what made him such a good journalist. "So what's the craic on it then?"

"You know I can't say anything about that - especially to a journo..." Charlotte's eyeballs darted around inside her eyes in mock indignation, and the sentence culminated with an eyebrow rise on 'journo', just for good measure.

"Anyone 'helping the police with their enquiries' yet?" said David, complete with air quotation marks and a slight air of mocking when he used the well-worn police trope. It hadn't gone unnoticed by Charlotte, who smashed the repost back with the vigour of a tennis player who was able to return a massive ace.

"Everyone is helping the police with their enquiries!"

David smiled at Charlotte. Their relationship was built on ribbing and mocking that only two like-minded people could manage. If either David or Charlotte tried that with older sister Jenna, then the metaphorical tumbleweed would twirl through the place.

A pause, as Charlotte mulled over something, was broken by the detective commenting "In fact, *you* can help me with my inquiries..."

"Oh really? What's in it for me?"

"A slap-up tea with the hottest detective this side of Catcliffe." she replied, playfully.

"Since you put it like that..."

❋ ❋ ❋

Doncaster wasn't known for its hills - mainly because it doesn't have many of them. But one it had is the hill Cusworth Hall is built on. Once a family stately home, the hall was now a museum and the landscaped grounds a country park used by the types of people the wealthy family who once lived here would have successfully kept out.

Charlotte and David were sitting on one of the several benches at the top of the hill, looking down over the view of Doncaster, as it descended into night-time. Lights of all colours illuminated the scene in the distance and the faint hum of the activity of a town carried across to where they were seated. David's wheelchair was parked to the left side of where he sat on the bench.

On the way there, they'd stopped off for fish and chips, at one of Charlotte's many locals, and they sat admiring this view, each with a box of this Great British takeaway. For Bronte, this was the perfect end to a lovely evening... a walk AND the delicious tit-bits of human food dropped both on purpose, and occasionally, by accident, by Charlotte and David. Bronte laid down at Charlotte's feet, keeping eyes open for fish falling from the heavens above.

David took a bigger mouthful than he should have, and with the food still being fairly hot, he did that 'blowing the inside of your mouth because it's burning you' dance with his head. Charlotte looked over to him, slightly smiled at her brother's discomfort, like siblings do somethings, and thought 'numpty'. After swallowing, David asked "Jeez, how can you eat this so quick? It's nuclear!"

Charlotte finished the mouthful she had by gulping it down quickly. "Years of only having 10 minutes for a lunch break before being back on the case. That and having an asbestos-lined mouth."

David took smaller mouthfuls from then on.

Charlotte was looking out at the scene of her hometown, and felt quite at sixes and sevens. Perhaps she should have asked David for his advice before deciding to quit. Perhaps he was a little put out that she didn't go to her elder brother for guidance? The thought never crossed her mind before, but now it had, she felt sorry for not letting him into her confidence. Her thoughts were broken by the sudden realisation that her mouth too actually felt a little burnt. That last mouthful was a little too hot to have gulped down so quickly, she thought. But she wasn't going to let David know that...

"So how's it going in Sheffield?" she asked, continuing to look straight ahead, and filling her mouth afterwards with a slightly cooler selection of what was left in her box tray. David took another mouthful, and looked across at her. He was sure they weren't here for such small talk. He waited to reply until Charlotte looked back at him.

"All good. No plans for leaving my job..."

They exchanged a look. Charlotte made the most infinitesimal nod of the head and bit on her bottom lip to show she knew David understood. He smiled a small smile full of love back at her, and turned back quickly to the vista in front of them - which was steadily darker.

Charlotte finished off her fish and chips, put the plastic knife and fork inside the cardboard box and closed the lid. She paused, clearly deep in thought, before asking "How did we all get here?"

"That's deep for a Friday night. Don't you be getting all psychotical on me." They both knew he got that wrong on purpose.

"Psychological..." she just had to correct - but in a playful manner - as she put the box on the bench to her right.

David wasn't too far behind in finishing his meal, and he passed his cardboard food box across to Charlotte, where she stacked it on top of hers.

After wiping his mouth with a tissue he'd drawn out of a small pack he had in his pocket, he replied.

"Well, it was fairly obvious how we'd all turn out, wasn't it?"

"What do you mean?"

David started with all the effervescence of a professor recounting their life's work. Each of the sibling's names was said with a definitive exclaim; his tone raised up at the end of each sentence and a small circular motion with his fingers were designed to elicit a verbal response - as if coaxing it from Charlotte.

"Jenna - always looking for someone to argue with and blame..."

Charlotte looked at him and took the cue with a small smile and a nod of the head.

"Lawyer..."

"Nessa - always clucking around us all and looking after every animal she found..."

"Mother and animal activist..."

"Me - starting a student newspaper at school..."

"Journalist..."

"And you - always wanting to find out what has happened and fight for the people who've been wronged..." He left the sentence hanging.

At this end part of David's thesis, he turned to look Charlotte straight in the eye. Her small smile had gone, as had the slight nods in agreement. When Charlotte didn't respond in the same way as before, David raised his eyebrows to encourage the reply. Charlotte decided, however, she didn't like this part of the dissertation, and turned once again to the view of Doncaster instead

- occasionally looking to the right at the young couple holding hands walking up the hill and laughing.

Still looking at Charlotte, David said “That's always been you; everything has to be right. Not necessarily happy, or pretty, or beautiful... but right; it has to be right.” It was said emphatically, but with heart and understanding; in a truthful, complementary and admiring way.

‘Jeez, how has he got it so spot on?’ Charlotte hated it when someone else hit the nail on the head... that was *her* job. “Since when did you become so astute?”

“Since I had a sister who studied psychoticology...”

His face lit up and the siblings exchanged a loving look.

Conversational handbrake turn.

“Anyway, you didn't invite me to the Savoy for a psychoanalysis, so what is it I can help you with?”

Charlotte suddenly came back to life at this point, her eyes widened and she turned her whole body to face her brother. “This company - Tempto Digital - what do you know about it?”

David frowned for a second, then his forehead rose up as he recounted what he could instantly draw up about the request. “God - they were big in the late 80s in 8 bit computer games. Set up by two brothers. When those went they switched to business software and then internet services for companies. Now they rival Amazon and Google in cloud computing services for websites and mobile apps.”

“Set up by two brothers?”

"Aye. Twins, actually." David stopped, and for a moment stroked his cheek in deep thought. "Can't remember their names; but I do remember they both died in rather suspicious circumstances."

The penny dropped for David, and he looked quizzically across at Charlotte. "Do you think the company is mixed up in that woman's disappearance?"

Bugger, Charlotte thought, there's no flies on him. "We're pursuing a number of lines of inquiry..."

David's smile said 'Always a copper!', as he turned to look at the view.

* * *

David pulled up on Charlotte's drive, and parked behind her Volvo. In contrast to Charlotte's vehicle, David's car was his pride and joy - for one reason only. It gave him the gift of freedom. It was a van-like Ford Grand Tourneo Connect specially-adapted to allow him to drive directly from his wheelchair. Granted, it wouldn't have been his choice of vehicle if he hadn't had the accident; at this time of his life, he'd have been looking at something more high powered and possibly a bit sporty - which no-one could say about his current drive. But the ability to wheel up the side ramp, and drive from his chair meant so much to David. He'd even put aside it was painted bright red - a colour he hated. Pragmatically, it made it easier to find in car parks, he convinced himself; so happy to have a car which gave him back the freedom the accident almost cruelly took away.

One of the big plus sides to the size of his car was being able to take Charlotte and Bronte places, which they did fairly regularly. So much so, Charlotte had her drive altered so he had a place to wheel himself out and in of his car from the ramp. The accessible walks he had done with Charlotte and Bronte since they moved back to South Yorkshire were amongst his most precious memories. Again, how different from before his accident, when going for a walk would have been one of the last things he would have wanted to do.

How life changes.

"Are you coming in?" Charlotte asked.

David thought about it, but then remembered he'd arranged to chat to someone later that night, and looking at the time decided he'd better get back. Explaining this to Charlotte caused her eyebrows to raise in interest.

"Sorry, I didn't ask you about your lovelife."

"Same as ever - complicated." he replied.

Charlotte unclicked Bronte from the seatbelt, and ushered him out of the car. "Is it still Tom?"

"No, " David replied wistfully. "No, we didn't want the same things."

"Ah. Sorry about that."

"It's ok."

"So..." Charlotte started to prompt for more new information. "...who is this one tonight?"

"Jessica." came the reply. Charlotte's eyebrows

raised again. "She works at that new club that's just opened in Sheffield. One great thing there is you know everyone's on the same page."

"Hope it's a good book you've chosen." Charlotte continued the metaphor.

"Oh I think so. Excellent cover at least. See ya sis!" David pushed his car into reverse and only just waited for Charlotte to close the side door before he moved at speed off the drive. Charlotte cringed slightly, at the possibility of a road traffic accident right outside her house involving her brother. There was a slight squeal of tires as he pushed the car Into first, and off; David might not have been able to have the high powered sporty number, but he wasn't going to let it stop his sense of adventure.

Charlotte opened her front door and Bronte raced in. Charlotte hovered for a moment, half expecting a crash; but when it thankfully didn't happen, she shook her head thinking about David. She knew he wasn't reckless - just playful.

Closing the door, she looked at the clock in the hallway; 10:42.

It had been such a tiring and emotional day she half considered going straight to bed, but she decided on staying up for a little bit longer. Bronte had decided to go to sleep, and was already working out which way he was going to face on his dog bed. Charlotte watched as he turned one way, then the other, and eventually settled on exactly the same place on it as he always did. '*Numpty*' Charlotte thought with a smile.

She went into the kitchen and looked in the fridge.

The light which shone back from the open door was glaring, but didn't illuminate much in the way of edible treasures contained within. Three strawberry yoghurts, two cans of dry cider, a 500 gram pack of closed cap mushrooms, two medium eggs - past their use-by date, five and a half pints of bottled milk, from the seven delivered this morning, a block of Extra Mature Cheddar Cheese and several tubs of Savers Cream Cheese.

Charlotte glared at the contents and thought not even Jack Munroe could do much with those. She needed to go shopping soon.

She relieved the fridge of its obligation to hold the cans of cider, and went back into the living room. As she turned the television on with the remote control, she looked across at Bronte, who was fast asleep, legs shaking with dreams.

The set came to life, part way through the late regional news.

"...helping police with their inquiries. There was traffic disruption in Doncaster today as police closed one of the main roads out of the town following an incident. The A19 over St George's Bridge was closed in both directions for around twenty minutes, with delays taking over an hour to clear. South Yorkshire Police thanked drivers for their patience." The presenter paused before the next story, which Charlotte took as her cue to open one of the ciders, take a long swing straight from the can, and press the buttons on the remote to see what was on the television to watch.

'When Harry Met Sally' was on one of the channels with a high number, as seeing as though it was

Charlotte's favourite film, and one she'd seen many, many times, she thought it seemed pretty apt for today. 'Let's think; it started at 10, and its 10:45 now, so it'd be around the...", her eyes widened with anticipation, "cafe scene..."

She switched over, to see the camera tracking to the left across diners in enjoying their meal to end on Sally and Harry. Impressed at her own deduction, she grabbed the remainder of the first can, and started to mouth all the dialogue a second before the actors did.

She was set in for the night.

Chapter 8

It was morning, and Charlotte was in bed - not completely asleep but was still prepared to give sleep a second chance. Those two cans of cider must have gone to her head. She thought back to how much she used to be able to drink at university, and wondered where that young lady had gone. All grown up, was the answer - although few would really level the acquisition of being grown up at Charlotte. Her Mum certainly wouldn't use that term to describe her… quite the opposite. Possibly Jenna wouldn't either; but that's the same as saying Mum wouldn't, anyway.

So sleep sounded good. Especially after the day she had yesterday. Bronte, however, had other ideas. Being the creature of habit he was, his habit timetable was telling him it was nearly time for a walk - so he dived on the bed and on the top of Charlotte.

"Morning, my boy! Is it that time already?" asked Charlotte, still half asleep. She looked over at the alarm clock, which today didn't have any alarming duties. 08:30 read the digital display.

Bronte barked. As much as a human and a dog could understand and communicate with each other, Bronte and Charlotte could.

"You know you had a long walk yesterday, right? You haven't forgotten that one, eh?" Bronte wasn't going to be fobbed off. "Ok, ok.. I'm getting up for the morning walk!" Charlotte said. Bronte jumped off the bed, a lot more energetic than Charlotte's slow movements. Bronte was already waiting downstairs in the utility room, ready to go out for his morning toilet break, and eventually Charlotte arrived to unlock the white back door. Bronte trotted out to do his business and Charlotte went back inside, closing the door behind her.

Switching on the radio in the kitchen, she emptied out the kettle - the first cup of tea in the morning *always* is made with a fresh, clean, rinsed-out kettle. Once on to boil, the distinct tones of a songstress from London battled with the sound of the kettle.

"Adele. Virgin Radio. Saturday breakfast, with me, Amy Voce. Now, I don't use Facebook much any more, I don't know if you do..." Charlotte shook her head. *"But I'm not sure whether I'll be able to use it again, because something odd happened this week, I don't know whether they are losing it. Basically I was trying to log into my account and I forgot my password, so I went through the whole Facebook verification. You know usually they'll send you an email reminder, or something? No! Facebook have gone next level; in order for me to access my account, they sent me a list of five Facebook friends; most of who I haven't spoken to for at least five years, and said you need to call at least three of these friends and get the verification code we've sent them for your account to work again! Sorry, what?! One of the girls on there, literally not seen her for a decade, I'm not going to call it and go 'Oh hi Linsday, sorry I;ve not spoken to you for a decade; how's your life; can you just go into your email and get a confirmation code for me?' That's ridiculous Facebook you've lost it!"*

'Well, that would be me locked out forever then.'

Charlotte thought, not that it would be a major loss. One of the beauties of having a non-smart phone is to be out of that constant social media bubble. Amy played 'Crash' by The Primitives; a top song for Saturday morning, as Charlotte opened the back door to welcome a dog with an extremely waggy tail back into the house. Sitting down at the table with a mug of tea - white, two sugars; two slices of toast - lightly toasted with several thick strips of mature Cheddar cheese arranged on top; and pot of thick and creamy strawberry yoghurt, Charlotte looked at the Yorkshire Post newspaper she picked up on the way downstairs. In this era of constantly updated news and push notifications on apps, Charlotte had the Yorkshire Post delivered every morning. She started the habit around five months ago - around the time of David's first front page story - and it was a distinct joy to open up one of the last remaining broadsheet newspapers in the UK.

Although she couldn't say that she always had the time to read it all on the day. Sometimes she had been known to go back to Mondays edition on a Friday - but she always tried to read as much of it as she could. Of course, the regular bouts of pride she felt every time she noticed David's name appear on a byline gave her the incentive to continue to scour each and every edition.

Charlotte didn't realise how hungry she was, and the toast disappeared in an instant. She opened the yoghurt, the metal foil lid making a distinctive sound as it tore off the plastic pot. It was a sound Bronte recognised immediately, and he came over to sit down Impeccably by the side of Charlotte. Because this was something that happened every time she had yoghurt, she lowered her left hand holding the lid down without looking, and Bronte licked the excess off from its underside. Allowing him all the time he needed to completely clean the lid, she multitasked and took a drink of her tea with her right hand.

It was a coordinated routine - but it wasn't completely clear which one of them had trained the other...

After breakfast, Charlotte went back upstairs to get dressed. Her pink striped satin pyjamas worked for around the house, but probably might attract *too* much attention out on a walk... Besides, she was pretty certain they wouldn't be waterproof either...

Charlotte wondered whether her wardrobe was amongst the most unique in the country. On one side was the walking gear. A range of lightweight summer and full-lined winter waterproof walking trousers and shorts, sweat resistant t-shirts including some with mosquito repellent, mid-layers including fleeces and jumpers. Not forgetting the thermals too.

Then, in the middle was the work gear. Two and three piece suits - mostly trousers - with a penchant for either greys or blacks with pinstripes or the whole hog with bold colours; burgundy, yellow and a lime green, for example. The red pencil trousers & blazer suit was her particular favourite. The work gear section also had a few crew neck midi dresses, of which were in subdued colours. All apart from the pink plunge neck sleeveless blazer dress, which got a warning as inappropriate for work one day in London. Probably right.

Then, there was the 'everyday clothes that aren't

walking gear' section. This wasn't that well furnished, because why would you really need clothes which *aren't* suitable for walking? Here was a collection of jeans and dresses, and her favourite, a sleeveless denim jumpsuit... which was completely impractical for walking, but which looked fantastic on her.

And lastly, was the evening wear. Charlotte had a great figure; everything nicely proportioned, extenuating by her height, and if the event allowed, she wasn't afraid to show it off. Particular favourites were the sleeveless backless sequin jumpsuit in blue - elegant yet practical, the long sleeve mesh bandage dress in black - stunning and classy, and the one shoulder burgundy fitted formal dress with two-thirds front split - sophisticated and ravishing. Her all-time favourite was her Elivia one sleeve mini dress in black, which looked all traditional and modest from the front but a turn around displayed an open back which extended to the base of her spine met with one sleeve from the right side. The effect, with her hair up, was mesmerising.

Right now, however, it was the turn of stretch walking trousers in khaki, along with a two-tone grey short sleeve baselayer top. Hot-footing downstairs, she selected her favourite walking boots and sat down on the enlarged bottom stair to put them on.

Bronte walked into the hallway from the kitchen, and saw his opportunity to give his human friend a good old fashioned doggie lick.

"Ok... Ok!" Charlotte managed to get out, between his tongue licking her face. "That's enough now! If we don't get out soon, we'll just have to have a short walk..."

That encouraged Bronte to stop, which in turn allowed Charlotte to finish tying her remaining shoelace in a double knot. She got up, grabbed her walking hat, and they were off.

Chapter 9

The weekend walks with Bronte were always long affairs. Partly because Charlotte had more time, and partly because of the guilt she felt from being out at work so much. It was true Bronte certainly wasn't hard done by; the run of the house whilst she was at work, and Toni regularly dog-sat too, but it didn't alleviate the guilt. Charlotte often heard working mothers talk about it in relation to their children... she'd never thought it appropriate to mention she felt it too, only about her dog.

She tried to find walks in different parts of the local area. If she had something else on in the day, she'd keep local, so a walk in Doncaster, Rotherham, Barnsley or across the county border into West Yorkshire. And when she had the whole day free, she'd take them both into the Peak District or up the North York Moors.

The walk she'd picked for today was in the south of the Doncaster borough, so she'd have to cross the River Don, and usually that would be using St George's Bridge. After yesterday, she decided to go the other way, and crossed over the river at Sprotbrough Falls, and headed that way to Bawtry Road and to the start in the former pit village of New Rossington.

She parked up on Grange Road, and after negotiating the similar streets and crescents of the village, they found themselves on a track called Hunster Flat Lane - a name Charlotte vowed to search for the meaning of another time.

Charlotte loved walking.

She loved the solace and peace of mind walking could bring.

And she loved walking with family or friends, be they the human or canine kind.

Her parents were big walkers, and so the family of five, plus the dog, were regularly taken out for walks on the weekend - whenever her Dad wasn't working. During her rebellious time, she railed against the outdoors, predictably, but it was always under her skin.

She discovered it for herself whilst at university; with the closeness of everything at Oxford, you could walk virtually everywhere you needed to go. From then, she'd walked in almost every part of the UK, and she'd been walking in Sweden, Italy and Ireland.

It was part of who she was; part of her DNA. And being able to share walks with her faithful best friend Bronte was always the best feeling in the world.

As they walked, Charlotte's mind started to wander back to the incident with Frank Drashler. It had been concerning her since it happened, although she wasn't entirely sure why it should.

Why didn't she talk to David about it, she thought - although she knew what he'd have said anyway. Something along the lines of "What are you worrying for anyway? It's been a year since Richard has gone - that's an acceptable length of time." And he'd have been right, of course. Well, what she imagined he'd have said would have been right.

The footpath veered right slightly, and up ahead

was the first person they'd met on the walk. It was a man; tall, fair hair, deeply tanned, who not only looked lost in the landscape, but also in life too. The green-based outdoor outfit he was wearing was fine in the countryside, it just didn't suit *him*. Arms out in front, he was holding an Ordnance Survey map open, and his face told a story that the lines on the map didn't really make any sense. He had an air of melancholy about him, which increased as they got nearer.

"Excuse me? Are y'alright? Are y'lost?" Charlotte shouted across to him.

The man looked up from his map. "Yes. Well, I'm not sure on which direction to go."

Charlotte stopped in front of him, keeping Bronte at a distance in case he didn't like dogs. There were people like that, Charlotte reminded herself. "That would depend on whether you're going to anywhere particular, I guess."

He agreed, and then realised Charlotte was asking whether he *did* have a place he was going to. "Tickhill."

"Tickhill's that way." pointing to the footpath behind him.

"Do you not need to look at my map?"

"No, I know." Charlotte said with confidence. "DCI Charlotte Walker, " she introduced herself, "and yes, Walker by name, walker by nature!".

"DCI Charlotte Walker...?" he repeated. "You're a detective?" He looked rather sceptical at Charlotte.

"My day off today, so we're out walking." she indicated to Bronte.

The man looked troubled by something; some inner turmoil he couldn't decide whether to bring to the surface. However, Charlotte had no desire to hang around chatting. She wanted to try and fix the outside tap before Toni picked them up for mantrailing, and so they needed to speed up.

"So, that way. Follow the footpath down to a junction." She closed her eyes to visualise the map in her head. "Turn right there, round the corner, right at the next junction, over the A1(M) and then you're in Tickhill. Ok? We're going this way." She pointed to her right; the direction he'd just come from.

"Oh. Ok. Thank you." he said, and as they walked away from him, Charlotte thought he'd probably forgotten all of that already.

The familiar ringing of Charlotte's mobile phone broke the quiet of the landscape. It was Jenna. She held the phone out in front of her, and scrunched her nose with a wince, letting it ring for a while. She considered not answering it, but eventually the distinctly shrill ringtone got the better of her.

"Hello Jenna." she said.

"Charlotte, it's Jenna." came the reply.

"Yes...I know."

"Oh." Jenna sounded genuinely surprised by this revelation.

"You're in my contacts. When you phone it tells me it's you." she explained.

There was a silence on the other end of the phone, and Charlotte imagined Jenna was processing this information.

Telephone conversations with Jenna ranged from difficult to extremely difficult. And that was because of a very specific reason - she was autistic. Well, more than likely autistic. She had never been diagnosed, but Charlotte knew. Her years studying Psychology (Experimental) at Worcester College, Oxford, told her that.

So, working on the premise she was autistic, Charlotte appreciated conversations on the telephone were challenging for Jenna. After all, she found face-to-face conversations tricky, and at least with those she could see all the non-verbal communication too; the way the eyes looked, what the mouth was doing.. At home, on the rare times they did chat, they used Skype, or such like, so Jenna could see Charlotte. On the telephone, Jenna had nothing to work on but the words.

And that's why Charlotte had considered not answering. Being completely selfish, she didn't feel strong enough to cope with an exchange with Jenna over the phone. Later, back home over Zoom, would be fine.

But she answered. And she was regretting it.

"Did you phone for a reason Jenna?" Charlotte asked, in the most neutral voice she could manage.

"Yes. Alexa told me I had to phone you."

"Ok." She sighed. "Did Alexa tell you why you needed to phone me?" She was trying so hard to remain calm.

"It was something about an anniversary." Jenna said

in a deadpan voice. *"So, happy anniversary!"*

This stopped Charlotte in her tracks. Not only had Jenna just congratulated her on something totally inappropriate, she'd also done it on the wrong day - and all because Alexa told her to.

As a rage started to mount inside her, she took a deep breath.

In fairness, she wasn't angry at Jenna. She'd made the effort to add an alarm to be reminded to call Charlotte; yes on the wrong day, and yes without reminding herself what it was for... but here she was, using a method of communication she found very challenging, and chatting to her youngest sister.

Which is why she very genuinely replied, "Thank you. That means a lot, Jenna."

"Bye then. Love you."

And she was gone.

Charlotte stared at her phone in wonderment. She knew now Jenna would be off doing something else; getting on with her Saturday, and wouldn't give that phone call a second thought.

No, it was *her* who would be mulling it over for the rest of the day. Typical. Such was the joys of Charlotte's eldest sister.

The rest of the walk proceeded without incident. No lost men; no sister's phoning having been instructed to do so by a robot; just Charlotte and Bronte enjoying the calm peace of the south Doncaster countryside. Along Egg Lane, right onto Carr Bank and then past the burial ground back into Rossington and to the car.

Charlotte opened the rear passenger door and took a water bowl out from the footwell and placed it on the pavement. It was a special type where the water didn't spill out, provided you didn't fill it too much. Bronte had a big drink and now it was the ritual of getting him into the car and onto the backseat, complete with harness attached to the seat belt. Perhaps, Charlotte wondered, whether with this change of car business ought to be to something larger? Perhaps something big like David's - but with a dog cage in it rather than the wheelchair mechanics?

But that thought went as soon as it came. She decided she wasn't a big car type of person. Even this Volvo was too big. No, something smaller; maybe something more sporty perhaps?

She closed the back door, got into the driver's seat and within seconds of travelling through Rossington, Bronte was laying down asleep.

* * *

Looking at the clock on the touchscreen display, she should just have enough time to get back home and fix the outside tap before going off to mantrailing. *'I mean, how hard could it be to fix a leak?'* Charlotte thought.

What she needed was not to be stuck in traffic at all on the way back.

She tapped the steering wheel out of boredom as she waited in what seemed like the longest traffic jam she'd been in for quite some time. She'd been waiting so long, the noisy inhalations through her nostrils she was doing in irritation had started to annoy herself.

She'd been so expecting the traffic to move any second now, she'd not looked out of the side windows. When she glanced across the road, she noticed she was outside a car dealer's forecourt.

As she was in the market for a new - or rather, new-to-her - car, she took an interest in what was on offer. From the road, she could only see the front row of cars, but she made out a Land Rover Defender, a Nissan Micra C+C - the rarely seen convertible - and a pink Mini Cooper.

Looking at the selection, she shouted "Oh yes!!"

Right there and then, as 'Drop Dead Gorgeous' by Republica was playing on the stereo, she'd decided on her next car. And it was right there in that forecourt.

"That is perfect!!"

Chapter 10

The constant moan of an old motorcycle idling over the fence on the left could only mean one thing; Helen-next-door's bit of rough had spent the night. His bike seemingly needed around thirty minutes of constant running before he could ride it; allowing the fumes to pervade the air. Thank heavens for the high fence and trees in between us, thought Charlotte.

It wasn't the audible accompaniment she perhaps wanted as she attacked the leaking outdoor tap. Stopping off at the car dealer had given her a lot less time than originally planned to attempt this procedure, but she remained confident.

"I mean, it can't be that difficult." Charlotte said to her faithful friend. As if he knew this undertaking wasn't a good idea, Bronte had decided to avoid laying down next to Charlotte, and was making short work of one of the dog chews she bought yesterday on a comfy bed a little way away.

Studying the tap, Charlotte tried to see where the leak was coming from - but the whole ensemble of the tap, pipe and the other gubbins seemed too complicated for its own good. She tried pushing the various sections closer together - but that didn't work.

It was time for proper tools. Charlotte lifted a wrench out of her toolbox. Looking at the tap, then at the wrench, she pushed the tool towards the pipes, in a hope the tool itself would know what to do.

It didn't.

"I've got a degree, you know..." she continued. Bronte stopped chewing, assessed the situation, and continued chewing.

At this point, the pipe came away from the bottom of the tap and sprayed Charlotte with cold water; completely soaking her. She screamed with surprise, trying at first to push the water away with both outstretched hands, which clearly was a fruitless policy. It took Charlotte more than a few moments to get over the initial shock and to realise she needed to turn the water off at the stopcock.in the kitchen.

Having done that, the noise of high pressure water spraying onto the paving slabs of the patio steadily died away, as what water was left in the pipes gradually ran out. She slowly returned outside, embarrassed that she made such a silly mistake, and sat down on the floor, in the middle of the water-soaked patio. *'I can't even remember to turn the water off first'* she chastised herself, and resigned to still needing Richard.

It was difficult to know whether the dripping from around Charlotte's eyes were tears or water dropping from her sodden hair. Bronte, however, was certain in knowing Charlotte needed him, and took advantage she was on his level to give her a pick-you-up dog kiss.

"Thank you! Thank you! Just what I need right now!" she said to him, between him licking her face. She warmed, and brought both hands up to him to fuss around his face. If she wasn't already crying, she could have started then. Just what would she have done without this wonderful dog?

Bronte only stopped his show of affection because he heard a knock at the front door. He barked twice, and so Charlotte knew what he was telling her. There was yet another thing on her long list of DIY jobs - the doorbell. She'd changed the batteries many times, but somewhere along the line, it still wasn't working.

* * *

Charlotte unlocked the front door, opened it and was surprised to see Ayesha standing there. Charlotte had caught her looking down the drive and she started talking before she'd turned back around. "Ma'am, I couldn't get you..."

When Ayesha had turned fully back to look at Charlotte, she couldn't help but notice the state she was in. In Charlotte's haste to get to the front door, she'd forgotten that she was absolutely sopping wet. So much so, a puddle of water had collected in the hallway as she stood.

Neither of them spoke, as they looked at each other - albeit with different feelings. One embarrassment but didn't want to show it and the other with interest but didn't want to show it either.

Ayesha's eyes dropped, and Charlotte was suddenly very aware how wet her grey top had become, how her sports bra was showing through the now transparent material, and how Ayesha seemed to be looking straight at that general area. There was an electric feel to the air.

"Come on in..." Charlotte said, hoping it would

break the moment.

Ayesha nodded, and stepped inside. But as Charlotte was holding onto the door, ready to close it, she couldn't get past without unintentionally brushing close as she walked in.

"Ma'am." Ayesha said, almost in an apology.

Charlotte tried to ignore it. "We're out the back. Go on through…"

With that, Ayesha walked down the hallway to the kitchen, leaving Charlotte to lock up and wonder what had just happened…

* * *

Ayesha looked around at the back garden. An oak tree looked Majestic halfway down the garden on the left-hand side, whilst a range of small trees stood guard along much of the boundaries with the neighbouring houses. Where the trees were absent, a high wooden panel fence took their duties. A path, which had seen better days, ran down the middle of the garden, creating two grassed areas. A selection of bedding plants were in various hanging baskets providing welcome colour. It was well tendered to, but it was clear Charlotte was no Monty Don.

"Oh hi there." Ayesha said to Bronte, as he trotted over to greet her. Somehow he knew she wasn't used to animals, and had decided to tone down his usual exuberant welcome to visitors to a more measured and calm greeting. He sat down nicely next to her, and within seconds she was giving his smooth fur a stroke without even realising it.

She looked around at the soaked patio, and then for Charlotte. She was right behind her, so should be outside by now. “Problem?”, she shouted back into the house.

“My attempt at plumbing. Not gone too well.” came the reply from inside the house.

“Ahh!”

“Should’ve known I’d be no good at it; my Dad flooded the kitchen once trying to repair the sink taps...”

Charlotte emerged from the house, now wearing a light blue knitted cardigan to hide her wet top. It wasn’t a look which would win her any fashion awards, but it was the closest thing to hand. Completing the look, a small hand towel was draped over her right shoulder.

Charlotte indicated for Ayesha to take a seat at the table. With Charlotte’s glass of something red on the table next to one of the chairs, Ayesha sat opposite, near the tap.

“You know I've got the day off today, Detective Constable... so what brings you around here?” Charlotte asked, whilst pulling out the bobble around her ponytail and towelling down the now free hair.

“Well, I was saying Ma'am, I tried to phone but I couldn't get through to you...”

“Yeah, I think it's dead, or I've left it somewhere... “ Charlotte employed her stock reply for why she hasn’t been watching her phone every five seconds, like the rest of the world.

"I just wanted to make sure you were alright. After yesterday, and everything?"

This made Charlotte stop for a while. She wasn't expecting that. "Yes. Yes. Fine, thank you. We had a good walk, cleared the cobwebs."

"I'm glad to hear that. It's just that after I dropped you off, I did some more digging and we've had a development in the case."

"Excellent! Would you like a cuppa? And you can tell me all about it." The inference was she was having one anyway, and that became clear when she stood up and walked back inside the house.

"Err, then, yes please. Coffee, please, if you have it." she said, straining her head in the general direction Charlotte went, as if to steer the words on the right trajectory.

Ayesha's phone pinged. Looking at it, it's a text message from 'DCI Walker'. *'Who sends texts these days?'* Ayesha thought, but then realised it was totally in keeping with the technophobe Charlotte Walker. She pressed to open the message. At first, she wasn't clear on what she was seeing... and then it clicked.

"Hey! You haven't lived until you've
received dirty texts in Latin!"

Had Charlotte - her boss - just sent her a dirty text in Latin??

'Virtus eius autem impulsus mirabilis erat.'

Ayesha held her finger down on the text to copy it, and pasted it into Google Translate. The English translation appeared...

'The strength of his thrust was wonderful'

Ayesha's eyes widened in surprise and amusement. 'God, she's brazen!' she thought , shaking her head both in disbelief and amazement that Charlotte is confident enough to send it.

From inside the kitchen, Charlotte opened one of the windows which looked out on the patio. Knowing full well what the text message was and who it was from, she acted all innocent and asked, "How do you have it?"

"White, no sugar please." came the reply - and in the light of the text message... "And strong..."

Charlotte smiled, understanding the reference.

"I'm not used to doing coffee, I'm afraid." she said, putting half a spoonful of instant coffee into the second mug.

"I'm sure it will be ok." the voice from outside said.

The ritual of making a hot drink was ingrained inside Charlotte, and without having to think about it, she grabbed the kettle, placed it beneath the faucet and turned on the tap to fill it up.

Nothing happened.

There wasn't the customary torrent of fresh water cascading into the kettle.

And then it hit Charlotte - of course, nothing would be coming out; the stop cock was still turned off.

She opened the door to the cupboard underneath the sink, bobbed down, and steadily turned it back on. The only problem was, she didn't know how much to turn it, so she just opened it fully.

The water, which had been held back for a while now, was allowed to continue its journey. Charlotte heard it hissing as it travelled around the pipework of the house, and into the various taps, where it would be ready to be called upon when needed.

But if, for example, there was a tap in the network the water now couldn't reach, because, say, the pipe which fed it had previously come away... well, the pressure would just spurt water over anyone who happened to be sitting in the general vicinity...

So, perhaps inevitably, there was a massive squeal from outside.

Charlotte stood up quickly from the cupboard to see an explosion of water everywhere outside from the not-fixed tap, and a completely drenched Ayesha trying desperately to get out of the way but slipping down on the soaked patio.

Charlotte clenched her teeth hard over her bottom lip to stop herself crying out.

Whoops!

Chapter 11

"There'll be something you can change into in my wardrobe. Sorry!"

Charlotte sent the soaking Ayesha upstairs. The younger detective seemed more surprised and shaken than upset and angry, and Charlotte was glad about that.

Ayesha's footsteps heading upstairs resonated loudly throughout the house. Apart from Toni and David, the old place didn't see many visitors, and it decided to make the most of it now it did.

Carrying the two mugs, Charlotte watched her start to climb the stairs, then moved into the living room, putting Ayesha's mug of coffee on the coffee table. Keeping her own mug in her hands, she sat down on the sofa and took a long sip of the tan brown liquid within - despite its temperature.

Charlotte suddenly realised she might have left something personal out in her room. "Ignore anything shocking pink that might be on my bedside drawers!"

From upstairs, Ayesha thought she heard for the first time the faint sound of embarrassment in Charlotte's voice. "I've not seen anything" she assured. Charlotte couldn't decide whether that meant she hadn't seen anything because it wasn't there, or that she had seen it and was being discreet. Charlotte hoped it was the former, but suspected it was the latter.

"So what had you come to tell me?" Charlotte

shouted upstairs.

Ayesha shouted down from upstairs in a determined voice. “Tempto Digital's founding twins, Scott and Carl Remington? Carl died in 2012, passing his share of the company to Scott. And Scott died in 2017, when all the company passed to his wife, Amber Remington.”

Charlotte, in the manner Amber corrected them yesterday, “*Ms* Amber Remington.”

“*Ms* Amber Remington - who since has sold off around 40% of the company...”

That was interesting, thought Charlotte. 40% of a multi-million pound company is certainly enough motive for someone to kill. “...making her a pretty tidy sum, I'd guess.”

“Yes Ma'am.” came the reply from upstairs.

Charlotte’s mind started to race. Thought lines appeared on her forehead. “So how did they die?”

Ayesha paused for a while, suggesting she was trying something on. “Carl from a heart attack; natural causes; Scott in a shed fire.”

“A shed fire? What, like a man shed?” Another long sip of tea.

“By shed, we’re talking something double the size of your garage.”

“Ah,”

“More like a games room, really. Had a mini cinema and a snooker table in there.”

Charlotte took a long gulp of her tea, finishing it

off in one go. That asbestos mouth in action again. "Snooker. Ok..."

"Mmm. Two other interesting things as well. Number one; parts of a remotely activated improvised exploding device were found in Scott's shed fire..."

Charlotte didn't expect that. "So it was murder? With an IED?"

"No-one was ever done. And number two, Amber, *Ms* Amber Remington, found both bodies." came the shouted reply.

"Really? That *is* interesting..." Charlotte's eyes developed her patented questioning look.

"Thought you'd think so, that's why I came around." The voice sounded as though it had made a choice on what to wear, and was just putting it on.

Charlotte heard Ayesha was at the top of the stairs, and so she swapped the empty mug she was holding for the full mug of coffee and walked into the hallway ready to hand it to her.

Ayesha came down the stairs wearing a loud baggy t-shirt with the word 'London' in large letters at an angle over the top of white and red line drawings of famous landmarks from the capital, all on a black background. The stonewashed dark blue jeans would have come down below her feet if it wasn't for the high-heeled shoes she wore to give her just that little bit of extra height.

Charlotte stared at her aghast.

"What's a matter Ma'am?"

“You went into the wrong room. They're Richard's clothes.” came the quiet reply.

“Richard...?” Ayesha tried desperately to understand the significance, other than that she'd Inadvertently put on some man's clean clothes. She remembered yesterday Charlotte talking about her siblings... Yes, that must be it. “Is he your brother?”

“No. He was my partner who died a year ago today.” she said flatly.

Ayesha’s head was in a whirl. So, let’s get this straight... Charlotte wasn’t in a relationship with Toni; they were good friends - but that didn’t explain the intensity of the embrace, but think about that later. Charlotte’s partner who was killed was a *bloke* - Richard. Now come to think about it, she could recall Charlotte being picked up by a skinny man outside the station, and she was wearing his clothes because she turned right at the top of the stairs and not left. And - most of all for Ayesha - this probably means Charlotte is straight.

It was a lot to process.

“Oh I'm so sorry Ma'am. I'll go and...”

“No, no - it's ok.” Charlotte interrupted her. She could see there was an unasked question on Ayesha’s lips, and she decided to answer it. “I couldn’t bring myself to get rid of all his clothes, so I kept some in the spare room.”

Ayesha walked past Charlotte and went into the living room. She sat down in one of the individual chairs and wished the comfy arms would swallow her up. Charlotte remained fixed in the hallway, and took another look at the London t-shirt from her position out of the room.

"I bought him that the day we went to see the Queen."

To say Ayesha was lost for words was an understatement. "Sorry Ma'am." was all that came out.

The wind had been knocked out of Charlotte a bit, as she realised she was still holding Ayesha's coffee. Gingerly she offered it to Ayesha, who got up quickly to take it off her.

Before Ayesha could take a sip, the front door burst open and Toni barged into the living room.

"Are you not ready?" she asked in her no-nonsense manner, looking straight at Charlotte, and not initially seeing Ayesha.

"Ready for what?"

"Mantrailing!"

Charlotte looked around the room to find anything which told the time - which was a vain hope as there were only three clocks in the entire house, and none of those was in the living room. "God, is it that time? Bugger. Errr, you've got the bag, haven't you?"

"Yes! And I prepared some treat pots too." she said to Charlotte, as she went to the back garden to fetch Bronte.

"God, you're a star Toni!" shouted Charlotte.

"Yeah! Yeah!"

Watching from the side was Ayesha, who took

advantage of the activity to finally take a sip of her coffee - and she instantly wished she hadn't. Try as she might, she couldn't hide the fact it was bloody awful on her face.

"Charlotte's coffee?" asked Toni. *'How did she guess?'* Ayesha slightly nodded her head. "Yeah... never agree to Charlotte's coffee." Toni took the cup of coffee off Ayesha and poured what loosely constituted a drink into the pot plant in the room - and then gave Ayesha the cup back. Toni smiled at Ayesha, just as Charlotte returned from the back garden with Bronte on a lead, giving him to Toni. "Come on boy, let's get in the minibus while your Mum gets her boots on."

"You finished already?" Charlotte asked Ayesha, indicating to the coffee cup, as she put one foot into a walking boot.

"Yes." came the rather meek reply as Charlotte hopped over to her, one foot in a boot and one foot out, to take the cup off her.

"You're coming with us."

"Well, I'm on duty, Ma'am."

"Then, you're definitely coming with us. That's an order." Charlotte said, finally putting the other walking boot on.

"Err, ok... Ma'am."

"But you'll need to change those..." Charlotte pointed to the dainty high-heeled shoes just visible beneath the borrowed jeans, which were the only part of the outfit she arrived in that she was still able to wear. "Those should fit you." pointing to a specific pair in a rack of walking boots in the hallway that wouldn't look out of place in an outdoor shop.

"Close the door when you come out." Charlotte said, leaving the house, but crossing over with Toni, as she came back in to check they'd got everything.

"Are you coming too?" she said to Ayesha.

As she grabbed the suggested pair of boots, she replied "I've been ordered."

Toni smiled. She pointed to Ayesha's t-shirt and quipped, "Let me guess… you're from the Met?"

* * *

Toni's dog-friendly taxi was pretty amazing. A custom-converted Ford Tourneo Custom minibus, with dog cages built into the back, and three individual coach-style seats in the middle row between the cages and the three seats up front. In orange, it looked very striking outside, with black vinyls saying 'Toni's Taxi' liberally applied around the body. Charlotte explained that she had told Toni that technically the vehicle was a minicab and not a taxi, but Toni liked the alliteration so she had called it that.

Despite the minibus having three seats at the front, Ayesha was sitting in the seat behind Charlotte, as the middle seat at the front contained a tote-style bag which was clearly important to today's activities. Something else very important for what they were going to do was Bronte - who was in the top row of the dog cages. Ayesha turned around to look at the dog, who was asleep and obviously was used to travelling. Ayesha studied the cages; they took up the whole of the back end of the minibus - where the third row of seats would have been - with two cages on the top and two on the bottom, each with separate doors But, as Toni had explained to her, they were designed so the divider which made two cages could be removed, to make one very large cage - and this was what Bronte was enjoying, spreading himself out and sprawled across where the divider would have been.

Ayesha turned back around to look out of the windscreen, and by now, she'd gotten over her initial embarrassment at seeing Toni so soon after mistaking her and Charlotte for a couple. She leaned forward, stretching the seatbelt to its limit like a child wanting to be a part of their parents' conversation. "So how do you two know each other?" she asked, either of them really.

Without taking her eyes off the road ahead, Toni said to Charlotte "She asks a lot of questions."

Charlotte turned to Toni to reply, with a smile. "She's a detective; what do you expect?"

It was a fair point. Toni was just about to talk, when coming along a side road joining theirs, she spotted a car which looked like it wasn't going to stop. Anticipating, Toni braked hard, but safely - and the car did indeed cut up in front of them. Ayesha had been holding on for dear life, whereas Charlotte took it in her stride, knowing Toni would be on it. Toni glared at the car now in front of her, and silent words of anger - possibly of four letters in length - seemed to be willing themselves to the driver.

Toni took a breath. When she was confident she was in full control again, she looked in the rear view mirror at Ayesha and said "This one saved my life."

Charlotte rolled her eyes and shook her head, as if she'd heard this many times before. "Oh please! Stop being so over-dramatic!"

"You did." Toni replied emphatically.

With Charlotte still shaking her head at what she thought was Toni's exaggeration, Ayesha inquired, "What happened?" Charlotte decided to look out of her window.

Toni had a tale to tell, and a willing listener. Mostly she kept her eyes on the road, but every so often, she glanced in the rear view mirror to look at Ayesha.

"I was going to agility classes with my dog Patch - you know like they do at Crufts with the jumping? Well, I wasn't really in any of the cliques there and was ready to pack it in, when this lady turned up with that dog." Charlotte smiled slightly at this point, as if recalling this time together. "They'd recently moved back here from *darn saurf*", she said with a mock Cockney accent, "and when we got chatting she persuaded me to stay and we became friends."

She looked across at Charlotte, who noticed the break in the story, and glanced across to see Toni's warm and thankful smile. She half shook her head as if to brush aside everything, but gave a radiant smile in return.

Charlotte turned back to the window, as if she knew what was coming next. Toni continued, but her tone had changed. "Then around two months ago Patch died from cancer and within a week I was diagnosed with breast cancer. I don't have any family and I didn't know how I was going to get through it - not having a dog 'cos Patch was my life. I didn't want to get another as I didn't think it was fair, so this one said I could look after Bronte whenever I wanted, and I could run him in competitions."

Charlotte turned back to Ayesha. "Got their first 'first place' last week."

Ayesha smiled at Toni, clearly impressed.

Toni continued her tail. "Then she came up with the idea of the dog taxi. Said to me there's no taxis in the area for getting people with dogs around; you know to the vets or such like; so she persuaded me to look into it and talked her dad into investing - and I've not looked back. Now I have loads and loads of dogs in my life!" Toni paused at this point to look at Charlotte. "She's extraordinary, this one."

Ayesha turned to look at Charlotte, who also had turned away quickly to look out of her side window. There, no one could see the embarrassment now. It was fine for Charlotte to help people; that's what she did, who she was... she just didn't want to have to listen to people thanking her. After all, she had to be talked into accepting the George Cross by all her family, friends and Richard, because she didn't want the attention.

"Yes... I've seen that." said Ayesha, full of quiet admiration..

It was then Ayesha realised why she'd read their relationship wrong through the window. They *were* in love; but as extremely close friends who had shared the highs and lows of life over the last couple of months. They were in tune, comfortable and there for each other beyond any platonic friends she'd ever known. And it was lovely.

"Taking a pause next week of course." Toni continued, checking in on Ayesha though the rear-view mirror.

"Why's that?"

"Op time Monday after next. I'm hoping they are cutting all of the big C out of this bad girl..." she said, bashing left breast.

That took Ayesha a little back. She didn't know what to say, and so "What's happening to the taxi when you're recovering?" so all she managed - which sounded a little thoughtless.

Charlotte looked up from checking her messages on her phone. "I'll have some spare time, so I've offered to help out. And my Dad said he'll stay with me and do some shifts. We got our Private hire driver's licence the same time as Toni - just in case."

"Spare time. Of course." said Ayesha, it all became clear... Charlotte has just quit and will be leaving next week. Then, she made another detective leap. "And you just told her that yesterday morning..." came what was a statement rather than a question, and what put the scene she saw from the car into proper context.

Charlotte turned back to Ayesha for a moment and flashed her a knowing smile. Almost as quickly, she turned back around; it's that recognition thing going off.

Toni slowed the taxi down for the next junction. For a moment, there was silence. It seemed an appropriate time, Ayesha thought, and looked at Toni through the rear-view mirror. “I'm sorry about the cancer.”

Toni caught her gaze and held it as she waited for the traffic. “Ahhh, don't be, love. In a bizarre way it's one of the best things to have happened to me. I wasn't living for years after my husband died, and now, I'm more alive than I ever have been. And I'll fight it - don't you worry!”

Even in the short time Ayesha had known Toni, it was the response she’d have expected from her. She wasn’t the type of person to be taking this lying down, and if you were to put money on anyone having a fantastic life after such an event, it would be Toni.

Looking out of the side window, Ayesha couldn’t help feeling both awe of and a little inferior to these two superwomen. Strong, confident and powerful females; she hoped she’d be like that one day.

Except better at making coffee.

Chapter 12

Of all the activities which can be undertaken with dogs, mantrailing was an odd mix of a very social affair for the humans, yet each of the dogs worked separately - making it perfect for any nervous or reactive dogs.

Charlotte had always found it a difficult activity to describe to people - many knew of agility from watching Crufts every year; the same of flyball - the relay race for dogs - because it regularly features at Crufts too. But mantrailing wasn't in the public's mind in the same way.

Charlotte eventually settled for 'hide and seek for dogs'. It seemed to do the trick.

Toni's van was parked in a layby just off a quiet lane which ran past a wood. There were four other cars also parked in the layby - a Land Rover Discovery, a Toyota Auris, a Kia - but all fairly big cars. *'Well, they'd have to be to transporting dogs'*, Ayesha thought. Each car had some sort of dog cage or crate in its boot, but obviously none of the other cars had the size of cages that were in Toni's minibus van.

All the cars present had their boots open, and all had one dog in them - apart from one.

Soon, a brown spaniel on a lead emerges from the trees, followed by her owner, and a lady who had the presence of a class teacher.

"That's Lucy, the mantrailing instructor." Toni said to Ayesha, realising she'd be needing a running commentary on proceedings.

"Great work Sam - and Tilly, of course! Coming on very nicely." Lucy said to the lady owner and the spaniel. As they went back to their car, Lucy turned to Charlotte. "Bronte - you're next."

Charlotte walked over to the minibus and collected Bronte, and a range of mantrailing paraphernalia. Clicking a normal lead on Bronte, Charlotte walked him over to the start area, where a ladies top was already on the ground. As Charlotte sorted herself out with leads and treats, Ayesha looked puzzled.

"So what exactly is this then?" she asked Toni.

"You know like Search and Rescue dogs? It's a bit like that. They're training the dogs to follow a scent and find a missing person."

"Oh a Misper." replied Ayesha.

Toni looked at her with a semi-glare. "Yes. I forgot you're a copper! The misper is already hiding in the woods, and that's her scent article there."

Charlotte already had Bronte on a shortish lead, which looked like it was made of two distinct thick strands of blue and purple wound together, but Charlotte also had another lead in her hand, which she placed on the ground. This lead was all black, a lot thinner in style and in a circular coil - and looked to be something like five metres if unravelled.

"That's Bronte's mantrailing lead." Toni explained, sensing Ayesha's wonderment." Charlotte puts that down on the ground next to the scent article - the top - and they both walk around it."

As she spoke, Charlotte led Bronte around the two items on floor of the wood.

“This is the routine to get Bronte to know that he's about to acquire the scent.” Toni continued.

Charlotte clipped Bronte’s mantrailing lead onto his harness and pointed with the gun shape for him to sniff the scent article.

“So, that's him acquiring the scent... and now Lottie will tell him to trail.”

“Trail!” Charlotte shouted to Bronte.

Bronte took a second or two to decide where the scent he’d been told to trail was, and then he was off. Charlotte followed confidently behind, holding the mantrailing lead and keeping it taught. An entourage of Lucy, Toni and Ayesha followed, a short distance away.

“Good boy.” said Charlotte, knowing Bronte needed reassurance throughout the trail.

The border collie was making good progress and good choices, turning down different cuttings in the wood, all the while following the scent of the Mispa. Every so often, he would stop for a wee and to check the direction.

The trail had gone on for a while, and Ayesha was amazed at the way he was sniffing around and managing to find the trail..

Suddenly, they reached a clear fork in the path, and Bronte stopped dead. The scent could go either way here, and he has to get this right. He tentatively sniffed both directions, and then decided on the narrowest, least-likely path.

“I'm not sure it's this way Bronte.” Charlotte said.

However, Bronte was sure, and started to lead Charlotte along the narrow path. It became increasingly overgrown and difficult to walk through, and so Charlotte decided Bronte had made a mistake.“No, it's not this way, boy. Come on.”

Against Bronte’s will, Charlotte took them both back to the fork in the paths, and tried to cajole him into going down the more obvious path.

Bronte took the instruction from his partner, and tried to believe it was this way; his nose desperately searching for evidence of the scent... but it wasn’t there.

Despondent, Charlotte said to Lucy, “I don't know what's a matter with him today.”

The reply from Lucy was unapologetic. “It's not him.” she replied, not flinching.

“What do you mean?”

“He had it. He was right.”

"Eh?"

“Take him back to the fork and try again.” the instructor commanded.

Back at the fork, Lucy offered some words of encouragement. “This time trust your dog.”

Charlotte dug deep inside and tried to sound positive for Bronte. “Trail!” she instructed.

Bronte immediately was on it, and headed straight down the narrow path once again. Charlotte still wasn’t convinced, but this time, Lucy’s words echoed in her head, and she's more supportive this time. The support passed down the lead and within a few moments, Bronte found the 'missing person' sitting amongst some trees.

"Good boy. Well done." said the Misper, giving Bronte his reward pot which was full of Bronte's favourite treat - cream cheese.

"That was amazing!" Ayesha shouted, a little too enthusiastic for their surroundings.

Charlotte ducked down to Bronte's height and said, "Good boy." It hadn't gone unnoticed that he was right and she was wrong.

"See? Trust your dog, Lottie. He's good; really coming on. He just needs you to trust him more." Lucy said, supportively.

Charlotte took a deep breath and tried to hide her feelings that she'd let Bronte down. "Yeah. Sorry. Bad couple of days at work and other stuff."

Lucy looked at Charlotte with a glance that said she understood more than Charlotte's words. "Don't be telling me sorry..." she said, indicating down to Bronte.

"Yeah..." Charlotte sighed, and kneeled down in front of Bronte. "Sorry boy, your mum was a bit crap there!" she said, fussing both sides of his head with her hands. Bronte responded with an "it's ok" kiss, or three.

"Anyway, you shouldn't be too hard on yourself... that's a five hour aged trail. Well done you two!" Lucy exclaimed, as Charlotte returned back to full human height and the party started to make their way on a more direct path back to the starting point.

Ayesha looked around and noticed Toni had set off first and was a little way ahead. As Charlotte seemed to be chatting with Lucy, she decided to catch up with her. "Aged trail?" she asked, when she was walking next to Toni.

Without looking at her, Toni replied, "The Misper went off into the woods five hours ago, and Bronte was able to follow the scent. The older the scent is, the harder it is for him to track."

Ayesha nodded in understanding. "They are very good, aren't they?"

"Yes. Quite the team. Bronte's helped Lottie get through the past year, since Richard went. They got him together, so he means an awful lot to her. "

Charlotte and Bronte were walking a little bit behind Ayesha and Toni; Charlotte enjoying Bronte's company, when Lucy eventually caught up. She'd been chatting with the Mispa, who was staying where they were ready to be found by the next pairing of dog and human. She caught her breath and decided to ask Charlotte what had been on her mind.

"Was that you yesterday?"

"What?" Charlotte replied, genuinely not getting what Lucy was talking about.

"On that bridge. With that man."

"Oh, yes. Yes, it was."

"It was incredible. I saw it on Facebook."

'Bloody Facebook' mused Charlotte. "Yeah, well, he just needed someone to listen to him. We all need that."

Lucy looked at Charlotte as they walked. "God, how can you be so calm about it?"

She turned towards Lucy and said, matter of factly, "It's who I am.", before returning back to her thoughts of why and where she ballsed-up that trail.

"Your girlfriend's nice." Lucy looked towards Ayesha. "Odd taste in clothes mind..."

"She's my new partner. Just come up from London." In her preoccupied state of mind, Charlotte thought it was clear she meant *work partner*. However, she didn't realise how the nine words of her reply could be interpreted rather differently.

"I can see that." Lucy said, referring to Ayesha's borrowed t-shirt and her tongue firmly in her cheek. "Well, good for you. All the times you've been coming to mantrailing and we've never heard about you dating or anything...so it's good you've found someone."

With that, Lucy ran ahead to set up the next trail, leaving Charlotte a little aghast at how that conversation went so wrong.

Ayesha looked around their surroundings. "It's a nice quiet wood this. Some lovely areas of wild flowers."

"You into your wild flowers?" Toni asked.

Ayesha thought about this question before answering. "I'm a bit of an amateur botanist, yes." She wondered why she was slightly embarrassed by mentioning this, when she'd already revealed to Charlotte she was also a comic book fanatic.

"Well, you want to get yourself into April Wood before it is shut off. There's tons in there."

"April Wood?" Ayesha repeated, as she nearly tripped over a very well hidden large fallen branch. *'Watch where you are going sometimes Ayesha Stoker, rather than who you are talking to'* she thought to herself.

Toni grabbed onto her arm, and stopped her from falling completely over. And then let go almost as quickly. "That's what it has always been called locally as it is full of bluebells in April."

"So why not Bluebell Wood?" asked Ayesha, puzzlingly.

Toni seemed to be astonished by this; as if no-one has ever voiced this perfectly logical question. "I don't know!" she said abruptly. "I didn't come up with the name!"

Ayesha smiled at her. She'd realised by now Toni's bark was worse than her bite.

"So what's happening to this April Wood?"

"Some company has bought it. Don't know why. They'd never get planning permission to change it anything else. Doesn't make sense. It's not the only wood either; from what I've heard, seems to be buying a lot up and then closing them off to the public." replied Toni.

Charlotte all of a sudden raced up to be between them, putting her hands on their closest shoulders, and said "That sounds rather intriguing, doesn't it?!"

* * *

"So why are you interested in who is buying that wood?" Ayesha shouted to Charlotte.

"I don't know; no real reason; just interested I guess." came the reply from Charlotte, who was kneeling down in her kitchen turning on the stopcock.

On the way back from mantrailing, they'd called in at Toni's to pick up a blanking plug for the outside tap that Toni just happened to have in her toolbox. Having fitted the temporary fix, the trio could have a hot drink, and Bronte could have some fresh water in his bowl.

"Curious as to who'd want to buy a wood that they couldn't do anything with..." Charlotte shouted into the living room over the top of the increasing roar of the kettle.

Charlotte's living room wasn't in the same size league as Amber's, but it was longer than it was wide, and so practically was divided into two rooms; a living area at the front end of the house where the sofas and the television was, and a music room-come-study at the back. An upright piano graced one wall, the type several generations of primary school children would have seen and heard played at assemblies in the hall. On the opposite wall, an open rack housing a Technics Hi-Fi separate system circa 1998, and a desk - which was where Charlotte kept her laptop.

And it was this desk Ayesha was sitting at, laptop open, investigating their unofficial case of the woods, with Toni watching her as she perched on one of the arms of the spare sofa which divided the two parts of the room.

"Ok. Let's see." said Ayesha, as she poked around on the Land Registry website. "Says 'Electrum Investments Ltd.'"

Charlotte returned from the kitchen with three cups filled with drink and a small block of cheese in her hands. Toni was very concerned. "Firstly, that's tea, right?" she asked.

"Yes." came the slightly perplexed reply.

Ayesha and Toni exchanged a look of relief. Ayesha had learnt her lesson with Charlotte's coffee.

"And secondly, the cheese?"

"Oh, well, that, my friend, is for me." said Charlotte, as she took a bite out of the block. "Mmmm" she said, appreciating the cheese. Toni looked at Charlotte with mock incredulity, as Bronte mops up the tiny morsel of cheese that Charlotte dropped.

"Extra mature?" asked Ayesha. Charlotte nodded. A smile crossed Ayesha's face as she looked back down at the laptop screen to study the new information she'd uncovered. "They've been buying up several other woods too. A few around here. Some in Lincolnshire, Anglesey, south Midlands..."

Charlotte pondered. She was sure there was a connection between those places, but at this time of night and after the last couple of days, she was unable to make it. Maybe in the morning...

"Makes you wonder why..." Toni said, after swallowing the first sip of her tea.

"We'll make a detective of you yet Tones!" Charlotte exclaimed, tapping her hands on Toni's shoulders as she walked behind to the sofa to sit on the other end.

Ayesha typed on the keyboard and visited the Companies House website. She searched for 'Electrum Investments' and scrolled down the page. She left out an "Mmm", as she clicked, scrolled, clicked some more, all following a trail of companies, but without finding any real clues. "Well, they certainly don't want you to find out much... shell companies and more shell companies, and directors registered in the Cayman Islands." she concluded.

Charlotte pondered. She knew there was something strange happening here when she overheard Toni talking to Ayesha earlier - and the complex web of company organisations certainly seemed to bear that view out. It was worth investigating some other time.

The mood of the evening was disturbed by the ringtone of Toni's mobile phone singing from her handbag. 'You Sexy Thing' by Hot Chocolate seemed *so* Toni. Flustered, she quickly found the phone and looked at the screen on the phone; 'Unknown Caller' it said. Toni gingerly answered it, as though she had an idea who it would be - and judging by her face, it wasn't someone she was happy about.

"Hello? Yes, this is Toni Madden." She listened to the caller, and got increasingly stressed and upset. "Listen, I've told you already that I'm not paying. I can't afford it." she told the person on the other end of the phone.

As Toni listened to the reply, Charlotte and Ayesha got increasingly worried for Toni. What *was* going on?

"But you can't take me off the map. Without being online, I won't have a business!"

Silence as Toni listened to the caller.

“But I've never had to pay to be on the maps before. I've told you I can't afford that!”

The voice on the other side seemed to get very agitated at this point.

“Please, don't do this!” she pleaded, breaking down.

Charlotte had watched from the sidelines too long and needed to do something. She grabbed the phone from Toni. “Who is this? Answer me!” she shouted into the phone.

The caller hung up immediately. Charlotte checked the call history - *Unknown Caller*.

Charlotte looked across at Ayesha, who was watching everything with a look of concern. Handing the phone back to Toni, she asked, “What was that all about?”

At first, Toni didn’t want to say, but by now she realised she couldn’t avoid it any longer. “I've had five calls this week from this man saying I now have to pay to be included on all the maps apps. But it's never been that way before? I can't afford it!”

Ayesha suddenly got up and looked intensely at Charlotte - this was their current case in the real world. Charlotte nodded back in acknowledgement.

“Why didn't you tell me about this before?” exclaimed Charlotte.

“Because I don't see you as police, but as my best friend.” Toni explained vociferously.

Charlotte accepted that, even though it didn’t make

any sense to her. In Charlotte's eyes, she *was* police - you couldn't have one without the other.

She grabbed both of Toni's hands and held them tightly with love. "Ok. Listen, this is what we're working on right now. This stuff."

"Right." Toni understood.

"And we're going to sort it, ok? These are blackmailers, and you shouldn't have to pay them. You did the right thing." she said, making sure she caught Toni's eyes, which were trying to look anywhere but at Charlotte.

"Ok."

"You need to give Ayesha a statement; tell us everything. What did he sound like? Can you describe their voice?"

"Well, I'll have recorded him." Toni said, matter-of-factly.

"What do you mean?" Charlotte asked, slowly.

"My phone. It's set to record all my conversations."

"Oh you beauty!!" Charlotte said, her face all lit up.

Ayesha got up and the two detectives gathered around the small speaker of Toni's mobile phone. When they were ready, Toni played the recording. A voice which sounded distinctly male was heavily disguised using some sort of modulation technique.

After it had finished, Ayesha looked intently across at Charlotte. "Well, even with that distortion you can make out some sort of an accent, don't you think?" the DCI said.

Ayesha nodded. “Yeah. I'll send it to the Tech guys. May I?”

With a flat open hand, Ayesha asked for the phone from Toni. “Yes, certainly.” came the reply, along with the phone, after unlocking it with her PIN code. The young detective studied the phone intensely and within seconds had sent it to her own work email address so she could send it on later.

Toni was quiet.

“Are you ok?” Charlotte asked.

Toni ignored the question, and instead asked one of her own to Ayesha. “Have I been taken off?”

Ayesha was on her phone forwarding the voice recording to the people who needed it. With Toni’s question, she glanced up and saw how distraught she was. She so wanted to give her a crumb of comfort, but when she looked at the various mapping apps she had installed, *Toni's Taxis* had gone from all of them.

“Yeap.” she replied.

“What am I going to do now?!” Toni said, breaking down.

Chapter 13

After a day off, it seemed incredibly cruel to have to go into work on a Sunday. A beam of light shone through the gap in the curtains where Charlotte hadn't closed them together fully, and it was hitting the exact spot she was laying.

She started to awake, and in her dazed mindset rolled over to run her hands over Richard's chest.

Except he wasn't there.

Then she awoke fully.

'Christ,' she thought, *'dreaming about him again.'* She wondered when this would stop. After the one year anniversary, she kept telling herself - but clearly that hadn't made a difference. It was all the little things in bed she missed. She missed laying her head on his chest; she missed his leg slung over hers; she missed him running his fingers through her hair.

And the sex. She missed that too.

At the moment, the CD player on her Sony Dream Machine alarm clock whirred into action, and 'Georgy Girl' by The Seekers played in an attempt to stir a sleepy Charlotte out of bed. She swung two legs out of bed, which clearly disagreed with the intended action.

Half an hour to get ready and get into work.

A quick cuppa, some toast, Bronte out for his morning wee and dressed - from the work outfit section.

The bonus about working on a Sunday was she could be fairly certain to be able to leave the house ten minutes before she was supposed to start work. And that was a theory she was putting to the test this morning.

* * *

The weather looked set for the rest of the day. The sun radiating down even managed to make the Doncaster Police Station look relatively attractive. The clouds present in the sky looked like they had been through a shredder.

Charlotte was sitting at her desk, a brew of tea in her left hand in a mug proclaiming 'World's Greatest Auntie'. It was more like a bucket than a mug, Ayesha thought; its size almost verging on it being a novelty mug for decoration only, than one to actually use in real life. Ayesha had a sensible - normal - sized mug, filled with a Vanilla Latte.

Charlotte looked at the clock on the wall - *'ten minutes bang on'* she noted..

"So, I think with knowing how Tone's phone call went last night, and the four previous ones, we can safely say there's blackmail going off at Tempto Digital."

"The company has access to a base map which affects most of the leading mapping apps..." agreed Ayesha

"And it has data on all the businesses included on

it... a ready made Yellow Pages to contact businesses and blackmailing them to paying up or be removed from the apps."

"Yellow Pages?" replied Ayesha, narrowing her eyes.

Charlotte looked across at her partner. How is she only five years younger than me and yet doesn't know of seemingly universal cultural references, she wondered. She considered for a moment an explanation of the once ubiquitous big, thick yellow directory... but then decided against it. "Doesn't matter... "

"How is she today?" Ayesha asked, assuming correctly Charlotte would have already talked to her.

"Still upset. I'm not sure whether more from the fact someone phoned her and talked to her like that; got her personal number from somewhere; or from not being on the mapping apps."

"It shouldn't really affect her not being on the maps anyway, should it?" asked Ayesha, voicing something she'd been thinking about all night.

"I wouldn't have thought so. Do people go on a mapping app looking for a minicab?"

It seemed a rhetorical question, but coming from the technophobe Charlotte, Ayesha thought she should reply. "No, they'd do a Google search probably for minicabs in a certain area. Or if you wanted a dog-friendly one, you'd search for *dog-friendly taxis*."

"Yeah." Charlotte agreed. "But for the pet food shop, not being on mapping apps I guess would be a big deal..."

Again, a seemingly rhetorical question, but Ayesha

replied, “Oh definitely, Ma’am.”

Charlotte nodded. “So, there's more than a high chance Sarah found out about this...”

“Do you think that's why she's gone missing?”

“I think this is looking more of a kidnapping than a missing person...” Charlotte said.

‘That changes a lot’, Ayesha thought.

“The CCTV from Tempto Digital has come through, Ma'am.”

“Now we might get somewhere!” she exclaimed. “Anything interesting?”

“Yes, but not in the way you'd might have hoped...” she replied cryptically.

Charlotte looked puzzled as Ayesha turned her monitor around to face the DCI; the cable to the desktop computer only just long enough to allow the direction.. On the screen, Ayesha had open a video file in the media player, and a window showing the files contained within a folder.

Using her mouse, Ayesha pressed the big ‘play’ button on the media player, and the readied video file started. It was a screen showing the security turnstiles in the reception area of Tempto Digital, from an elevated viewpoint somewhere above the reception desk. Charlotte closed her eyes for a moment, and rotated a 3D model of the reception area in her head, so she could fully grasp what she was looking at.

“So, Ma’am, Sarah Knight entering the building for work at eight thirty am as we already knew...” Ayesha tapped on the monitor near Sarah's figure on the footage.

"...from the key card logs, right."

The filming position of the camera doesn't show a clear image of Sarah walking through the turnstiles; that is until she turned around to talk to someone. The built-in date and time on the bottom right of the footage confirmed when it was recorded.

"Yes. Then out again at one pm for lunch..." Ayesha double clicks open a different video file from the folder she had open. The date and time confirming 13:00 and this time the video shows a very clear image of Sarah, as she was walking towards the camera position and through the turnstiles.

"...back again at quarter to three..." Again, the video Ayesha opened endorsed this.

"...but watch what she is wearing and her hair when she leaves at 6pm..."

Ayesha moved the mouse and clicked a few more times to bring the footage timestamped 18:00 to the fore. Clicking on the play icon, the video showed a very different looking Sarah Knight - the light grey suit of the previous video files had changed to a dark, pinstriped one. But the most striking difference was the length of her hair - a short cropped cut on the previous videos, but then *longer* hair in a ponytail on the video supposedly later in that day.

Charlotte's eyes widened with the discovery. "Bloody hell!"

Ayesha turned to Charlotte. "So unless she had a

change of outfits and hair extensions at work..."

"... that "6pm" footage has come from a different date!" Charlotte jumped in. "So there's nothing here to support the idea it was Sarah who logged out with her own key card at 6pm on Thursday..."

"Well, ANPR has Sarah Knight's car driving away from Tempto Digital at 3:30pm..."

She closed the previous open virtual folder, and double clicked to open another. For a moment, Charlotte was lost in awe at the dexterity Ayesha had around the computer. Suddenly, footage from a traffic camera showed Sarah's car driving along a road, at 3:30pm.

"Really? So where was she going, so soon after just coming back from lunch?"

"Well, her husband never said she went home. But her key card logs have no record of her swiping out of the building until 6pm..."

"Mmmm..." was the sound a pondering Charlotte made in response.

"And one more thing... I ran all the vehicles Tempto Digital owns through the ANPR too..."

In bewildered wonderment, Charlotte asked, "When have you had time for this??"

"Just eager, Ma'am! And look at this... a van registered to the company heading away from Tempto Digital at 4:25pm..."

More clicking, and Ayesha showed Charlotte a traffic camera clip with a white Transit-sized van driving fairly recklessly at 4:25pm down the same road Sarah drove on.

"How many large vans does the company own?"

Ayesha checked on her computer. "Just the one; that one."

Charlotte leaned in across Ayesha and clicked on the 'Play/Pause' icon of the media player window with the mouse. She'd paused the CCTV footage of the white van going past just as it reached the centre of the frame, making a still image to study. She narrowed her eyes in concentration, staring at the dots on the screen which went to make up the picture of the driver.

"Do you know, even though that's blurry... I think I know who that is..."

Chapter 14

Charlotte's car wasn't the only vehicle in the Tempto Digital car park on this Sunday morning, but you could have counted those there on two hands. *'No sign of a white van here though'*, thought Charlotte, as they walked to the entrance.

Unsurprisingly, the automatic doors were switched off. Ayesha tried to open one, but it wouldn't budge. She stepped back and looked around the giant glass building.

"Well, he said he'd be here." she murmured.

"Be nice if he'd have been here to let us in." Charlotte replied with clear consternation. With a hint of irony she continued, "Hey, ring the doorbell..."

For a brief moment, Ayesha started to move forward towards the doors, and then stopped when she realised there was a distinct lack of a doorbell. She turned around to see a playful grin on Charlotte's face.

Just then, they could see the burly figure of Frank Drashler had entered the reception area, together with a group of men who were dressed so similar, they could have been some sort of clone race. Charlotte waved to catch his attention through the glass of the doors.

With a puzzled look on his face, he leaned over the reception desk and pressed a button, opening the two doors into the glass-lined atrium. As Charlotte and Ayesha walked through into the main building, Frank leaned back from the desk to greet them. "Can I help you Detectives? You know it's a Sunday, right?" he asked with a grin.

Charlotte smiled back at him. "Unfortunately crime doesn't stop for the Sabbath, Mr Drashler."

"Kelvin Thomas told us he was here today." Ayesha batted the comment back, without any humour.

"Ah. Well, please, come inside, Detectives." Frank led the two past the reception desk towards the Security turnstiles.

"Do you normally work on Sunday, Mr Drashler?" asked Charlotte.

"As and when, Inspector, as and when." he said, turning to face them as he walked on. "We're undertaking a full security sweep today, and as Head of Security, that's my domain." Just to emphasise the phrase, he ran his hand underneath his name badge.

"Anything serious?"

"Could be a potential data breach. Some of our information has been copied and we need to find it."

"Could this be a police matter?" asked Ayesha, helpfully. Well, they *were* already there...

That stopped Frank in his tracks for a moment. And then he recovered. "Let *us* conduct our search first, and if we need the police, I know where to find you lovely ladies..."

Charlotte acknowledged his complement, whilst it hit a note of smarminess with Ayesha. Charlotte wasn't sure whether it was the thought of the job ahead of him that made him hesitate, or the mention of police involvement...

“If you'd excuse me, I must get on. You know your way to Kelvin's office?” It sounded like a question, but actually was more a statement, as before they could answer either way, Frank had left them both and was moving at pace on his mission, together now with some heavies in black suits. Men In Black, thought Charlotte, wryly.

* * *

This time, Charlotte and Ayesha used the stairs to the first floor - entirely at the request of Charlotte. “It’s only one floor.” she commented. “Come on DC Stoker, it’s good for you!”

As Charlotte held the door for the first floor open for Ayesha, who was distinctly unimpressed and clearly a little bit out of shape, she said “Perhaps you should come out walking with Bronte and me? That’ll do wonders for you.” It wasn’t the stairs on their own that caused Ayesha’s breathlessness, but the desire to match Charlotte’s three steps up at a time stride. A match Ayesha, with her shorter legs, found extremely difficult. Charlotte noticed the slight look of disdain at that moment, and so added an infectious smile to help smooth the sea.

They turned right down the corridor, past the lift, and eventually reached Kelvin Thomas’ office. Ayesha knocked on the door.

No response.

She knocked on the door again.

No response.

She looked through the small but tall window which ran the height of the top part of the door. "He's in there..."

Charlotte wondered whether it would work again. "Try the doorbell."

Ayesha stood back and looked around the door for a second or two, before realising Charlotte was messing *again*. She threw a rueful glance at Charlotte, who just smiled back.

"I'll phone him." Ayesha said, in a self-congratulatory tone.

"Good idea." replied Charlotte, who started to do a little tour around the corridor as Ayesha dialled. She looked at the door marked 'Meeting Room' which was to the left of Kelvin's office, as she looked at it in the corridor. It had the same type of door and Kelvin's, and so she gazed through the window. The room contained a massive pine table around which many chairs were situated. To the right - on the wall next to Kelvin's office - hung one of those electronic white board screen things Charlotte had never got the knack of using when she needed to, and they were presumably powered by the two desktop computers sitting on a desk near to the window.

She tried to open the door, just out of curiosity - but it was locked. It needed one of the key cards to open it, of course. So the contents in the room were safe - no-one could get at them, thought Charlotte. It seemed an obvious thought, but somehow she thought it could be relevant.

“Ma’am?” shouted Ayesha, her head poking into the corridor around the open door to Kelvin’s office, before disappearing inside. The slowly-closing door had just about closed by the time Charlotte had dragged herself away from her deliberations outside the Meeting Room, and she just managed to sneak in.

* * *

Kelvin and Ayesha had already taken up their seating positions from the other day, leaving Charlotte to stand - not that she minded.

Charlotte glanced across at Kelvin. She didn’t think it could be possible, but he looked even more dishevelled than on Friday. Today, he wore a black T-shirt with the main character from ‘Lethal Force 7’ and a pair of ripped jeans. The ensemble would probably work on somebody fifteen years younger, but they looked out of place on him. Charlotte smiled with astonishment about the notion that he’d actually put more effort into the way he looked on a regular weekday.

“It's a bit hectic today, then? For a weekend?” Ayesha asked.

“No idea what they are trying to find but I have to be in.” he said disapprovingly. “I'd rather be at home gaming. Still at least I know the update to ‘Lethal Force 8’ will have downloaded when I get home.”

Charlotte perked up. “Oh yes! Is it out now?”

“Yes, last week.”

“Oh fantastic!I…” she stopped mid-sentence after seeing Ayesha's ‘Let's get to the point’ face and reverted back to a Detective and not a gamer. “Mr Thomas, you told us there wasn't any problems between Sarah Knight and Amber Remington, but the diary entries on her phone we found seem to suggest otherwise.”

“What do you mean?”

Charlotte indicates to Ayesha to begin. Sorting through the papers she was holding, she started to read from the copy of the diary entry in front of her. "’8/4/17 - Confronted Amber about the delay to releasing TimeSMS. She still won't give me a straight answer as to why. That woman is so infuriating."

Charlotte looked seriously across at Kelvin, whose face told her he had nowhere else to go to deflect this. Ayesha continued “Fast forward to four days ago; Wednesday; ‘Amber refuses to see me about the maps issue; says I have to go through Kelvin. But he might be involved.’”

Kelvin’s eyes darted around the room, as if looking for some secret time-space wormhole that he could escape through. He then looked genuinely disappointed when one didn’t materialise...

“So, a couple of things here seem to spring from this... one, how and why did Ms Remington delay the release of the app?” asked Charlotte. “Two, why did Ms Remington refuse to see her about whatever she found, and three, why did you tell us Sarah hadn't discovered anything about the mapping issues, but she clearly had."

Kelvin looked pensive. He took a deep breath and he started the story.

"Back in 2017, Amber was Head of Product; it was a notional position Scott gave her after they got married a couple of years before, but by then, she'd started to believe she actually knew more than the rest of us; started to wield power. The text app was Sarah's baby - the first time we'd gone into apps, and the first time we'd returned to software to the general public - like how Scott and Carl started the company originally. Scott was really excited about it, and was spending a lot of time with Sarah on developing the app - and Amber got jealous. She tried to stop the development anyway she could, and when she failed, she did the only thing she could and stopped the release - saying the app hadn't been tested thoroughly enough, and that she'd better test it herself. It only came out months after Scott's death, and only then because the investors Amber sold parts of the company to pushed for its' release."

Charlotte took this on board with great interest. "So what about the mapping issues?" she continued.

Kelvin shifted in his seat, and looking to the floor started. "You're right, Sarah did discover the issue, and she wanted to go right to Amber to report it. She didn't know who was involved in it."

"This is about the fact that someone at Tempto Digital was blackmailing companies into paying to be on the base map?"

This stopped Kelvin in his tracks. How did she figure it out so quickly? “Yes! Yes,” he said. ”She'd discovered a load of evidence showing all the companies who had paid up and those who hadn't. The ones who paid, stayed on the map; the ones who didn't got erased from the map. But the documents didn't show who was behind it. Sarah suspected I might be involved and so wanted to go straight to Amber.”

“Why would she think that?”

He sighed. “I've got some fairly large credit card debt, Inspector - gaming is an addictive hobby. I guess she thought I was involved to help pay them off.”

“And are you?”

“No!” he exclaimed. “I'm certainly not. No, I knew nothing about any of it. I didn't even know things were going off the map until we got the reports coming in.”

Charlotte studied him for a short while.“And presumably you told Sarah this at your meeting on Thursday?”

“Yes. But anyhow, she said she'd just discovered more files the night before that proved I wasn't involved. She said the documents contained a list of everyone involved. And she said now Amber would *have* to see her.”

Charlotte’s eyes narrowed as the super computer of her brain went into overdrive. “Did Sarah show you these new documents?” she asked.

“No, she said she'd got them on her laptop and had a backup copy too.”

“Did you tell anyone else about this backup copy?”

Kelvin looked deep in thought for a second. "Well, Amber, of course... I told her Sarah had said she had a copy on a USB stick stored away safely."

'Stored away safely.' Those three words echoed around Charlotte's head. She closed her eyes and tried to think how she imagined Sarah would. Needed a safe place. Could be anywhere at home. Except, there'd be a logic to it. So probably in her office - she spent a lot of time in the office. There was an obvious place there, of course - locked up - but that might be *too* obvious. Almost like leaving a calling card - especially if you thought someone might end up being after it. So possibly not at home at all. *'Stored away safely.'* Has to be somewhere she'd got ready access to, that wouldn't raise suspicion. Somewhere safe; locked; needing a key... needing a key...

Charlotte without warning broke from her trance-like state back to the here and now. She looked around at the other two in the room, to see whether she'd make an obvious show of possibly solving a part of the case - but fortunately she hadn't. That was something she'd worked on over the past few years. In the past, she'd literally jumped with joy when coming back from her 'internal deliberations' as one of her former partners put it.

'Ok. So now to get out to check if I am right.' Charlotte thought.

Then, all of a sudden, Charlotte seemed to be experiencing massive pain. Wincing, she moved her hands to hold around her middle and rubbed them around in a circular motion. With the discomfort plain in her voice Charlotte asked, "Err, Mr Thomas, I just wonder if I could use the toilet please?"

"Oh, yes, of course. Are you alright?"

Charlotte whirled through a list in her mind of possible causes for her sudden upset; appendicitis, ovarian cysts, a kidney infection, Crohn's disease, but looking directly at Kelvin she decided she had found the perfect one.

"Women's problems..." she part said; part mouthed, like Les Dawson in his character Ida.

The condition had the desired effect. "Oh, my word, yes." came Kelvin's very embarrassed reply. "Here's my card..." He offered it unquestionably to Charlotte.

"Thank you."

Doubled up, Charlotte took the key card from Kelvin and walked out of his office, closing the door behind her. Ayesha looked on, very concerned, and then looked back at Kelvin, smiling uncomfortably.

* * *

It was a miracle how Charlotte managed to open the door. The pain was excruciating; she had to hold her stomach tight and move very slowly to be able to cope. Steadily, she closed the door to Kelvin's office and was out again into the corridor.

And then the pain stopped.

Or rather, she didn't need an excuse to leave the office for a few minutes, whilst Ayesha kept Kelvin busy.

Knocking her teeth together in thought, she looked around the corridor. In the distance to the left - the direction of the toilets - she saw Frank and his Men In Black leaving one office, chatting, and then entering the opposite office. The office door closed shut. They obviously haven't found it yet then, she thought. By now Charlotte had pretty much sussed out what they might be looking for, and if they were, it put a lot of this case into perspective.

Another gang of Men In Black exited from the lift on the far right side of the corridor, which broke Charlotte from her thoughts. She might only be 33, but years of experience had taught her that the best way not to be caught in a place you shouldn't be is to act as though you owned the place. After all, she was an official visitor, but perhaps not doing what she was officially there to do. They were marching towards and starting to look interested in her, so she thought *'they are men, I'll go with flirting'*.

She flashed them one of her famous smiles and said "Morning boys! Looking smart today!" A rise of the eyebrows helped sell the patter. As they walked past grinning ear-to-ear and craning their necks to still keep sight of her, Charlotte thought she'd add a shift of weight from one foot to the other; model-style. To which they all instantly reverted to being schoolboys and started to chatter presumably about her amongst themselves.

They disappeared into the same office Frank and the other heavies were in, leaving Charlotte thinking it was almost criminal, the power she seemed to have sometimes. Almost.

The way was clear now. She knew from her sweeps of the corridor before there were no CCTV cameras in it; possibly Kelvin's doing.

Charlotte turned right and was on a mission. It was clear she wasn't going to the toilet.

* * *

They'd been travelling for a while, and still there had been no explanation of Charlotte's sudden illness. Was she ok now? Should she be looking for a doctor? Ayesha needed to find out. In the best concerned voice she could muster, she asked "Are you alright, Ma'am?"

Charlotte, however, was already five or six jumps ahead. The case was moving along and she was sure she had started to get a good grasp of the main threads. *'Oh did she ask something?'* Charlotte thought, having to think back to know what to reply to. "Er, yes, of course." she offered.

Ayesha waited a while for any follow up explanation... but one wasn't forthcoming, so she decided to leave it there. "Do you believe him that he wasn't involved in the blackmail?"

"I think I do. I don't think he's got it in him to carry out something so complex and..."

"And what?"

Charlotte paused. "And... well, something so offline!" Ayesha chuckled. She had come to the same conclusion, so it was good to have it affirmed by her superior. Just then, the police radio bursted into life and mentioned the registration plate of a blue Ford Focus for failing to stop and which had given traffic the slip.

“So,” Charlotte started, wanting to work through some of the elements they already knew. ”...we know Sarah left the Tempto building at 3:30 on Thursday, but we don't know where she went after that…”

“...and her car was left abandoned.” her partner added.

“...with no prints on the steering wheel.” continued Charlotte. “Wiped clean. Laptop; wiped clean. But mobile phone - covered with only Sarah's prints.” Ayesha looked across at her. “So chances are they never found her phone...?“ Charlotte deduced with a question.

“Maybe, Ma’am.”

Pondering for a second, Charlotte looked across at Ayesha and said, “Come on.... I'll buy you dinner.”

Chapter 15

Dinner, Ayesha mused, has the connotations of civility. Of good times spent with friends, in pleasant surroundings and with the best food imaginable.

It does not, she continued, have anything to link the word to the place they are right now; a lay-by off one of Doncaster's main roads, with what can only be described as a truck serving what *it* labelled as food.

Now Ayesha didn't see herself as a snob, but she did feel she shouldn't be here. Not because there were a few people - men, really - who looked rather undesirable (actually, in her line of work, that would make this a prime place to be) but more because this looked to be a place where anything which left that truck would only have a passing relationship to 'food' as she knew it.

Still, her boss had brought her here, and both as the newbee and as a passenger in her car, she wasn't really in a position to disagree.

From the picnic bench she was sitting at, Ayesha could see Charlotte was near the front of the queue at the cafe truck. Watching her for a while, Ayesha wondered whether she'd ever have that confidence; that presence Charlotte had in buckets. She was standing there, in a queue completely of men, who were loud, brash and in some cases rowdy, and yet she didn't seem to be phased by it at all. She seemed to give off an aurora; *'don't mess with me, buster'*. At that moment, one of the men in the queue must have made a quip, and Charlotte turned to face him, put her hands on her hips and must have delivered the most amazing put down, as all the others in the queue laughed and giggled at him.

Ayesha's phone pinged; another text message. A wry smile of anticipation crept across her face of who it could possibly be from. 'Charlotte', of course. She opened the message, to see another Latin quote...

'Ex quo ostendit illa quid eum facere,
iustus amat iactantem sem.'

Copying it and pasting into Google Translate again, the Latin became the English translation...

'From the moment she shows him what to do, he just loves tossing salad.'

Ayesha shook her head with a smile on her face, her eyes rolling in mock indignation.

Charlotte by now was at the head of the queue, leaning on the side of the van which was 'Harry's Caf'. The 'Caf' had no 'e', as it was supposed to rhyme with 'gaff'

Harry, the café owner, passed the two sausage sandwiches to Charlotte, and she picked them up, along with two polystyrene cups of tea, with lids on them.

"Thanks Harry. If you hear anything..." Harry nodded, winked at her, and moved to the next customer.

She started walking back towards Ayesha when a large man who barely fitted his own circumstances blocked her way. "I'm wearing a magic watch, and by my watch, you're naked!" he said to Charlotte.

'Jeez' she thought, knowing how this chat up scenario was supposed to go in the bloke's head; she was to say 'I'm not naked,' and he would say, 'Oh, it must be an 1 hour fast.' Except it didn't quite go like that for him this time.

"That's funny," Charlotte said with her head cocked to one side, "'cos I've got one of them too. And by my watch - which is 30 seconds fast - you've got my knee between your legs..." She stared at the man, eyebrows raised, who took only another three seconds to realise he had made a bad choice and moved very quickly out of Charlotte's way.

"Problems?" Ayesha asked, as Charlotte put down the teas on the table and then climbed over the seat of the picnic table in an incredibly un-lady-like manner.

"Naw. Just someone mistakenly infatuated with me. It's understandable, I guess." She smiled at Ayesha. Adding two sweeteners to her tea to make it more palatable for a coffee drinker, Ayesha smiled back.

"Sausage and tomato." said Charlotte, handing her the sandwich she'd asked for. As if she'd read Ayesha's misgivings about where she'd brought her for food, she continued "Now, ignore the location." she said, her free hand gesturing across the vista of the lay-by with a flat palm. "Harry does the best sausage sandwich for miles." Her hand returned from the outstretched position to a single finger pointing upwards.

Ayesha tried not to show her lack of belief at this statement on her face, and realised she'd probably failed in that attempt. She took a bite, tentatively. But she need not have worried; Charlotte was right, this was a taste sensation. Well, as much as sausages, tomatoes and two pieces of bread could be, this was perfection. *'Mental note'*, thought Ayesha, *'trust Charlotte more'*.

Charlotte had been watching the change of facial expressions on Ayesha's face as she tucked into her sandwich, and satisfied that her new partner seemed like she was enjoying it, she took a big bite out of hers. "And, he's pretty useful to know to find out if anyone knows anything, if you know what I mean..."

"And does he?"

"What?" replied Charlotte, mouth mostly full of sausage and mushroom, with one small mushroom escaping to the ground.

"Know anything?"

Charlotte looked across at her and admitted "No.". Ayesha gave a wry smile, between mouthfuls. "But that means something in itself." the DCI continued. "If Harry's not heard anything, then it's likely not to be any of the local players."

Even when faced with nothing; no information at all, Charlotte manages to make a deduction, thought Ayesha. "Right. Someone moved into the area then recently?"

"Possibly..." said Charlotte, slightly distracted by the arrival of a car in the far end of the lay-by behind Ayesha. A blue car. A blue Ford Focus. A blue Ford Focus that had just been mentioned on the radio as being pursued by traffic. As Ayesha was talking, Charlotte watched the driver of the Focus, a man in his mid 20s, get out of the car and swagger over to some other lads of a similar age in another car. As the Focus drove in,

Charlotte spotted it had the driver's side window down - possibly to dissipate any smells of any substances the driver may or may not have been smoking, Charlotte surmised. But the driver moved to the other car without pulling up his window. Perhaps Charlotte had an opportunity here...

"You got your radio?" she asked Ayesha, who was just finishing her sandwich.

"Yes Ma'am..."

"Tell Traffic we've got their Focus."

Ayesha looked at Charlotte as if she'd just said the last sentence in a different language. "Ma'am?" is all she could offer.

With more force, Charlotte repeated, "Tell Traffic we've got their Focus!" This time Charlotte indicated behind Ayesha, who turned around to see what she was talking about - only to also see Charlotte entering into her eyeline walking very casually but confidently up to the Ford Focus. There she goes again, thought Ayesha; that confident *'don't f**k with me'* attitude.

By the time Charlotte had reached the Focus, she'd put on a glove on one hand; a trick whilst walking she'd developed over many years. Dropping the pen that she'd been fiddling with over the past few days - on purpose of course - Charlotte bent over to pick it up, and ducked down around the side of the Focus, away from the sight of the driver and the lads in the other car.

She looked casually into the open window of the Focus. *'Well, well, well'*, thought Charlotte, *'the numpty has left the keys in the ignition. Anyone could just lean through the open window here..'*, doing the deed as she thought, *'and half-inch those keys'*. With her gloved hand, Charlotte took the keys from the ignition, and walked in the same manner back to the picnic table, and an astonished Ayesha.

Putting the keys on the table, Charlotte proclaimed, "Traffic's Focus."

In the distance, the driver of the Focus returned to his car - only to find someone had taken his keys. He straightened up, and with the gusto only a certain type of person can muster, shouted "Oi!! Which one of you's nicked my keys?"

If a lay-by can become all quiet - like in the movies when a stranger walks into a bar in the Wild West - then this lay-by did. It was quite a question. There were probably several men there at the moment who probably had nicked some car keys in their time, but for once, they were all innocent.

The devil in Charlotte just couldn't resist it. "I don't know, you can't have 'ought these days." she said to Ayesha, in a voice loud enough to carry over to the driver. "I'd phone the police."

As if right on cue, from out of no-where, two traffic police cars skidded into the layby, brakes squealing. The lads in the other car tried to scarper quickly, but one of the traffic cars had blocked them in - and officers were out of their car so fast, they had no place to go.

The driver of the Focus - so full of bravado a few seconds ago - decided that legging it was his best option, and headed straight past the table where Ayesha and Charlotte were sitting. In an effortless move, Charlotte shuffled over from the middle of the bench to the side, stook out a leg, and the man tripped over it, collapsing on the ground in an unceremonious heap. He looked around at Charlotte from his vantage point on the floor, and before he could say anything, Charlotte chipped “I think you might be nicked” - indicating to the two uniformed officers who were in pursuit. They grabbed him off the ground and one started to lead him back to their car reading him his rights as they went past Charlotte. A sudden dawning came to the man as he spotted his set of car keys on the table.

The other officer walked over to Charlotte’s table, by which time, Charlotte had already bagged up the keys, by turning the glove inside out, and held it on her right outstretched arm for the officer to collect - rather like a bag on an old-fashioned mail train. “Thanks, Ma'am.” said the officer as the glove was collected.

“Your round next time, I think...” said Charlotte. The officer walked backwards for a while in order to smile at Charlotte - who raised her polystyrene cup of tea up to him as if to say ‘Cheers’. Charlotte watched the man intently as he was helped into the police car, and then, all of a sudden, her focus shifted back to Ayesha - to whom she wiggles her eyebrows at.

Ayesha just stared back at Charlotte, almost unable to comprehend what just happened... and the casual way Charlotte coped with it all. Was this what happened to her everyday? Catching a suspect by nicking his keys and tripping him up? Oh, and talking down a possible jumper - let’s not forget that. She was in so much awe, she almost forgot what she needed to tell Charlotte; what had just come in from control...

“Ma'am, there's been a break in at the Knight house!”

Chapter 16

There was an invasion in the village of Norton. An invasion of beings in all-over white suits, surgical-style gloves and rubber boots. They were from the planet SOCO, and had descended on the Knight house looking for clues and evidence surrounding the break-in. The invasion was supported by a number of uniformed police officers from an entity called South Yorkshire Police.

The extra vehicles needed for this invasion made it even more difficult parking near to the Knight house on the main road, so Charlotte decided to leave the car on the nearest side road and the pair walked up to the house. Dodging their way under the police tape and past uniform, they headed to Jason, who was standing in the front garden. A uniformed officer had just finished talking to him as Charlotte asked "What happened?"

"We stayed last night at my Mum's, and when we got back, the front door was broken open." said Jason in a daze.

"Did you go in?"

"No, I phoned the police and we stayed in the car." He indicated with his head towards Daniel, who was sitting in the passenger seat of their car parked on the drive. Charlotte turned in that direction and saw the passenger door open with two female officers squatting down talking to the lad. "After everything he's been through I didn't want him to see his home like that."

Charlotte understood. “Good thinking.”

Jason took a deep breath, looked around in agitation and helplessness. “Look, do you need me for a while? I think I'll take him back to my Mum's.”

Charlotte looked across at the officer who had been chatting with him as they arrived, and they nodded their head. “No, that's fine. We'll have officers here outside now that this is a crime scene. You can come back later to check if anything has been taken - but I suspect nothing has.”

“Then what is this about?” Charlotte looked at Jason. His face said he desperately needed answers - and his wife back - but now wasn’t the time to be getting into the details of Charlotte’s theory, such as it was. She indicated to Jason’s son. “Look after him first. We'll talk later. And you'd better get someone organised to fix that door.”

“Yes, thank you Detective.” Jason said, agreeing this was the best course of action.

Just as Jason started to walk away, Charlotte shouted to him “Mr Knight? Did Sarah have a hair cut recently?”

It seemed such a strange thing to ask straight off that it stopped Jason in his tracks. Having a couple of seconds to think, he replied, slightly puzzled, “Yes, on Tuesday. She had long hair before, but decided to have it cut short because it was taking too long for her to get ready in a morning.”

Charlotte smiled. The curse of the long-haired female. “I know the feeling! Thank you, Mr Knight.”

She watched him walk back to his car and saw the relieved look on Daniel's face. She took a deep breath and stiffened her resolve to find his mum. At the front door, Ayesha looked to be finishing off from talking to SOCO people, so they could compare notes soon. The talk of hair, however, had made her realise her ponytail was working loose, and she was in the middle of shaking her hair free and refixing it when Ayesha walked over. Waiting until she was in clear ear shot, Charlotte let her know the hair revelation. “Sarah had a hair cut on Tuesday.”

“So the footage supposedly at 6pm on Thursday came from at the latest Monday?” replied Ayesha. Charlotte nods in agreement. “I think it might be time I had one.” she added, realising she’d not managed to get those irritating frizzy straggly bits around her ears through the bobble. Ayesha waits to see whether Charlotte has got anything else, before reporting her findings. “Neighbour saw a white van pull up in the early hours of morning, but thought nothing of it. Also saw someone looking over the front wall the day before. They ran off down something called a ‘snicket’?”

Charlotte smiled. “A snicket. It’s a gunnal, a gynall, a ginnal... “ Ayesha looked just as confused. “An alleyway…” Charlotte elaborated.

“So why not just say ‘alleyway’ then?!” retorted Ayesha.

“I can see we’re going to have to give you lessons in Yorkshire dialect, Ayesha.” Her new DC nodded, bewilderedly.

“Entry through the broken door; no prints

anywhere. But there's nothing obvious taken.".

"I think we can guess what they came for…" came Charlotte's measured reply.

"Ma'am?"

Charlotte's eyes narrowed. "'The new documents on 'a USB stick safely stored away'..." she replied, using Kelvin's words exactly.

It suddenly dawned on Ayesha what Charlotte was getting at. "That locked drawer in her office!" Before Charlotte could say anything, Ayesha raced to the nearest SOCO person, asked permission, and then bounded into the house to check Sarah's office. Charlotte watched on, whilst playing with something between her fingers. A few minutes passed before Ayesha left the house, in a much slower manner. "Yep. That drawer is busted open." she said, short of breath and sounding very disappointed. "They'll have taken it."

Charlotte still had a look of *'you should have listened to me'* on her face. "I'm not so sure. This is a super intelligent person... is she really going to keep a USB stick with documents somewhere as obvious as a locked drawer?"

Ayesha considered herself told off by this remark. A locked drawer seemed a perfectly good place to keep something you didn't want anyone to get. "You don't think there was a USB stick in that drawer?"

"No, I think there was a USB stick there, but it wouldn't have the documents they wanted on it. She'll have hidden *that* somewhere else…"

"So, where?"

"Well, the best place to hide something you don't want found is in plain sight. If it was me, I would have hidden it where it wouldn't be noticed... where it wouldn't cause any suspicion..".

Ayesha's mind starts to work the way Charlotte is thinking. "...like being in with other USB sticks somewhere?"

Charlotte nodded in general agreement. "...or, say, plugged into a computer.. No-one would take a second look at something *already* plugged into a computer..." Again, Ayesha agreed. "...and if you choose a room which is normally locked; needs a key card to get in; and that you could gain access to before someone else..."

The penny has dropped with Ayesha as to where Charlotte is alluding to. "The Meeting Room! That's why Sarah went in the room before Kelvin!" she exclaimed.

"It's just a theory..." Charlotte replied with a half smile and a shrug of the shoulders. If Ayesha hadn't been so focused on the implications of what Charlotte had just apparently figured out, she might have picked up on the complete lack of sincerity in the reply. Because it was clear it was no mere 'theory'.

"It's so obvious now. We have to get back there to check..." Ayesha's words had a growing sense of urgency.

"No need..."

Ayesha looked at Charlotte to ask 'why?'

"I didn't go to the toilet..." Charlotte pushed forward the item she'd been playing with all this time - it was a computer SD card.

Chapter 17

The world had seen some amazing double acts throughout history; Laurel and Hardy, Morecambe and Wise, French and Saunders. But the new double act on the block was Walker and Sheldon. It didn't frequent the various comedy clubs around the country, but did provide regular performances in one of the interview rooms of Doncaster police station.

However, these performances were relatively easy to get tickets for, and there seemed to be a constant flow of people wanting to be in the audience for these exclusive gigs. This performance, for instance, was ready to be seen by an audience of only two; the man who ran from the Ford Focus, and the man who was the solicitor of the man who ran from the Ford Focus.

Charlotte sat across from the arrested man; Dean opposite the solicitor. They'd been sitting down across from each other for a while now, as Dean sorted the official housekeeping with the tape machine. Then Charlotte did her customary 'I'll read through various papers first for a little while' thing.

When she was ready, Charlotte looked directly across at the man she tripped up. He was leaning so far back on the chair, his bottom must have been resting on the edge of the seat. He was agitated, possibly suffering from the effects of withdrawal perhaps, but at least he and his car turned out clean - from drugs, at least.

He needed a wash, that's for certain, thought

Charlotte. His clothes looked like he'd been wearing them for days; black jeans and a T-shirt proudly proclaiming 'The Smiths' - although she wondered whether he knew who they were. An earring punched through his right ear - not that there was anything wrong with men wearing earrings, of course. Not thinking of anyone in particular. Or having any type of body piercings. She brought herself quickly back from this flight of fancy. The long hair of the young man hid a rather innocent face - or rather what would be if it didn't have a look of defiance and hostility. Perhaps he just hadn't had the right chances in life... or the right role-models?

Then again, his solicitor was hardly the positive force you'd expect a man in his position to be. His brown suit looked straight out of the 1970's and Charlotte couldn't decide whether he was wearing it for a bet. And then she could decide whether he'd win the bet by wearing it, or had lost a bet and that's why he was wearing it. Either way, *dreadful* was the word for it, win or lose. He was in his later forties and had a face of someone who life had passed by.

They were a motley pair, but one of them hopefully had some answers Charlotte was interested in - which was presumably why Dean had asked for her to join him.

It was time for the Walker and Sheldon show.

"So, why am I sitting in on this interview with this fine upstanding member of the community, DI Sheldon?" Charlotte started, in an exaggerated manner.

"Well, DCI Walker, this gentleman has just told me

something interesting I thought you'd like to hear..."

"Well then, young man.... " she said, leaning into him more across the desk, as if to invite him to tell her a story. "I'm sitting comfortably."

The man just continued to lounge on his chair, but said nothing.

"Hmmmm, he doesn't seem to be very forthcoming at the moment, DI Sheldon. Does the chap have a name?"

"Yes." said Dean, smiling. "Trevor Potts."

"Well then..." she said, again addressing the young man, as before, but this time adding great ironic emphasis on his name. "Trevor...."

Trevor had had enough of this show and decided the fastest way to end it was to start talking. "I'm here doing a bit of couriering." he said, in a heavy London accent.

Charlotte leaned forward, with a renewed interest. "Oh yes? What is it, and who to?"

Whatever he had already said to Dean, he was a little reluctant to say it again in front of Charlotte.

Charlotte followed up. "I think we can take it by the lengths you gave our Traffic boys the run around that you didn't really want to be found with it in your car? Ehh? Oh, and there's the small matter of a couple of thousand pounds in your pocket..."

He looked across at his brief, who continued to be as much use as a chocolate fire guard. "Well, I'd delivered it. But I didn't want no coppers having me or my car in.

So I scarpered... until you turned up."

Charlotte's eyes narrowed. With a half smile on her face she said, "Yeah... imagine that? Caught by a woman tripping you up... That'll go well for you in prison... Trevor..."

Trevor didn't see the funny side of that. But she was right. If word got out of the almost slapstick way he'd got caught, he wouldn't have much cred to trade on in jail. He closed his eyes and shook his head for a few seconds.

"So.. Who and what?" asked Charlotte.

He sighed, and said "Stuff for IDEs. And Oleg Petrov."

Walker and Sheldon looked at each other.

* * *

"Oleg Petrov. Russian national. Not the kind of bloke you'd want to get on the wrong side of. Having said that, he is known to be very charming, and especially to be quite partial to the ladies... Form as long as your arm however; extortion, explosives..." said Dean, who was controlling the computer back in the Incident Room.

Gathered around the monitor were Charlotte, Ayesha and Vernon. A photo of a pretty unsavoury character was on the screen; obviously tall, stocky, built like the proverbial brick poo house. The text mentioned distinguishing features being a tattooed upper left arm.

"Murder?" Charlotte asked, thinking she wouldn't

have put it past this character. Even to her, he seemed to be the type of person you'd cross over the road for on a dark night.

"Possibly... " replied Dean, "though no-one's made that stick."

"Doesn't mean he hasn't done it, just that he's been very clever." chipped in Vernon.

"Hmmm." agreed Charlotte. DS Price *does* come up with valid points - every so often. "And he's now in our neck of the woods?"

"Must be. Delivery boy in there just had an address to drop off, but we've had no sightings at all." Dean said.

"No," Charlotte pondered, "no-one's told me 'owt either..." She looked again at the photo on the screen. "Well, we need to be on our guard if he's planning anything on our patch."

"Gov." replied Dean, just as he moved back to his desk.

"Oh, and that address Amazon man dropped his stuff off at? You've checked it out?"

Dean smiled at the delivery quipe. "Yes Gov. Stuff already taken. Roads in and out no CCTV."

"Of course. Anyway, good work."

Praise from DCI Charlotte Walker was certainly not scarce, but it still felt great and it was given.

Chapter 18

Charlotte was never one for a lot of light in her rooms. No particular reason; she couldn't say it was to 'help save the planet' by reducing her energy costs... more that she just preferred mood lighting. Tonight, Charlotte's mood lighting was provided by the solitary table lamp on the large coffee table next to the long sofa. To be fair, it wasn't exactly like living by candlelight anyway; the lamp had a decently bright aspect - but it certainly provided more ambiance than the barrage of ceiling lights the room had been fitted with by the previous owners.

The table lamp illuminated a part-eaten tub of honeycomb ice cream, with a spoon stuck in it rather like a murder weapon, and a part-drunk can of cider. The Cs. Well, **ci**der and i**ce** **c**ream.

The lamp provided just enough brightness to allow Charlotte to be looking through her record collection at the other end of the room. Seven proper boxes - the ones with the flip top lids - were out, and they were just the twelve inches ones. Charlotte had lost track of how many boxes of singles she had.

Her collection started when her Dad bought her a record deck as a going away present to uni. The first album she bought was a very decent copy of Blondie's 'Parallel Lines' from a charity shop in Oxford. Since then, collecting vinyl had become a bit of a passion - and she'd got some gems in the collection too.

Flicking through the albums to see which one matched her mood this evening, she realised vinyl for her must be like comic books to Ayesha. Each one of us has a passion; a desire to collect something - be it records, comic books... or possibly dogs.

Every so often, her fingers would linger over an edge, as she mulled over whether that would be the perfect accompaniment to the rest of the evening. Eventually she got to the S's and black cover of Stevie Nicks' 'The Other Side Of The Mirror' cried out. Pulling out of the box, she cast her eyes over the beautiful cover; Ms Nicks looking stunning in the dark red dress. Charlotte looked at the dress enviously, and then tried to talk herself out of coveting it as it would be completely impractical for dog walking...

She slid the thin black vinyl disc out of the inner sleeve, blew on it, and then positioned it on the record deck's platter. The careful placing of the perfectly-balanced tonearm resulted in the crackles and pops all lovers of vinyl appreciate. The opening words to the first track, 'Rooms on Fire' leapt from the speakers.

Content she'd made the right musical choice tonight, Charlotte walked back to the sofa, only to find Bronte had sprawled out and was taking up virtually all of the available space. Charlotte looked at him, and he turned to look at her. There was a reticence to move on the dog's part, so he offered his appeasement behaviour of a massive tail wag... that should do it. Charlotte's resistance lowered and a smile appeared, which only made the tail wag even more. Charlotte gave in. "Utch up then" she said to him. Charlotte moved to sit down in her spot on the sofa, next the little table, and for a second, it looked like she'd be sitting on Bronte... until he moved his outstretched legs at the last moment to allow her just enough space.

She grabbed her laptop from the coffee table and opened the lid. The machine powered up, and after going through the inevitable Windows Update ('God, I hate technology!' came the thought) she was connected to the net. Opening her browser, the screen filled with three previously opened tabs. One was Facebook, one was eBay and VW Campervans for sale and the other was the webmail page for Charlotte's email address.

Clicking on Facebook, she saw she had an inordinate amount of notifications. Wincing, she clicked on the icon, to see more than a few birthday notifications. *'Well they can go.'* she thought, ignoring them. There were a few from some of the various groups she was a member of, and she thought she'd look at them another time - knowing full well she never would. Then she decided rather than look through all of them, it would save time to ignore the rest of the notifications too, and took a deep satisfaction in clicking on the "mark all as read" menu option. *'That'll sock it to Zuckerberg'* Charlotte thought, ironically.

She did decide to click on the chat icon, which had fifteen new messages showing in the red box. Scrolling down, most seemed to be from Friday evening and they were all asking variations of the same question; 'Was it you on that bridge with that man?' Charlotte's face dropped in a frustrated frown. One caught her eye - from Mum. Opening it, she read 'Hope you've been ok.. Blah blah blah.' Charlotte gave up on it. *'Why send me a Facebook message when you know I don't have it on my phone?'* she wondered. With everything that had happened over the past few days, she didn't have the capacity to enter into a discussion with herself about why her and her Mum didn't seem to see eye-to-eye... so she just sent a very large 'thumbs up' in reply. *'That would do.'* she thought, and then added 'xx' as an afterthought, just to make sure she didn't say 'You didn't send any kisses!', which she had been known to...

Taking a deep breath, as if to close that messaging chapter, she noticed one of the messages from an old school friend had a link to a post in a Facebook group, which Charlotte made the mistake of clicking on. When it opened, it was a full account from an eyewitness of everything that happened on Friday afternoon, complete with a zoomed in photo of Alistair standing on the side of the bridge with Charlotte talking to him. At first glance, Charlotte thought no-one would be able to identify either of them from the blurry image, but when she scrolled down she saw several comments naming both her and Alistair. "Bugger." thought Charlotte, and she closed the Facebook tab completely.

Many thoughts started to race through her head seeing that post. The detailed description of the events on the bridge and that photo brought it back all again. And if it had done that for Charlotte, what would it have done for Alistair and his family? God she hoped none of them were on social media. She didn't read any of the comments on that post, but she could imagine some of them wouldn't be supportive of a human being who's world had just come crashing down.

She grabbed the can of cider and drank the rest of the amber liquid in one go; squirming a little as the deliciously sour taste overwhelmed her mouth.

Amongst the inevitable emails from supermarkets pushing their latest special offers on products which cost less a year ago was an email from David. Clicking on it, he'd put *'Did some research for you... hope it helps. You might find the last one particularly interesting. Love David.'*

'Aww bless him!' Charlotte thought, clicking on the first link.

A newspaper cutting opened up, with the headline 'Games Master dies of heart attack'. She recognised the photo was of Carl Remington before she read the caption. Further down the article was a smaller photo of Amber in tears, with the caption 'Girlfriend was with him at the time he died'. Scanning through the text, a piece in larger writing stood out to her, 'Remington was diagnosed with heart condition three months ago' said the paper.

She clicked on the next link; it was a feature from Hello magazine, with several glamorous photographs of Amber in Lady of the Manor-style poses, under the headline 'I thought I'd never find love again - until I met his twin'. Further down, a photo of Scott and Amber's wedding day had the caption 'The pair got married earlier this year'. She noticed a larger piece of text which said 'Couple work together at Scott's software company'

This was all very interesting background, mused Charlotte, as she picked the cider can from the table, and disappointingly realising she'd just finished it.

The third link was a tabloid newspaper story with a photo of Scott and Amber together, but the photo had a 'shattered' effect added; the headline "Software boss splits with wife over affair". The large paparazzi-style photo below it was of Amber in a posh car leaving a building, trying to shield her face from the photographer. The car was being driven by a man, but because of the angle the photo was taken, only his stocky hands on the steering wheel could be seen, with the caption underneath "Wife Amber with mystery lover".

Closing that image, Charlotte clicked on the last link in the email, which opened a page from the Yorkshire Post website. 'Detective saved our son' read the headline and it was written by someone called 'David Walker'. *'Oh it's not!'* Charlotte hoped it wasn't about the incident on the bridge - but after she'd read a short section, of course, it was. The large photograph was of an elderly couple, who Charlotte assumed, without reading the caption, were the Mum and Dad of Alistair. She decided not to read anymore, apart from the text in larger letters saying 'We'd have lost our son as well as a daughter-in-law'.

Charlotte closed the laptop lid in anger, and threw it onto the other sofa; only just enough to make sure it didn't fall on the floor. *'What's he playing at?'* Charlotte thought about David, *'showing me that I'm good at my job... the job I'm leaving...'*

Charlotte went into the kitchen. What she needed right now was a good cup of Yorkshire Tea. But, on opening the fridge, she discovered she was out of milk. *'How can one person get through seven bottles of milk in less than three days'*, she wondered. She closed the fridge in despair.

Instant hot chocolate it was then.

The rest of Stevie Nicks.

And bed.

Chapter 19

5:21am.

'*Why?*' Charlotte wondered. '*Why am I awake at 5:21am?*'

She looked across at Bronte, who was taking up more than his fair share of Charlotte's double bed. He was sparked out. That's because he is sensible, Charlotte mused. Perhaps I could get back to sleep for a while...

5:39am.

Charlotte decided to give up trying to go back to sleep, and to embrace the morning. The big question would be whether she could get up and out of bed without disturbing Bronte? She rolled back the edge of the duvet, and slid herself out of the bed. In the end, that wasn't difficult at all... he must be tired.

To be fair, so was she... so why the hell was she awake at this time? And not just awake; wide awake.

She went downstairs. What would be good right now would be a top cup of tea. Nothing like that first brew to set you up for the day ahead. Remembering she had run out of milk, she opened the front door to eagerly collect the milk - except what greeted her were the empties she put out last night. Not a bottle full of milk was to be seen. '*I thought milk deliveries came very early in the morning*' she questioned. To her, 5:41am did seem very early, but for some reason she assumed her milk was delivered in the wee small hours of the morning, possibly by some kind of milk vampires that had to be back at the dairy caskets before the sun came up or they'd burn up and die.

Instant hot chocolate it was then.

There was only one thing to do, it seemed to Charlotte, at 5:45 on a Monday morning - FIFA.

She grabbed the PS4 controller from its charging station next to the television, and pressed the middle button to power up the console - which in turn switched on the TV. As the Playstation home screen appeared, she moved the left joystick across to FIFA21 and pressed the cross button.

As she repeatedly pressed the cross button to get past the inordinate numbers of animations and copyright licensing screens there seemed to be before the game actually started, Charlotte's mind went over the links David had sent over; not least the last one. Was she doing the right thing? Leaving the force? Does it not seem a little ironic, no, a cruel even, to leave the police *after* Richard was dead - when she wouldn't have ever entertained it when he was alive?

She tried to put those thoughts to the back of her mind as she took on two players from Japan and one from Australia, beating all three comprehensively. *'Take that world!'* she thought. But it was a hollow victory.

Getting up and peering through the living room's closed curtains, she noticed the sky's lightbulb would soon be changing to morning light mode.

Yawning, there seemed little point in going back upstairs to bed, so she decided to rest on the sofa until it was a proper time to be awake. She pulled out the huge fluffy throw over Vanessa had bought her the previous Christmas, and settled down on the sofa.

'I'll probably not fall asleep anyw...'

******

7:05am.

Charlotte was awoken with a jolt by the clinking of glass bottles outside. She took a moment or two to realise where she was.

Yes, on the sofa. So she must have dozed off in the end. And she definitely felt better for it. She stretched and got up, folding the throw over neatly and lobbing it onto one of the oher sofas.

She went outside to collect the milk. *'Jeez'*, she thought, *'they've done it again! Semi-skimmed instead of the full-fat I ordered! Another thing to have to sort. And they hadn't left the bottles in a milk crate either.'*

She grabbed two bottles and pushed them into her chest, then grabbed the other two and carried all four full bottles of milk inside. With her free hand, she closed and locked the front door. It was a well-practised move. She might not have been as eco-conscious as sister Vanessa, but having milk delivered was one of the ways Charlotte thought she was doing her bit. Although if they maintain these shenanigans of sending semi-skimmed, she might have to consider going back to the supermarket.

The closing of the door awoke Bronte, who responded to the sudden loss of his human with a slightly panicked bark. "I'm down here." Charlotte shouted, and within seconds, her canine companion had raced down the stairs and was wagging his tail in front of her. Knowing he wanted his morning fuss, she said "Ok, ok, let me put the milk away first…"

After fusses had happened, breakfast, a shower and an appropriate selection of clothing - the dusty yellow two piece suit with cream shirt was the preferred choice today - Charlotte was on her way.

She pressed the key fob to unlock her Volvo. This was the last journey in this car. Charlotte knew she was doing the right thing trading it in, because she didn't feel any regrets. Sure, it was a nice car and all, but it never felt like *her*. Hell, she'd not even given it a name - like she had with all the other cars she'd owned since learning to drive. Perhaps being the car she'd just got a month before the accident didn't help with her bond with the vehicle. Still, it had been there throughout the ensuing year, so it wasn't all bad.

It was just a bit too fancy for its own good.

And didn't have a CD player.

Chapter 20

By the time Charlotte walked into the Incident Room, Ayesha had already been there several hours.

"Morning, Ma'am."

"Jeez, What time did you get in?" Charlotte asked, a mixture of acknowledgement and disdain in her voice, as she sat down at the opposite side of the desk to Ayesha.

"Eager to get moving on things." she replied, with the same 'needing to please' look a young puppy has.

"Well, then.. 'Good morning'." Charlotte exaggerated. This raised a smile from Ayesha, whose focus then moved back to the computer she was working on. Charlotte then remembered she had news...

"Hey, I've got a surprise for you outside!"

"Oh yes?"

"Show you later!" With that, Charlotte sat down and tried to make a start on a mountain of paper which was trying quite successfully to take over the desk.

Ayesha was in danger of letting her curiosity run away with her, so she forced herself back into the job. Then she remembered she had something for Charlotte.

Ducking down to the floor, she picked up a medium sized blue 'bag for life', which was scrunched up so as to keep the contents safe inside. "By the way, Ma'am, here's your clothes from the other day…"

"Oh thank you." she said

"Washed, and everything…" Ayesha said proudly.

Charlotte indicated her approval, but didn't fully appreciate the implications of someone who didn't have ready access to a washing machine and a tumble dryer having processed these clothes so quickly.

She reached over to take the bag from Ayesha, but she grabbed the wrong side. The bag unravelled and its contents dropped onto the desk; Richard's London top… his jeans… and a purple thong that was definitely not Richard's.. Charlotte raised her eyebrows, picked them up and held them in the air stretched between her hands.

"Ayesha?" she said, eager to get the Detective Constable's attention. Ayesha looked up from her desk, and immediately glowed a shade of scarlet. It was at this moment Vernon walked into the Incident Room.

"Oh good God! They're mine!"

"I figured that! They aren't mine! Mine are red and a bit skimpier!"

Vernon had a look of outraged disgust on his face and was frankly appalled. "Have none of you got no shame!" he exclaimed, leaving the Incident Room in a frenzy.

"What's his problem?" asked Ayesha.

"Time of the month…" replied Charlotte.

Ayesha sniggered at the thought of DS Price having PMS, as Charlotte bundled the thong into a small ball and threw it over at her. Taken by surprise, she tried to catch it, but it unballed in middle air and instead of landing in Ayesha's hand, it landed on her shoulder.

Charlotte and Ayesha looked at each other, and then burst into a fit of giggles like school girls… just as Assistant Chief Constable Sharon Tate walked in behind Charlotte.

Ayesha managed to stop laughing, and tried to indicate with raised eyebrows and a slight forward motion with her head there was someone behind Charlotte.

Charlotte took the hint and turned around to see Sharon only just managing to maintain her professionalism.

"DCI Walker…" she said curtly. It was an invitation to follow Charlotte knew she couldn't turn down. She watched as Sharon walked efficiently out of the Incident Room.

Charlotte turned back to Ayesha and gave her a look of 'oh no, I'm going to see the headmistress'. Ayesha tried to hold back more giggles; as if she'd better behave or she'd be next...

Charlotte pushed the chair back to get in, forcing it to make an excruciating scraping noise on the floor, and walked out - head drooped as if she was heading to the naughty corner.

* * *

Sharon was already sitting back behind her desk as Charlotte walked in. Having been indicated to sit down, Charlotte drew the chair back, sat down, then looked across at Sharon.

There was a silence for a while, as Charlotte waited for Sharon to finish off writing a note. Charlotte took this opportunity to quickly write a text message - which was no mean feat without a Qwerty keyboard on the phone. She tapped away furiously, the actual keys making a noise which prompted Sharon to glance up at Charlotte, albeit without moving her head. Once completed, Sharon took a deep breath, looking intensely at Charlotte, as she pressed to send the text. The phone went away in a pocket.

"So, how are you?" she asked the detective.

Charlotte took this question in the only way she was thinking at the time; on the case. "Ok... the case is heading in the right direction; making good progress..."

Sharon interrupted her. "No, how are *you*?"

It still hadn't dawned on Charlotte what Sharon was talking about. She scrunched her face up and said jovially "Errr, fine, yes."

Sharon was getting a little frustrated. She wasn't sure whether Charlotte was being deliberately obtuse, and decided to spell it out clearly. "After Friday? The bridge?"

Suddenly it clicked. "Oh right! No, fine, totally fine. I've seen Bronte since then; been on some walks, so I'm spot on."

Sharon nodded with approval. She took a deep breath before saying, “I'm supposed to tell you off for not waiting...”

Charlotte looked back at her. It was this part of the relationship they’d both had challenges with. Yes, they had been work colleagues who had become close friends, but when all was said and done, Sharon *was* Charlotte’s superior officer; several ranks more superior. And occasionally - very occasionally - there had to be uncomfortable conversions involving Charlotte’s conduct.

This one one of those occasions.

But despite how challenging Sharon thought these occasions were, it was nothing compared to Charlotte’s view of them. They reminded her of how much her friend was part of ‘them’ and not part of ‘us’. And that troubled her. Which led to the slightly defiant reply of “Tell that to his Mum and Dad...”

Sharon looks across as sternly as she could muster at Charlotte. The DCI considered explaining just what she thought of the ‘rules’ - but decided against it on this occasion, and simply said “I'll consider myself told off.”

That eased the pressure slightly. “I'm supposed to offer counselling...” Sharon continued.

“Naw, no shrinks for me, thank you. Bloody psycho mumbo-jumbo...” She threw Sharon a knowing glance, as they both were very awarded what subject Charlotte studied at university, and they shared a smile.

Sharon broke the smile first. Knowing her job here was done as the superior officer, she tried to move into 'friend' mode. "Look, if you ever need anyone to talk...

"...you're at the top of the list." Sharon noted the comment with quiet satisfaction; both that Charlotte was happy to talk to her, and that she was at the top of any list Charlotte might have had. As if spotting this, Charlotte added - with a glint in her eye - "Well, towards the top... up there... at least..."

Sharon realised Charlotte was teasing her. Sharon raises a smile.

"Can I go and catch some bad guys now?" Charlotte asked. Sharon shook her head in mock disbelief of Charlotte's disrespect, and waved her to go. As Charlotte opens the office room and steps outside, Sharon shouts after her.

"Have you changed your mind yet?"

"Nope. Still leaving!" came the reply from down the corridor as the door slowly closed.

Chapter 21

Ayesha had been waiting outside the station for ten minutes now. She looked again at her phone, and the text from Charlotte received fifteen minutes ago saying to meet her outside in ten minutes.

She had begun to realise that the genius crime detective did have her faults… organisation being one of them. Time-keeping another. And quietly, she was slightly reassured by that.

And besides, if they were going anywhere now, how were they going to get there? Ayesha looked around the immediate vicinity for Charlotte's Volvo and couldn't see it anywhere. In the place around where Charlotte normally parked in the car park opposite was a 4x4 pickup, a pink Mini and a light blue car equally as small, which she couldn't make out.

She looked behind her again to see if she could see Charlotte coming out of the station. No sign. Then her phone pinging. It had to be Charlotte. Perhaps it was to say 'sorry for being late'.

She opened the message...

'In momento, she madefacta est, et suave olens succus crura ejus destillavit.'

'Copy and paste' Ayesha thought as she performed the actions on her phone. The resulting translation caused her to let out a shocked, surprised sound - which was so loud , it made her look around to see if anyone had noticed.

Moments later Charlotte descended the steps to join Ayesha, who was shaking her head at her in mock disgust. Charlotte blinked with feigned innocence.

"What?" she exclaimed, with her playful manner, as she started to cross the road to the car park. Ayesha waited for a car to go by, before chasing after her.

They walked to the place where Charlotte parked, and Charlotte suddenly stopped between the pink Mini and the light blue car.

"Where's your car, Ma'am?" asked Ayesha.

"It's here..." Charlotte said, enthusiastically.

Ayesha looked. As they were standing between two cars, she wasn't sure which one Charlotte meant - but she was *really* hoping it wasn't the pink Mini... Nothing against anyone who liked the colour, but it certainly wasn't her taste. Not that it would be her car anyway, of course.

Charlotte's smile was full of mischief. It was as though she knew exactly what Ayesha was thinking - and she played it for all it was worth. She extended her left arm in a gesture to say 'here it is' towards the pink Mini, and enjoyed seeing Ayesha trying noticeably to hide her true feelings about the colour of the car. She couldn't do it any longer, and pointed to the light blue car; it was the convertible Micra.

The look of relief on Ayesha's face was a picture. "It's times like this I wish I had a camera phone!" Charlotte ribbed.

"I really thought you'd gone completely crazy then!"

"As opposed to only partially crazy with this?"

Charlotte smiled.

Ayesha looked around at the car. It was a 59 plate and looked very neat and tidy; the light blue colour really suited the curvy lines of the small car. From the front, the bulbous headlights and the chrome-lined radiator grill looked like a cute smiley face.

"So you really did it?!"

"Yeap... needed to change - and this is it. Much more..."

"..you!" Ayesha finished off.

Charlotte nodded her head in agreement. "Yeah... I think so." She opened the driver's door and pointed inside to the central console of the dashboard. "And look...!"

."... a CD player?" Ayesha guessed.

"A CD player!" Charlotte confirmed with a huge smile whilst getting in and closing her door. Ayesha walked around the car to her side, shaking her head a little and smiling at Charlotte's slightly bonkers decision.

As Ayesha opened her door, a mechanical whirring noise started, and the roof began to steadily retract back into the back of the car. It wouldn't win any prizes for speed, Ayesha thought, but she had to admit it was pretty cool to see such a little car topless. With the roof completely folded away, she got in and closed the door. Fastening her seat belt, she looked across at Charlotte, who was waiting for the look. With her audience watching, she put on a pair of mottled brown tortoiseshell sunglasses, pulled her hair out of the ponytail - and with a wiggle of her eyebrows, pulled out of the car park complete with a trademark Charlotte wheelspin.

* * *

This was the first time Charlotte had the opportunity to really drive her new car. She'd sat in it on Saturday, and had driven it around the block, but now on this sixty miles per hour section, she could open her up and see what she could do.

Pushing down on the accelerator, the car had a nice little bit of power, but with only a hundred and eight brake horsepower, she was never going to be a speed machine. But if she wanted that, she'd have bought something else. What this car had, Charlotte decided, was character.

Character and personality.

And a CD player.

Which she could have been using now, if she had remembered to bring some CDs from home this morning. It didn't matter. The roof of the car was down, and to be honest, she doubted whether she'd hear any music at all over the sound of the air rushing around the vehicle, as it pushed its way forward.

Charlotte was loving it. She had the proverbial wind through her hair, making it dance in wild patterns; her sunglasses changing the light blue sky to a hazy shade of sepia brown; and she had good company. This could make even the most mundane journey into an adventure, she thought.

"Where are we going Ma'am?" Ayesha quizzed Charlotte, raising her voice slightly to be heard over the added noise of the topless car.

"*Ms* Amber Remington's humble abode. I need to ask her more about her husband's death..."

Ayesha figured Charlotte must have taken them a different way, because she didn't recognise any of this landscape.

"Do you think that is relevant to Sarah?"

"It could be..."

Ayesha had already learned to trust Charlotte's hunches, and was prepared to do so on this - even though she didn't think there was much to be gained in talking about a decade-old case.

Charlotte looked across at Ayesha. "Breadcake." she said.

"I beg your pardon?"

"Breadcake. It's what we call a bap."

"Right." replied Ayesha. "But it isn't a cake..."

Charlotte felt a little battered by this. "Well, come to that, what is a 'bap'? I mean, that makes no sense for small shaped bread product."

"Fair enough." bounced back Ayesha.

"Don't you come up here mocking the way we speak, young lady!" Charlotte retorted with mischief in her eyes. "That's got to be near a world record, surely?"

"What is, Ma'am?" Ayesha was getting used to the

conversational handbrake turns.

“Five thousand, two hundred and seventy?”

Ayesha suddenly realises why that number was significant to her; her comic book collection. “Actually, no. The record is over one hundred and one thousand.”

“Good grief.” exclaimed Charlotte. “American?”

“Yes.”

Charlotte scrunched up her nose. “Figures.”

Chapter 22

Charlotte's new car glided down the tree-lined driveway and onto the gravel in front of Amber's country house. Ayesha was the first to get out. Looking around, she thought she saw something white in the garage on the right - just as the only opened door automatically closed shut.

It happened just as Charlotte had started the process of closing the roof on the Micra - and the sound overlapped. The new owner was clearly pleased with her purchase, as she climbed out of the car to see the roof marry up with the windscreen. She put her sunglasses on the driver's seat, and with a bobble she had in her hand fixed her windswept hair back into a ponytail - complete with the inevitable straggly bits around her ears.

As she walked around from her side of the car, she looked down the long drive to the more modest houses facing the estate on the other side of the main road.

"I wonder if any of those houses have any CCTV which might just catch the ins and outs of Ms Remington's humble abode?" she said, pointing in their general direction.

"Possibly, Ma'am."

The call-to-action Charlotte had offered seemingly didn't have the desired effect. "Well, go on then!" she said. Eventually the penny dropped with Ayesha that Charlotte meant for her to go and see *now*.

"Right-o, Ma'am." she replied with a frown, and started the long walk down the drive.

The benefits of a superior rank, smiled Charlotte. Ayesha should be thankful she's got a boss who's not giving her all the crappy jobs, Charlotte mused. And she then went on a brief trip down memory lane remembering some of the tasks 'entrusted' to her - or rather dumped on her - by senior colleagues when she was a newly-qualified DC. All the tasks she promised she wouldn't be so nasty with any newly-qualified DC under her charge. So Ayesha *should* be thankful she's got an understanding boss; someone who has only made her walk back down one of the longest drives in Doncaster, when she could have stopped at the top and let her get out then. Only Charlotte hadn't thought about the possibility of CCTV at the top of the drive.

Still, the exercise will do her good, she thought.

Charlotte turned around, headed towards Amber's front door and pressed on the door bell ringer.

* * *

Ayesha waited outside number 47. She'd been unlucky with the previous dwellings - no CCTV on any - but she was slightly more confident about number 47. Not least because the doorbell was one of those posh video affairs, and also that she could see a range of CCTV cameras around the property. This was actually the best position, because if she was lucky, there might be a camera pointing all the way down Amber's driveway. If she was lucky...

A man in his early thirties opened the door; tall; hair brown enough to be called brown and not red - a sort of auburn, she thought; and skinny - very skinny. “Yes?” came a deep voice which really didn’t seem to be at home in this frame.

“Hello, sir, I’m DC Stoker, of South Yorkshire Police. I noticed your CCTV and I wondered whether any of them capture anything of the main road? We’re investigating an incident and any footage you may have of the main road outside could be very useful to us.”

“Err, yes. That one out of the front on the corner does. I had to turn off the notifications on the app for that one ‘cos it triggered with every Tom, Dick and Harry going up and down hers across the road..” He pointed over at the gates to Amber’s drive.

“That could be of great help, sir, thank you.”

The man looked Ayesha up and down, but not in a sinister way, more of a ‘trying to work you out’ kind of way. And then he asked, “You’re not working with Charlotte Walker by any chance? I used to go to school with her.”

This wasn’t what she’d expected. Perhaps an offer of a date - that’s happened on house-to-house before - or arresting someone else they’d wanted on another case - also happened before. But not ‘I went to school with your DCI’.If it was a chat-up line, it was an inventive one.

“It’s all a bit ironic that she’s a high-up police officer - after how she was in school.” the man followed up.

Now that did pique Ayesha's curiosity.

"Do you want to come in, and I'll get that footage for you?"

* * *

Amber showed Charlotte into the living room, their feet echoing on the wooden floor. It was a large room; a very large room, with a high ceiling and two gold chandeliers - which Charlotte thought to be a bit over the top. The imposing stone fireplace provided a focal point to the room, with enough oil landscape paintings on the walls to fill a small gallery.

"Please, have a seat, Inspector." Amber said, indicating to a sofa which could well have been the big sister to the one in Amber's office; same design, only larger. But still as low down. Charlotte couldn't help thinking this was all part of Amber's mind games with whoever found themselves in this room, as she collapsed into the clutches of the sofa.

Amber walked over to a drinks cabinet - this one larger and more well stocked than the one in her office. "Drink, Inspector?" she offered, not looking at Charlotte and knowing full well the request would be turned down.

"No, thank you. Still on duty..." came the reply.

Amber tilted her head to one side, as if to say 'suit yourself', and poured herself a large whisky - neat. She turned around on her heels, causing the floor to protest, and then Amber sat down on another sofa - possibly the eldest sister in the sofa family - opposite but slightly to the right of Charlotte, and looked directly at her. She took a few sips from her glass before asking. “Where's your partner in crime today, Inspector?”

With a smile, Charlotte replied “She's busy on another matter.”

Sensing an opportunity for a tease, Amber said “You two make quite the cute couple, don't you know?” keeping her bottom lip on the rim of the glass as she hoped Charlotte would rise to it.

Charlotte was busy getting her notebook and a pen out of her jacket pocket, and so almost without thinking said “You’re not the first to have said that...”

Amber was disappointed she didn’t get the response she expected from Charlotte, and took another sip from her drink to hide what her face said.

Suddenly, a familiar voice boomed in from another room. “Amber, do you know where...” And then Frank Drashler walked into the living room. Wearing just a pair of white boxer shorts, he clearly wasn’t expecting anyone else to be in the room, let alone a Detective Chief Inspector. His question tailed off as he saw Charlotte and he moved slightly to the right, although not before she noticed something on his left arm. “...my clothes are?” he eventually finished.

Now it was Charlotte’s turn for a bit of gentle ribbing. “Talking of cute couples...” she said, aimed at Amber.

The lady of the house managed a look which

straddled both embarrassed and annoyed. The detective wasn't supposed to know about them.

"Inspector! What a pleasant surprise!" came the familiar Cockney accent.

"Mr Drashler. Perhaps more of a surprise to see you here."

"Well, I am Head of Security."

"Yes... was it the grounds or Ms Remington that needed a little securing?"

"Oh yes!" Frank replied in a way which suggested very clearly the answer, looking away in fond memories.

Amber instinctively rubbed her left wrist. She turned to look at Charlotte, suddenly flustered beyond belief, as the detective raised an eyebrow and an interesting smile towards her. *'Well, well, well...'* Charlotte thought.

"They're in the games room..." Amber pushed the words fiercely out of her mouth as if to get rid of Frank faster.

"Ah yes... on the snooker table..." Frank said, looking at Charlotte with a wide grin which told a story about what had just been going on in Amber's house before she arrived...

"Before you go, Mr Drashler." Charlotte interrupted. "I just wonder whether you like hammering your balls into the pocket?"

Amber turned to Charlotte with shock. "I beg your pardon?!" she exclaimed, as Frank returned a devilish smile.

Charlotte continued, “Or are you a more gentle type; caressing the balls... in snooker...”

“Oh, I'm a hammerer...” replied Frank, knowing full well the meaning behind the question as he maintained eye contact with Charlotte throughout their exchange.

“I rather thought you might be...” she replied, eyes narrowing.

It was at that moment, Charlotte decided from now on, a little flirting was fine. She realised the words of ‘imagined David’ were right, and it had no bearing on her relationship with Richard or that somehow she was being disrespectful of his memory. After all, Richard always loved her flirty nature. So, bring it on!

However, for Amber the flirting had gone on long enough. She lept off her sofa and rushed over to Frank. “Go... GO!” she exclaimed to him, pushing him out of the room.

Charlotte had relished this exchange... especially seeing as though Amber had tried to make her feel uncomfortable about Ayesha only a moment ago.

When Amber re-entered the room, Charlotte caught her brushing down her blouse, as if someone had just spent a few stolen seconds getting their hands on something contained inside. Then Charlotte noticed the unbuttoned top of Amber’s blouse, and she felt it her public duty to point that out to her. Amber again looked rather embarrassed, as she fastened up the buttons and tried to gain her composure.. “Why are you here, Inspector? I'm sure it wasn't to make snooker innuendo at my expense..."

"No, Ms Remington, that was just a fortunate happenstance..." replied Charlotte with a grin. "I'm looking to refresh my understanding of what happened the day your husband died..."

"Oh really, Inspector! Do we really need to go over that yet again? Don't you think it's hard enough getting over something like that?!" Amber said, sitting down on the same sofa as before.

"Yes. Yes, I know, believe me," Charlotte said, with a raise of her eyebrows and a dip of her head, "but if you could just go over where you were when it happened..."

Amber was about to protest, but something in Charlotte's manner gave away something she wasn't saying. This took Amber by surprise, and rather disarmed her - for a second or two.

"Well, I was at a conference that day - all day. And the night before actually." she said, quietly.

"Presumably there were some witnesses?" she asked with a sagacious frown.

"I was actually on stage as part of a panel talking about the rise of mobile apps in the future. So, just a few; only around 600 witnesses..." she said with that usual smug look of hers. She took delight in sharing her story. "I believe the Inspector at the time called that my cast-iron alibi..."

Charlotte's eyes told of her scepticism, but she tried to hold it in. "Alibi - that's another Latin word..." she said, seeing Amber couldn't quite know what to make of that comment. "And you found Scott when you returned from the conference?"

"Yes. What was left of him." she replied, ice cold.

"That must have been very hard..."

"Yes..."

Charlotte studied her closely. Was that sorrow or remorse in her eyes?

"Well, thank you again Ms Remington; I'll see myself out."

* * *

Charlotte walked out of the doorway and down the stone steps to meet Ayesha, who was just returning from her fishing expedition and was a few hundred metres away down the drive.

"That was good timing." Charlotte shouted, as her partner took the final steps to meet up with her. "Any joy? she asked Ayesha, who was now in earshot enough for a more conversational level of volume.

"Yes, only one mind, but number 47 has a camera with a clear view of the road and the to this place. I've got the footage from Thursday and Friday transferred onto my phone."

"'Your phone'" Charlotte said with disbelief. "Jeez... you young people!"

Ayesha smiled. "Easiest thing I had to hand!" She looked at Charlotte. "The occupier was a Mr. Chris Davis?", the inflection at the end of the sentence designed to raise Charlotte's interest.

Charlotte stopped, frowned and looked to her left - and eventually the name clicked. "Ohhhh!" she exclaimed. "From school? THAT Chris Davis?!"

"The very same, it seemed." Ayesha had the look of someone who knew something.

"Wowzers, that's a blast from the past!"

"Yeah, he said they'd all missed you at the 10th Anniversary Reunion a few years ago?"

"Well, I was a bit busy, you know..." Charlotte said vaguely, and then it came to her why she didn't go - well, one of the reasons she would admit to anyone else why didn't go did. "It was on when we had that nasty triple murder at Holborn..." she said, slowly at first, but then faster as the memory came back to her, pointing the index finger of both hands skywards at either side of her head to emphasise the reason.

Ayesha looked intently at Charlotte, and eventually Charlotte returned the look. That was all she was going to get on the matter.

"Find out anything, Ma'am?"

"Much more than Ms Remington would have liked me too, I think. Her and Frank Drashler are having a relationship. He was there playing snooker..." Charlotte smiled to herself at the joke that Ayesha didn't get.

Charlotte paused before she got in the car. "What do we know about Frank Drashler?"

Chapter 23

"Nothing." announced Dean.

Charlotte, Ayesha and Dean were all looking at a monitor screen in the Incident Room at the station. As usual, Charlotte had delegated the operation of 'tech' to someone else; this time to Dean, who was sifting through the information they had on Frank Drashler.

Or rather, didn't have.

"What do you mean nothing?" replied Charlotte curtly

"I mean nothing." Dean moved the mouse around some more and pressed some keys on the keyboard. Charlotte thought this was to make sure he hadn't missed anything - although if it was, he hadn't.

"No previous?"

"Not only no previous; but no address - turns out it's a mailbox number - no passport..."

Ayesha had pushed her seat away from where she was, and wheeled back to her desk, looking through information on her computer. "I can't find any trace of him before 2017..."

"So... Where was he before 2017?" Charlotte pondered.

Dean nodded his acknowledgment of the quandary, but left it with Charlotte.

"Anyone for a glass of Tizer?" Charlotte shouted.

There wasn't a reply, just as Charlotte expected. She headed into her office saying "Suit yourselves..."

Ayesha had been feverishly typing and moving her mouse for several minutes now, and shouted, "Ma'am, the report has come back on Sarah's laptop..."

"Go on..." Charlotte shouted from her office.

"Wiped clean."

"Of prints?" Charlotte enquired, returning to the Incident Room with a glass of Tizer, to stand next to Ayesha.

"Of everything; prints and files, Ma'am. The hard drive was completely empty; not even an operating system on it."

"So... whoever had the laptop found what they wanted, and then wiped the whole hard drive to make sure no-one else could?"

"Would certainly fit."

"And they wouldn't know we've got the back-up copy Sarah said was on a USB stick..." Charlotte for a moment was deep in thought, until a realisation broke the spell. "Oh, while I remember, could you pick me up tomorrow, please?" she asked Ayesha.

"Of course, Ma'am." came the reply. "You've not got problems with your car already?"

"No! She's fine... just got somewhere I need to go after I finish... Last day and all that."

"Ok. No problem." Ayesha tailed off quietly, realising their time is coming to an end.

"Thank you." Charlotte replied, with her infectious smile.

As she turned towards her office, the smile disappeared. Over the past few days, she'd started to wonder whether she'd done the right thing; in quitting. It had been tough at times, sure, but maybe the love she'd always had for the job was coming back... And it was no coincidence it had happened with the arrival of her new DC.

As she went to open her office door, she cast a quick glance over to Ayesha and thought how she'd really miss her.

She entered her office, only to be greeted by an astonishing aroma. On the desk in front of her was layed a large bouquet of flowers and a card. Charlotte wasn't great on plant identification, but she spotted lilies, orchids, gerbera daisies, hydrangeas and a few roses. It was a profusion of colour and beautifully presented. She opened the card, which had the words 'Thank you' in a hand-written script on the front; inside it read...

'To Lottie,

Words don't exist to say what you did for us on Friday. Having just lost a lovely daughter-in-law, we wouldn't have got through losing our only son too. We know you probably just see it as doing your job, but we'll always be grateful for how you affected our lives that day.

Thank you. Mr & Mrs Cowal.'

She let out a deep sigh, and carefully put the card on her desk. Removing the fake flowers from the vase on the window sill, she arranged the bouquet the best she could. Looking around the office, she spotted her water bottle, and poured the remaining liquid into the vase, along with the contents of the little plant food sachet that she opened with her teeth.

She replaced the vase on the window sill. God, what a lovely thought, Charlotte mused.

Although it didn't help her feelings of doubt about whether she was doing the right thing...

* * *

After work, Charlotte took Bronte out for an early evening walk - just for an hour - and then he was happy to lay down on his dog bed in the garden chewing on a bone, whilst Charlotte had another attempt at fixing the outside tap.

This time, she was serious.

The stopcock was turned fully off; she'd got a full range of tools at the ready - and she was wearing an anorak. She wasn't taking any chances. Her secret weapon this time was her laptop on the patio showing a YouTube video from a female vlogger explaining exactly what to do to fix the problem.

"This time I will not be beaten!" she said to Bronte, who was watching her progress intently from his safe distance away.

Charlotte played a part of the video, watching and listening intently, then paused it. With a dogged determination, she tried to apply what she'd just learned to the issue she had. Then, she performed the same action on the tap.

There was a range of jiggling and pushing and "Get in there, you ..." from Charlotte, but finally the tap and the pipe which fed it were reunited, seemingly against their will.

Charlotte pushed herself up and stood back to admire her handiwork.

Now, for the moment of truth - turning on the water.

She cleared away the tools into the toolbox, pushing it away from a possible water attack with her feet. The black plastic box made an uncomfortable scraping noise against the paving of the patio. She removed the laptop with rather more care, taking it inside after drying her hands on a towel.

Looking out of the kitchen window to check, she swore she saw Bronte visibly duck.

'Here we go', she thought. She knelt down at the already open under sink cupboard, and steadily turned the faded red stopcock.

Silence.

She turned it some more. The whooshing of the previously pent up water started to echo around the house. But there was still nothing coming from outside.

She turned it a little bit more and decided to leave it there.

She slowly lifted herself up and peered out through

the window, as if in a cartoon.

Nothing.

No water spraying everywhere. She'd done it!

"Yes!! Yes!" she shouted, extremely pleased with herself. The excitement caused Bronte to race inside.

"Time for tea!" she said, which was followed by a large bark from Bronte.

The euphoria was tempered, however, with a look inside the fridge. Amazingly, the shopping fairy hadn't delivered a full week of food for Charlotte without her knowing, and so the fridge was empty - still.

She closed the door, and said "Fish and chips it is then..."

Chapter 24

Tuesday morning.

A Tuesday morning like no other.

When she handed in her resignation on Friday morning, Charlotte had wanted this day to arrive fast. The start of her new life away from the force couldn't have come quick enough.

Now the day was here, it was difficult to put the mix of emotions she felt into words. Fear was certainly there, especially as she'd not given any real thought about what she was going to do next. She had some money saved but that wouldn't last forever, and as a recipient of the George Cross, she received an annuity too, but she was the sort of person who needed to *do* something. Funnily enough, the excitement she felt on Friday for a new life had started to recede. Perhaps she'd come to the conclusion that she *was* a copper - and that was that.

Anyway, it was done now. Regardless of whether she'd changed her mind, she couldn't if she wanted to. The decision was made, and if she wanted to go back to the police, she'd have to look at a different force.

'So, you've quit, only now to think maybe you shouldn't have, but instead of talking to Sharon, you've talked yourself into applying to another force that you don't know. Great move Lottie.' Her internal monologue was both cutting and correct, as usual.

By now, she'd done all the usual morning routine,

and was standing in her matching white bra and knickers in the bedroom. As it was her last day, she decided not to wear the usual suit, and instead considered wearing something from one of the other sections of her wardrobe. Sliding one of the doors to the built-in wardrobe revealed the work gear section. There were some possibilities here. How about the red pencil trousers & blazer suit, with a white top underneath? Ok, that was pulled out of the rail and hung on the curtain rail as an option.

The next door was to the 'everyday clothes that aren't walking gear' section. Blue jeans and a white t-shirt? Possibly too casual - she'd not feel able to arrest anyone wearing those. Section discarded.

Now, the evening wear. On first glance, there could be some options here... although they all would probably be responsible for giving DS Price a heart attack. And she wasn't keen on the guilt from that for the rest of her life...

So, it's either the red suit or strike a blow for her new life of walking and go for some traditional walking gear. In the end, the walking gear won out, and the red trousers and suit went back in the wardrobe for another day... back in its correct place, of course.

Rebecca, Charlotte's cousin who was a detective in the RAF Police, would have said she was demob-happy - the sense of elation in anticipation of demobilisation from the armed forces. And in a way, she'd have been right. There was a sense of freedom flowing over her as she put a pink sleeveless base layer over her head and pulled up the cream walking trousers. *'After all, what are they going to do? Fire me?'* she thought. The rebel was never too far away from the surface with Charlotte.

* * *

Ayesha pulled onto Charlotte's drive, and parked behind the Micra convertible. She turned off the engine and kept her hands on the steering wheel.

Deep breath.

Today was it; DCI Charlotte Walker's last day. Ayesha had been dreading this day coming since she found out her detective mentor was leaving. Was that only five days ago? Seemed a lot longer in a way. By now, Ayesha had come to terms with having moved all this way from London to start a new life. Although she hadn't been told who'd be replacing Charlotte - they probably didn't know themselves yet - the group of people she'd be working with all seemed ok. Mostly. Excluding Vernon, of course - but then there's always the one or two you try to stay away from, if at all possible.

Digs wise, she'd seemed to have got sorted with a house share with two other ladies from uniform; so that would be better than a B&B. Finally, she could look at getting some of her stuff brought up from London. Not the comic book collection, of course, that would have to wait until she had a place of her own - which was a lot more affordable up here than in the capital.

'No, it'll be ok', she reassured herself.

Still, the prospect of a Charlotte Walker-sized hole

in this new world was something she'd have to get used to.

Ayesha got out of her car and walked the length of the drive to the front door, pressing the doorbell - then knocking on the door when she remembered the doorbell doesn't work.

Charlotte walked out of the house, collected the wheelie bin, and dragged it past Ayesha to the road. Walking up the drive back to the house, she raised up her eyebrows to see 'hello' to Ayesha - and promptly went back inside, closing the front behind her. After a while it became clear Charlotte wasn't coming out anytime soon.

'Right. What now?' she thought.

At that point, the front door opened, but instead of Charlotte standing there, she was very surprised to see Bronte. The clever boy had opened the door by himself, and walked over to Ayesha, tail wagging.

"Who's a clever boy?" she said to him in the exaggerated fashion she'd heard others use with animals. Ayesha wouldn't call herself a convert quite yet, but seeing Bronte in action over the past couple of days had helped her understand the appeal of pets, and dogs in particular.

Without realising it, she had again been hoodwinked by Bronte into fussing him, which is what she was still doing when Charlotte came through the open front door looking for a dog. She was in the middle of a call on her mobile, and gave Bronte a roll of her eyes when she saw the scene.

The person on the other end of the phone had clearly stopped talking, as Charlotte said “That's fantastic! Thank you.”

There was a pause.

“Yes, I've got all that. Left straight after the phone box; yes.”

Another pause.

“Tonight at 6:30. See you then. Bye.”

Charlotte removed the phone from her ear, and checked the call had finished, before saying hello properly to Ayesha.

“I see he collared you again...” she smiled as Bronte had a look of innocence about him.

“Yeah, he’s very good at that!”

Charlotte looked down at him, and ordered him back inside the house. “Bye, Bronte. See you later.” Bronte’s head visibly dropped, as he obediently but slowly trotted back inside the house. “Tones will be around later.” Charlotte said cheerfully, whilst at the same time trying to hide her guilt for leaving him.

Charlotte locked the front door, and the crime busting duo made their way to Ayesha's car.

“What was all that about Ma'am?” Ayesha asked conversationally.

“All in good time, my dear! All in good time!”

The path of the ladies crossed over in front of Ayesha’s car, for Charlotte to make her way to the passenger’s side - for a change. As they climbed in,

Charlotte asked "New Corsa? She gave the car the once over with her inquisitive eyes.

Ayesha agreed, and as she shut her door said "It was my present to myself for making DC."

"Nice." replied Charlotte.

Ayesha entered car-sale mode. "Heated seats; heated steering wheel...but... " she pointed to the central console, "...no CD player!"

Charlotte shook her head and in mock disgust said "Outrageous! Send it back!"

Ayesha smiled as she started up the car. The stereo, tuned to Absolute Radio, was part-way through 'Every Little Thing She Does Is Magic' by The Police, and both of the coppers smiled at how apt this was. Only one of them smiled also because of the title of the song, and she reversed the car off Charlotte's drive, and drove it along Melton Road.

* * *

Charlotte returned to the Incident Room from her office with a glass of Tizer. Looking around, it was quieter than usual, and she liked it that way. She sat down at her usual desk and winced as she remembered why she'd got up in the first place; to give herself an excuse to not to fill in the countless forms she had in front of her.

Ayesha was looking through the CCTV footage from the house across the road from Amber's. It would have been a mammoth task but the system Chris Davis used segregated each time the camera was triggered by movement into a separate video file. So, it was a case of opening every file to see what had triggered it. Sometimes it was passengers walking by, other times vehicles she wasn't interested in.

But then, she struck gold. "I've got a result from the CCTV camera from across the street at Amber's, Ma'am...

Charlotte welcomed another excuse to avoid the forms. "What have you got?" she asked, as she walked across to lean over Ayesha's shoulder.

The Detective Constable played the open video file, which clearly showed Sarah's car pulling into Amber's driveway.

"When was this? Is there time stamps on this?"

Ayesha clicked on an icon, and it confirmed it was 4:03pm on Thursday.

"Bloody hell! The quality of these cameras is amazing!" commented Charlotte.

"And clearly show Sarah pulling into Amber's drive..."

"*Ms* Amber..." corrected Charlotte. "If only everyone had ones like these."

"That Chris Davis seems to be a bit of a tech nerd." Ayesha said, straining out of the corner of her eye to see whether Charlotte was taking the bait.

"Yeah, he was, as I remember. Probably why it would never have worked."

Ayesha bit her teeth over her bottom lip at this revelation. Returning to the job in hand she said, "So Sarah pulled into *Ms* Amber's drive after she left Tempto Digital's offices on the Thursday."

"And how long does it take to do that journey?"

Ayesha clicked onto another tab of the browser showing Google Maps. "Around 35 minutes." came the reply.

"So she went straight there. And what time did she leave?" and then added, jokingly, "Or is she still there?"

Cocking one eyebrow, Ayesha replied, "Well, you might have something there…" Charlotte turned slightly to look at her with a mix of doubt and disbelief. Surely not? "Sarah's car leaves at 9am Friday morning... but look who's driving it…"

Charlotte turned back to the screen. The footage showed Sarah's electric car stop at the end of Amber's driveway - windscreen wipers working to dispel the rain - waiting for a space in the traffic before it pulled out onto the main road. Then, Ayesha clicked back on the footage to pause it on a lovely still, clearly showing Frank Drashler at the wheel as the car turned right onto the main road..

"Well, well, well... so either Sarah is in the boot of her own car, or still at *Ms* Amber's…"

"...or she'd already been moved…" Ayesha introduced a third option.

Charlotte looked interested in this possibility, as Ayesha clicked to open another CCTV video file. The now familiar vantage point looking towards Amber's drive was devoid of vehicles, until a white Transit-sized van pulled in.

"The white company van driving like a maniac to *Ms* Amber's house? Left Tempto Digital's offices at 4:25 - gets here at 4:51".

"Bloody hell. That's some driving."

"And look who's driving it..." Ayesha clicked back on the footage to pause it just as the van turned left down Amber's drive, and the lovely sharp still image clearly showed Frank Drashler at the wheel again.

"And then, Friday morning 3:30am..." Ayesha said, opening a further file. Even though it's pitch dark, the video quality is certainly good enough to see the white van pulling out of Amber's driveway in the rain. Frank is clearly driving again, but this time pauses when he reaches the junction with the road to remonstrate with someone in the back of the van.

"3:30am... Frank's driving again, but who is that in the van..."

"Can you zoom into that?"

"With these cameras I can a little..."

Ayesha clicked on the mouse a little, and a closer-up image of the van displayed on the monitor. It's fuzzy, as images are when they are zoomed in, but it clearly shows a figure with blond hair.

Charlotte's eyes lit up. "That's got to be Sarah!" she exclaimed.

"That's what I thought Ma'am!"

"So where is he taking her?" Charlotte wondered out

loud.

“Well, I did some wider ANPR checks on the CCTV cameras but I lost him after 4:30 Friday morning. I think he was just driving around to trying to throw us off the scent, before going to wherever he went.”

Charlotte moved closer to the monitor and ran her finger around the image of Frank on the screen. “Frank Drashler is involved in this up to his neck.”

“Maybe more so, Ma'am… The Tech Guys managed to demodulate the caller to Toni... guess who it is?”

Ayesha clicked on an audio file on her computer. It played the conversation from Saturday night recorded on Toni’s phone, only this time the caller’s voice isn’t Disguised - and it is Frank Drashler. Charlotte let off a wry smile.

“And then…”

“You mean there’s more??!” Charlotte exclaimed.

“MmmHmm... Tech Guys have also been busy decrypting the files on that SD card from Sarah you found... She was quite the detective... loads of documents pointing to people involved - mostly Tempto Digital employees... including one…”

“...Frank Drashler.” concluded Charlotte.

“Yeap.” Ayesha confirmed.

Charlotte tapped on the image of Frank on the monitor. “Right, let's get him in.”

Chapter 25

As interview rooms go, this one was fairly standard. It was of a decent size, allowing for movement inside, and was large enough not to make the occupants feel claustrophobic. A window, the lower part made from frosted glass, looked out onto the road outside; the walls painted a dull blue colour and plain apart from a large map of the Doncaster borough on the wall opposite the window. An average sized table was positioned in the middle of the room, with the usual recording equipment at one end. Two plain padded office chairs were arranged on one side, and were sat on by Charlotte and Ayesha, and on the other side, the same type of chairs found themselves sat on by a gentleman and a lady.

Frank Drashler sat across from Charlotte, and looked rather tasty she thought in a shiny light grey suit, which appeared silver in certain light, nicely contrasted with a deep burgundy shirt underneath the jacket. Opposite Ayesha was his solicitor; a tall, powerfully built blond lady with strong features and a jaw line to match her unquestionable large hourly rate. Her suit undoubtedly was the most expensive item in the room, and she stared across at Charlotte and Ayesha through very dainty designer glasses.

"Do you know, Inspector, it's almost a pleasure being caught by you..." Frank said.

Charlotte took the compliment and asked "If I'd have been on your case from the start, would you have given yourself up earlier then?"

Frank smiled loutishly. "Now, I wouldn't say that... but I might have contemplated it..."

Charlotte flicked him a respectful smile.

And now down to business.

"So... this blackmail...?" she prompted.

Frank sat back in his chair, ready to tell his story. "Decent screw really. No need for violence; easy blue-collar stuff."

"Until Sarah Knight got in the way..."

"Believe it or not, Inspector, I didn't want to do anything to her. I suggested buying her out; she's got a kid; would she've said no to hundred K, for example? I mean, would you?"

Ayesha shifted in her seat and started to look uncomfortable - was that a bribe?

Charlotte knew it was banter, and so decided to be honest. "In her situation, I'd have given it serious thought..."

A congratulatory smile crossed Frank's face. "Wise, Inspector, wise. But I was overruled."

Charlotte's eyes narrowed and she leaned in towards this tower of a man. "Who by, Frank?" she asked softly.

Frank leaned in similarly towards this impressive detective. "You and I both know you know." he replied, mirroring Charlotte's tone.

That wasn't enough, thought Charlotte. She needed

something a little more concrete. She smiled as she worked out a phrasing that he might appreciate. “Is it your snooker-loving friend with the pocket?”

Frank smiled. Continuing the snooker metaphor, he replied “You've got a 147 there, Inspector.”

“Thank you.”

The two were only about thirty centimetres away from each other across the table, and Ayesha didn’t like this development at all. She needed to break them out of this.

“Have you any proof of this Mr Drashler?”

Frank glanced across to Ayesha without moving his head, and for a brief moment flicked her a look of irritation she’d interrupted his flirting. “I've actually got some recordings of us... she knew everything, down to the last detail; all her idea. I hope it will help…”

“...you?” Charlotte continues Frank’s unspoken word.

“Of course.” he replied, unashamedly. Charlotte smiled wryly.

Charlotte had Frank’s attention once more. Ayesha tried again. “And the break-in at Sarah's house?”

“I left it as long as I could; waiting for them to be out of the house long enough. No-one innocent needs to get hurt.”

“So, where is Sarah, then?”

“I genuinely don’t know.” he said coldly.

It was the first time Charlotte had seen something

really nasty in him. His words sounded hollow and he had developed a distinctly chilling look in his dark eyes. She swallowed back and decided to keep her questioning in the same light as before.

"Oh, come now, Frank, surely you know roughly where she might be?"

"Sorry, no." The abrupt answer wasn't in keeping with his seemingly cheery demeanour. She was sickened by the thought Frank knew where Sarah was but wasn't going to tell her. But she shouldn't have been that surprised. They knew he was so mixed up in all of this, so what did she expect? Her priority now surely had to be bringing Amber in, then questioning them both, Independently, to find where Sarah was.

Frank paused for a while, as if to accept his fate. Then a wide smile broke out across his face. "We should have that game sometime Inspector. What's your highest break?"

"67." came the reply, with Charlotte unable to resist wearing her proud face.

"Not bad..."

"Thank you. I'll see if we can organise a Police-Prisoner championship for where you are going..." she replied. Frank bowed his head with acknowledgment.

Charlotte ran her tongue over her lips. "So I suppose you could say you are under a-rest..."

A look of amusement crossed Frank's face - he'd always liked this Inspector. Charlotte indicated to Ayesha it is time to go, and the younger detective left first, holding the door open for Charlotte.

"Oh, just one more thing, Mr Drashler..." Charlotte turned from the door to look at Frank again. "I wonder if you could roll up your sleeve and show me your left arm please..?"

Without looking at Charlotte, a bad-boy smirk appeared on Frank's face; *'well played Inspector'*. He rolled up his left sleeve, and then turned to look Charlotte directly in the eye.

* * *

There was a reason why Charlotte drove herself everywhere. Two reasons actually. One, she relaxed knowing *she* was in control. And two, she made a terrible passenger.

Not because she got car sick, or anything like that, she was just a genuinely terrible passenger.

She'd thought about this before, on the rare occasions someone had to drive her somewhere, and the conclusion she'd arrived at was she's a terrible passenger because as a passenger she's *not* in control.

She wasn't in control as the car in front had started to brake around two seconds ago and Ayesha hadn't responded by slowing down... yet.... *'Ok, that was too late.'* she thought. It was all Charlotte could do to stop herself from throwing her hands onto the dashboard in front of her, as if bracing herself for an impact. Ayesha eventually slowed down with plenty of time for the car in front to speed up again, so Ayesha didn't have to stop. It was, Charlotte told herself, sensible and responsible driving, truth be told. The only thing wrong was Charlotte wasn't in control.

It was taking all of Ayesha's concentration to drive at this present time. She'd nearly missed the fact the car in front was braking, and it was only thanks to him speeding up quickly that she didn't have to do a full-blown emergency stop. Which certainly wouldn't have done her confidence any good.

She couldn't put her finger on why. True, she wasn't the most confident driver in the police, but she was driving her own car - not someone else's like when she drove Charlotte home on Friday. So why was she like this?

Charlotte decided she should talk. "There's a reason we didn't have anything on Frank Drashler before 2017..."

"Ma'am?"

"He didn't exist before 2017."

"What?" Ayesha wasn't in the right frame of mind for riddles.

"He was somebody else..."

To Ayesha who is concentrating, this didn't make any sense.

Turning down the now familiar driveway to Amber's house was welcome, because it meant Ayesha could take a break from driving. She pulled up behind Amber's Mercedes, which was parked right outside the front door, where they usually stop. The boot and the rear passenger side door were open, as was the front door to the house - which had captured Charlotte's interest. As the two detectives got out of the car, they were joined by the marked police car Charlotte had requested, kicking up gravel as it stopped behind them.

“Ma’am?”

“Yes?”

“147?”

“The highest break possible in a game of snooker.”

Ayesha looked satisfied now she knew, as the duo were joined by two uniformed officers.

“Afternoon.” Charlotte welcomed them. “Give me a couple of minutes and then come in.” Charlotte raised her eyebrows and smiled theatrically, and before Ayesha could say anything, the DCI had trotted up the steps and into Amber’s house.

The two uniformed officers looked across to Ayesha, who smiled politely at them.

* * *

There was an agitation to the atmosphere in Amber’s living room. Three large suitcases and one smaller one were packed and ready to go, and Charlotte only just avoided walking into them as she quietly wandered into the room.

Her arrival was unnoticed by Amber as she was on the phone, and the ringing tone seeping from the handset’s tinny speaker was getting her more and more angry. By the time the call was transferred to the default voicemail ‘leave a message’ announcement, her lips were pressed firmly together with rage.

Waiting for the obligatory beep, Amber proceeded to leave her curt message.

“Where are you? You're supposed to be here by now! We *both* need to be away from here, remember?! Call me when you get this.” Amber scowled as she threw the phone onto one of the four sofas in the room. Turning around, she was startled by the presence of Charlotte.

“Oh Inspector!”

Knowing she was inside Amber’s house without invitation, she offered “The front door was open, Ms Remington...”

Amber was sufficiently flustered with events not to have the presence of mind to ask the detective to leave. “Yes, I'm loading the car.” she said, instantly regretting it.

“Are you going somewhere?”

“Just for a night.”

Charlotte acknowledged the reply. “Just for a night, eh? On your own? There's an awful lot of luggage there for a night. Or does that include Frank's as well?”

Without thinking, Amber said “No, Frank's bringing his own...” Amber realises what she had well and truly let the cat out of the bag. So Frank was part of this plan to escape, seemingly for a night, but with more than a night’s amount of clothes; much more. Charlotte was pleased she’d been able to sneak around Amber’s defences, but she knew she’d be unlikely to get anything else out of her without her noticing. Especially as Amber had already shook her revelation off and was wearing her poker face again. “I'm sorry, Inspector, but I'm due to be at a conference this afternoon.”

“Oh really? When was this arranged?”

“Oh it's a last minute thing. I'm on a panel at 3:45.”

“I see.” said Charlotte. “Just like the day Scott died”.

“Yes. Well, I've been on many panels since Scott died and no-one has died, Inspector.”

“Maybe so. But maybe you hadn't needed to get rid of anyone else since Scott.”

Amber was getting more than a little annoyed at this. She’d been exceptionally helpful, she thought, but this was enough. She leaned on the back of the leather sofa, and in a low, rather menacing voice said, “You've got nothing on me for my husband's death... or the disappearance of Sarah Knight.”

Charlotte was a little pleased by Amber’s indignation. Another chink in her defences, perhaps? More cheerily than it deserved, she replied, “Well, you're probably right at the moment Ms Remington.” as she noticed Ayesha and the uniformed officers enter the room and stand by the door. Amber is smug personified, and as Charlotte had hoped, she was so concentrating on her duel with her that she failed to notice them.

“So with that, Inspector, I'll be on my way…”

“...to meet up with Frank?”

“Yes. When I find where he is…”, she said almost under her breath.

That was the cue Charlotte had been waiting for. With the gusto of a performer, she delivered “Ah, well,

I can help you there, actually... He's in one of my very comfy holding cells down at my nick…"

The smug grin was suddenly wiped from Amber's face… around about the time the colour drained from it.

"What?!"

Charlotte continued with, "Mmmm. Yes. And he's expressed a wish for you to join him. I mean, it's not the Ritz, but there's some pretty soft pillows in there these days…"

"What are you talking about?" Amber retorted, failing to hide her indignation.

"It seems I came across a large number of documents on memory card a couple of days ago, and thanks to *my* computer tech team here...", she pointed to Ayesha, "...I was able to clearly see the wide spread blackmailing of businesses - coordinated by a chap called Frank Drashler. And then, someone - let's call him a snooker-loving individual - told us in fact, it was actually YOUR idea. He's got some recordings which make for interesting listening…

Amber was livid - Frank has betrayed her. "What the…?!"

Charlotte jumped in, "So, I might not be able to pin murder and kidnapping on you at the moment, but I **can** charge you under section 21 of the Theft Act 1968. More commonly known as blackmail."

Charlotte walked up close to the seething Amber to get in her face and said "I'd say you've been snookered…"

With a glance of her eyes, Charlotte looked at

Ayesha and indicated to her to make the arrest.

Ayesha tried hard to put a lid on her excitement, but her chest puffed out with pride at her first arrest as a *Detective* Constable. She moved across to Amber, who was still standing defiantly opposite Charlotte, and said the words she knew off by heart. "*Ms* Amber Remington, you are under arrest for blackmail. You do not have to say anything, but it may harm your defence if you do not mention now something you later rely on in court. Anything you do say may be given in evidence."

Ayesha instructed the two uniformed officers to lead Amber away, and they had got within metres of the living room door, when Charlotte channelled her inner-Columbo… "Just one more thing, *Ms* Remington…" The officers stopped and Amber turned to watch Charlotte walk theatrically over to her - this time getting so close in Amber's face that the ends of their noses almost touched. "I know you killed your husband and I'm fairly certain you at the very least didn't help save his brother when you could."

Amber smiled slightly, only marginally hiding her pleasure that she knew Charlotte couldn't prove it. "And when I find Sarah Knight, I'll be charging you with kidnapping too.", the detective continued.

Amber took a breath, and leaned to her right to whisper in Charlotte's left ear. "Kidnapping implies you'll find her alive. I wouldn't count on that, Inspector. She'll be dead by I V."

Amber took a step backwards, and without the two of them breaking their stare, the two uniform officers led Amber out of the room.

Just as Charlotte turned to Ayesha, a cry from the corridor came Amber's parting shot... "Vale Inspectorem!"

* * *

Charlotte walked down the steps of the house onto the gravel driveway in time to see Amber's face shooting daggers at her from the rear window of the police car as it drove off. She guessed a police Volvo wouldn't have been the method of transport Amber had in mind for today.

She sighed a deep, troubled sigh. She now had the two central people to this whole affair, but she was still no closer to finding Sarah Knight.

"And what the hell did she mean by 'I V'?" Charlotte continued her thought process out loud.

Ayesha walked over to Charlotte. "Intravenous? Killed by an injection? Perhaps she's held at some medical facility?"

"Mmmm." Charlotte wasn't convinced.

"I can make enquiries, Ma'am. Hospitals, errrr GPs...?"

"No. No. It doesn't make sense."

Charlotte kicked some of the gravel on the driveway, and because it relieved some of the frustration, she did it again.

“I am missing something here, and it's just there in front of me.” She thumped her forehead with her fist, much to Ayesha’s shock. “What did Amber say again?”

" ’She'll be dead by I V.’ - that was it 'verbatim'.” Ayesha was pleased with herself for including a Latin word...

Latin.

Could that be it?

“Verbatim... Latin... THAT'S IT - it's not the letters I V; it's the Roman Numeral - she meant 4; that she'll be dead by FOUR O CLOCK!” Charlotte had cracked it.

Ayesha and Charlotte exchanged a horrified look, as the clock tower on top of the stables rang out for 1:30pm.

The clock really *was* ticking now.

Chapter 26

The incident room was a buzz of eagerness, anticipation and nerves. There must have been around twenty officers, a mix of detectives and uniform, all waiting and collecting into small groups. Ayesha was standing at the front of the room next to the incident board, which had been moved to a point where it partially obscured the window to Charlotte's office. Ayesha looked out at officers, talking Amongst themselves. If they were a class of smart, but unruly kids, then she was the teaching assistant who they knew they didn't have to behave for.

Just then, the teacher pushed open the double doors at the back of the incident room with such force, the hinges regretted being there. Stoney-faced, she barged through the class, turning the volume down on their chatter as if with a remote control as she walked between them..

As she reached the front, she turned on her walking boots and faced the class. They had all turned to look at her. *'That was the power of Charlotte'*, thought Ayesha.

"Ok, let's gather round!!" she instructed; the frown she was wearing a meer hint of her inner commotion. Gradually, the collective moved towards the front and congregated around the incident board, or as close as they could.

"Ok, settle down and listen up! We've got a deadline here people: 4pm." she exclaimed, writing a big '4pm' on the board with her dry-wipe pen, and then circled it for added emphasis. She looked around the room at the gathered officiers. “We need to work out where Sarah is and then get her out of there before 4pm. If our hunch is right, we'll be finding a body after 4 if we don't get to her.”

That caused some unsettled chatter between the crowd..

Charlotte brought them back to the matter in hand. “Ok! Because of the time available, we've got to work to a theory. We know Amber and her associates have been removing any businesses from the base map that don't pay up to their blackmail. So, let's work on that they'd do the same for the place they have taken Sarah...” She looked at everyone individually. “Let's look for anything that has been taken off the base map in the last couple of days, that wouldn't be explained by a blackmail threat.”

From the back, Vernon had been thinking over this premise, and couldn’t wait to point out a problem. “What if the place where she is has been taken off the map weeks ago?” he shouted. Everyone turned to look at him, mulled over his point, and then looked back at Charlotte. Surely he had a point?

Charlotte took a deep breath, and gravely replied, “If we believe that, we'll just have to wait to find a burnt body in a random fire by the end of today... and a kid will have lost his mummy.” This thought sobered the room slightly. “So I prefer we look for somewhere taken off the map in the last couple of days...”

A general murmur of agreement swept across the troops.

"Ma'am?" came a voice from one of the uniformed officers. "Shouldn't we be getting the Bomb Squad?"

"Not much point if we don't know where she is, Constable Giles." Charlotte rightly pointed out.

This reply generated another ripple of agreement, but no movement.

Charlotte looked at them, gave them adequate time to act, then yelled, "So come then!"

Teacher had spoken, and the class went quickly back to their desks. The mood had changed to one of quiet optimism, as they went about their tasks.

Charlotte studied the room in front of her. Whilst she had complete confidence in these people, they faced a Herculean task. If the blackmail operation had been running for months, there could be thousands of businesses removed from the base map. And this was happening all around the country, so there was no guarantee Sarah Knight was even still in the Doncaster area.

But, her instincts told her she was. And whilst there was a chance, she was determined to do all she possibly could.

Ayesha was still standing next to the incident board. Something had been troubling her, but unlike Vernon, she didn't want to say it in front of the class.

"Ma'am? But if it is Amber, we've got her in custody - she can't do anything."

Charlotte walked over, and rested her bottom on the spare desk pushed up against the wall next to the incident board. Once there, she indicated with her head for Ayesha to join her.

“Remember her husband's death?” she quietly said to Ayesha, who nodded. “There was evidence of some sort of device which they suspected triggered the fire…”

Ayesha frowned in thought. “An IED? But she had a cast-iron alibi - almost as good as hers now.”

“Yeah… hundreds of people. I know.” Charlotte paused. Ayesha knew she was deep in thought, as she’d now got her pen out of a pocket, and was running it through her left hand. “But I think that's what she was banking on, and she scheduled a text message to be sent when she knew she was going to be on stage.”

“Could you do that back then? Was that possible?”

“Remember one of the projects Kelvin Thomas told us Sarah worked on?” Charlotte raised and held her eyebrows for a moment waiting for Ayesha’s memory to catch up.

“A text scheduling app! Released as their first app…” she exclaimed, almost too loud for their breakout meeting to go unnoticed any longer.

“...in 2017…” Charlotte confirmed.

Ayesha’s face showed she was sure everything fitted together. Charlotte lifted herself off the desk, and looked closely at Amber’s photograph on the incident board. It appeared to be looking back at her, teasing her.

Without saying a word, Charlotte bounded out of the Incident Room.

She had an idea.

* * *

It's an inevitable progression of any double act that sooner or later, one of the duo wishes to branch out on their own and see if they can make it solo.

And so the Walker and Sheldon partnership was paused, to allow Walker to undertake a solo career. And he had her first gig already. Just like the duo's gigs, this one was a sell-out. In fact, half the audience was so looking forward to the gig, they were pacing around the venue - the usual interview room in Doncaster's Police Station.

Charlotte walked in and smiled at Amber as she sat down next to the constable, who had been acting as a chaperone. Amber did one more lap of the room before she sat down opposite Charlotte. The ladies smiled coldly at each other, before Amber opened and her smile slipped.

"I hope you don't expect me to tell you where Sarah is, Inspector..."

"I'd be very disappointed if you did." Amber leaned back in her seat and showed a wry smile.

"So what's this? A social call?"

"You could call it that."

Amber suddenly sat forward leaning as far over the desk between them as she could. "Are you threatened by me, Inspector? An older woman in control?"

Charlotte studied her, and steadily moved to adopt

a similar position across her side of the desk. They were inches away from each other now. "I'd say the more pertinent question is, are you threatened by me?" she asked, throwing the question back and tilting her head to one side.

Amber's cheeks wavered, every so slightly.

Charlotte continued, "You see, I've taken your motto and actually done good with it. Made society a better place. You? You've just sown negativity and deceit." She paused, for dramatic effect, "And murder, of course."

Amber moved back to a normal sitting position on her chair, and Charlotte did the same. Amber studied the detective for a while. "You know nothing of me, Inspector! Nothing about my life." she said, with a visible curl on her upper lip; the bile evident.

Charlotte took a moment, then replied coolly and steadily. "Well, I know you were unhappy as a child; moving around to the various places your Dad was billeted at. I know you had very few friends growing up, and so you've struggled to make positive connections to people throughout your life." Charlotte narrowed her eyes. "And I know you still resent your Dad for making you have to live the way you did."

It was more brutal than a pounding sledgehammer and took more than a little of the wind out of her sails. For a moment, the tall figure of Amber looked lost; naked against Charlotte's summation.

"How am I doing?" Charlotte asked, with a little wrinkle of her nose and holding her left hand out, palm up and fingers splayed. Amber looked around the room;

anywhere to avoid Charlotte's gaze. And was that a small tear forming?

It didn't take long for the normal Amber to return. And when it did, it came with forty years of anger. "Not resent, Inspector.... Hate." she said, slamming her clenched fists down on the table. "I hated him for what he put me through. All because of his wonderful job!" The bitterness seeped from every fibre of her being.

"He couldn't help where it took him." replied Charlotte, seemingly defending someone she'd never met.

"He could have left! Done something else. Thought more about his family; thought more about ME! He should never have had a kid. My first lesson in rejection. I guess some people are just born to do a job and nothing else."

For a moment, Charlotte wasn't quite sure who Amber was talking about. It sounded a little like a certain red-headed detective not too far away from this room... The point wasn't lost on Charlotte as she shuffled around in her chair.

When she returned from this wanderment, Amber had been busy boiling up another mug of hostility. Her forehead seemed to now have a burnt-in frown.

"Do you know, everywhere we went, I just found myself watching other kids playing; playing outside in the street; in the woods... I was an outsider." she said, eyes blazing.

"Didn't you want to go to play with them? Join them outside?"

“Actually, no. I wanted to stop them playing. Close it all down. Why should they enjoy themselves when I couldn't?”

The squint and frown from Charlotte revealed how appalled by this she was; but it did explain an awful lot.

Amber continued, “Do you know, one year, he even told me on my birthday we were moving? Birthday in one place; a week later, Easter in another.”

As if someone had just given Charlotte a script, she took up the story from here, filling in some of the blanks. “So, by the time your family settled down, in Oxfordshire, you were just about to start your O Levels... one of which was Latin - hence you *‘studied Latin at Oxford’*."

Amber smiled at her own cleverness.

“So, it was then you decided you were going to take control of your life.... *Faber est suae quisque fortunae*" Charlotte continued.

Amber quietly under her breath translated, "Every man is the artisan of his own fortune.”

“Or woman.”

Amber smiled in acknowledgment.

“So, after the chance meeting of Carl Remington, you decided on the future you wanted, and went after it.”

“It was love, Inspector.” Amber said, as sincerely as she could manage.

“It was greed, Ms Remington.” Charlotte replied curtly.

Amber started to develop a face to protest, but decided there was little point, so her poker face returned.

Charlotte had what she came for, and it was time to go. She stood up, pushing hard on the desk as she did so, in a grand gesture. All animated and loud, she said, "Anyway, lovely to chat. Shame I can't stop longer, but I've a missing person to find."

"I hope I haven't helped you at all, Inspector." she said, the glee in her voice was self apparent. Charlotte walked around to the side of Amber, and leaned in next to her ear.

"Actually, Ms Remington... , " she said both softly and with force, "you have!" and with that she left the room, closing the door behind her. Turning to look briefly through the window in the door, she watched as Amber desperately tried to maintain her poker face.

* * *

There's a measured hum of work being undertaken in the incident room. Everyone is busy working on the task at hand, when Charlotte bursts in.

"Well... anything?" she shouted curtly, to anyone who was brave enough to respond..

"Nothing Gov." Dean replied after realising no-one else dared to answer, and that he was the most senior officer.

"Jeez, how are you all going to cope when I'm

not here?" It was almost a lesson in 'How to alienate an entire room in one easy stroke'. A wave of mild indignation swept across to Charlotte. She chose to ignore it.

"Sarah's in April Wood!!" she exclaimed.

The statement caught everyone's attention. How the hell did she know that?

"Did Ms Remington tell you?" Ayesha asked.

The speed at which she ran the length of the building back to the incident room caught up with Charlotte, and she paused for a moment. "No, well, not in as many words."

The room looked puzzled.

"Check your mapping apps... April Wood... Only the outline is there, isn't it? No paths, tracks, buildings..."

The room en masse turned back to their various devices. Mice were moved and clicked on; keyboards were typed on; mobile phone screens were pressed and pinched. It was all going too slow for Charlotte...

Eventually there was a wave of agreement, but the excitable Charlotte needed a more positive confirmation. "It's been taken off the map, hasn't it?!" she said in exasperation.

"Yes!" replied Ayesha, helping her partner.

"Thought so!"

Ayesha found herself aghast, yet again. "Ma'am, how did you...?"

Vernon, however, is not impressed. He thought he

could see through Charlotte's amazingness. With clear consternation he exclaimed, “She'd already checked on her phone!”

Charlotte pulled out her Nokia 3310 and shook it in the air towards Vernon with relish. “Not on this, I haven't!” Charlotte had skewered Vernon again.

There was no time to gloat. Charlotte pointed at a select few uniformed officers. “You four; with us. Come on. And bring some bolt cutters just in case.” Then aimed at the remaining, “We need the dog section to April Wood as a matter of urgency. Get on it now. And round up the others on those documents doing the blackmailing; I need them all banged up.”

With that, the posse of Charlotte, Ayesha, Dean, Vernon and the four uniformed officers left the Incident Room at pace.

Chapter 27

The entrance to April Wood was set back off a side road from one of the more quiet suburbs of Doncaster. At the turn of the 19th century, it was part of the estate of the nearby country house, but it was sold off when the then owning family couldn't maintain all the grounds. Since then, it had always been in private hands, but with the public allowed access at all times.

That was until now.

It hadn't taken the new owners long to board up the side of the wood which buffered up to the road. They were the sort of boards you find outside buildings being renovated - often decorated with 'artist impression' drawings of what the new finished project would look like. Except all these boards had on them were "Keep Out" and "Private Property" in big red letters. Every so often, the phrase "Property of Electrum Investments" was repeated.

The monotony of the boards was broken solely for two metal mesh-style gates blocking the once open right of way through the wood, locked together with a padlocked chain. The only evidence this was a legal thoroughfare was the green faded Public Footpath finger sign pointing beyond the metal gate.

Four cars descended to park in the empty lay-by, and the police team made their way to the now blocked entrance to the wood. Charlotte studied the gates and wondered whether they could climb over the top - but then noticed the particularly nasty-looking barbed wire on the top.

Dean pulled at the locked gate, with inevitable futility. The chain and gate rattled almost sarcastically at him. So he kicked it, and then regretted that course of frustration straight away as winced in pain.

"I think we can take it as red that it is locked, DI Sheldon?" asked Charlotte, with a wry smile on her face.

"Gov." agreed Dean, rather sheepishly.

"Well, that's it. We can't go in there without a warrant." said Vernon, happy to have done as little as possible and maybe go back to the station for something to eat.

Charlotte wasn't going to let something as inconsequential as a locked gate and the need for a warrant stop her. They were on a mission and time was of the essence. As a child, she was an avid watcher of the children's television series *Blue Peter*, and their famous phrase of 'here's one I made earlier' stuck with Charlotte throughout her life. In fact, her whole police career was almost built on that adage - to have something up your sleeve ready for the next situation. And she had just the right 'something' here - thanks to being a walker.

Smiling, she knocked his negativity away. "Ahh, you're forgetting about the Countryside & Rights of Way Act 2000. It is an offence to block a public right of way, and a walker can use any reasonable measure to gain access..."

Vernon looked at her aghast. *'Surely she wasn't trying to use THAT as a defence for getting in the woods?'*

he thought. But almost as the thought had finished forming in his head, Charlotte had gone to the boot of Ayesha's car and pulled out the bolt cutters and an evidence bag containing Sarah's top. Handing the evidence bag to Ayesha on the way, she walked over to the locked gates, and studied them for a short while.

"Well, I certainly am a Walker!" she exclaimed, enjoying both the double meaning of the word and the cutting of the locked chain with the bolt cutters. She yanked the now snapped chain off the gates and pushed the gates open with relish. "Come on!" she shouted, as Ayesha offered her hand for the bolt cutters, before Charlotte threw them on the floor.

The party entered into the woods, led by a charged-up Charlotte - with Vernon the rather unwilling and unhappy person bringing up the rear, who looked shocked at the damage to the gate.

They walked for a while, but without a clear plan of where they were going, it was a bit of a rabbit warren.

At the junction of several paths, Charlotte stopped - and the rest of the party fell in behind her. She pondered "It's no good. What we need is a map..."

"But the wood has been wiped from all the mapping apps..." reminded Ayesha.

"No.. What we need is a *map*." she said, pleased with her own cleverness. She knew why there was a reason she'd worn walking trousers this morning - big pockets designed to hold a proper OS Map.

She pulled the physical map from her leg trouser pocket. Ordnance Survey Explorer 279 Doncaster,

Conisbrough, Maltby & Thorne read the title on the front of the tattered, well-used map. Charlotte smiled at the map as though she'd just seen an old friend.

Opening up the map to its fullest extent, Charlotte laid it down on the floor, and then dropped to her knees, using herself as a paper weight. Ayesha noticed she'd come alive now, as she looked around for April Wood, finding it by following the road they drove here on. However, Charlotte's enthusiasm for involving an OS Map soon turned to dismay as the realisation of the task ahead dawned on her.

"Christ. I didn't realise it was so big." Charlotte's eyes darted around the part of the map where the wood was. *'She needed a plan'*, she thought. "Well, if we are assuming Sarah's here somewhere, you'd think she'd be in some sort of building." she said, as she looked for support from the others on this.

"Makes sense. Somewhere to keep her tied up?" replied Ayesha, helpfully.

"Yes." Charlotte was thankful for the validation at this point. "But there's nothing marked on even the OS map."

Charlotte knew she was running out of options and out of time. Time. She asked anyone what time it was. Five minutes past three came the reply.

"There's no chance we'd be able to search woods this size in time without the dogs." she surmised, grimly. "Where is the bloody dog unit?" Charlotte bellowed to anyone listening.

Dean had just come off the phone to headquarters, knowing Charlotte would need the answer. His face though, said it all. “They're saying could be another two hours, Gov.”.

“Jeez, we need them NOW.“

A gloom descended on the group.

There was an increasing danger of them being in the right woods and hearing an explosion before they could get to Sarah.

Charlotte dropped backwards and laid down on the ground; her head looking up to the heavens for divine inspiration. Her breath had become shaky and shallow and she tore at her own hair in frustration.

She had to admit it to herself… she had failed.

Chapter 28

Several minutes had passed.

Several valuable minutes, and Charlotte was still laying down on the ground, her face hidden by her two hands pulling and pushing the skin of her forehead around on her skull; her thumbs doing the same on her cheeks.

Because of her, someone will lose their life; a man will lose his wife and son will lose his Mummy. And what did she promise that little boy?

For a while, no-one said anything. What could they say?

Then Dean said quietly, "We could split up. There's eight of us, let's search; we could still find her."

Charlotte replied slowly. "What if one of us did find where she was, getting the rest of us there for backup could take too long. It's not safe for us."

This was a Charlotte none of the people in the wood had seen before; broken, beaten and without hope. They looked at each other in turn, as though trying to comprehend a new world order; one DCI Charlotte Walker had failed.

If only the dog unit could get here faster.

They'd be able to track Sarah.

Ayesha had an idea, and it was so bloody obvious...

"Ma'am? What about Bronte?" she asked. In such a

short question, she'd gone from confident, to 'forget it, it's a silly suggestion' to 'it might just work'. But that didn't stop her visibly wincing after she'd said it.

"What? Who?" enquired Dean, seeing for the first time in a while some degree of hope.

"DCI Walker's dog, sir; Bronte. They do mantrailing together..." Seeing Dean's puzzled look, she explained, "they search for mispers... for missing persons!"

"Gov; that's the answer!" Dean exclaimed.

Still laying down on the ground next to the map, Charlotte considered it for around a second or two, and then dismissed the idea. "What? No, he's not trained for this." Her left hand outstretched and being waved in the general direction of what Charlotte assumed was the centre of the woods.

However, the more Ayesha thought about it, the more she was convinced it could work. "From what I saw, Ma'am, this is exactly what he's trained for."

Charlotte started to tap her teeth together. *'He couldn't do this... **They** couldn't do this.. Could they?'* Ayesha had sown the seed in Charlotte's mind, and she was beginning to think it might just work...

Ayesha kneeled down next to Charlotte, and said, "What have we got to lose, Lottie?"

Charlotte turned to Ayesha and looked directly into her eyes.

Ayesha watched as the twinkle started to return.

Then, in one swift movement, Charlotte lifted herself at the waist to be sitting up.

DCI Charlotte Walker was back.

The team looked on with growing anticipation as Charlotte dialled on her phone.

"Tone? Can you bring Bronte, please... April Wood. We've got a job for him. Oh, and bring cream cheese..."

* * *

It was 15:40, and Toni had brought Charlotte's mantrailing bag, the long line, the cream cheese and a dog. If they were going to do this, they'd have to make it fast.

But Charlotte's confidence in the endeavour was ebbing away fast. "I don't know about this. We've only done aged trails up to five hours, not five days!"

Ayesha could see her partner needed some moral support here, and so worked through the logic. "Ma'am, we know the van was on the move in the early hours of Friday morning before we lost it..." she said supportingly, and then looked across at Toni for anything she could add.

Toni took up the batton. "And don't forget, it rained on Friday morning, so the scent will have stuck to the ground..." she said positively, hand pointing towards the ground.

The negative voice of Vernon had been quiet for too long. Even he couldn't bring himself to say anything when all hope had gone, but now he could resist no longer. "I thought rain washed scent away? They always go through a river when trying to escape being tracked in the movies."

Toni stared at Vernon for a few seconds, in a way someone would to decide whether they were being genuine, and when she decided he was, she turned to look at Charlotte. "Is this guy for real?" she said. "No, you fool, it sticks it more to the ground when wet!!"

Vernon looked incredulous at being spoken to like that, and moved out of the way. Charlotte tried to hide her giggles, but the levity was short lived... This was scary.

Toni returned to her reassurance of Charlotte... "And the wood's been fenced off - there'll hardly be any contamination."

Ayesha looked at Charlotte - a 'you've got this Ma'am' look. Charlotte took a deep breath, dropped down to her knees at the side of Bronte and whispered in his ear. "Time to shine!"

Pouring Sarah's top out of the evidence bag onto the floor, she placed Bronte;s mantrailing lead next to it, and the duo walked around them both. Charlotte picked up the mantrailing lead, clipped it onto Bronte's harness and instructed him to acquire the scent from Sarah's top.

"Trail!" came the command.

Bronte took a while to decide which direction he needed to go. The trail was laid down days ago, not hours like he was used to, but eventually he's got it. He confidently heads off along the main path, with Charlotte following, holding the mantrailing lead and keeping it taught.

Bronte was tracking the scent steadily and confidently, and whilst there's some apprehensive looks between the party following, Charlotte was remaining positive.

"Good boy." she told him continually.

Bronte stopped for a wee and to check direction. Sniffing around, he's convinced the trail turned off the main public footpath, and looked to be heading down a narrow track to the left. Charlotte followed Bronte, and the rest followed Charlotte.

All apart from Vernon, who stopped before leaving the path, and shouted to the others. "If we come off the main public right of way, we'll need a warrant, Ma'am."

'That bloody man', thought Charlotte. *'Even in the situation they found themselves in now, with a missing person gone five days; who we suspect might be in mortal danger, he still prattles on about procedures in order to be pedantic.'*

She paused for a moment, causing Bronte to eventually stop too when he reached the end of the long mantrailing lead Charlotte was holding on to. Within seconds, she plucked the following out of the air... "Fine. Arrest *Ms* Amber Remington on the suspicion of kidnapping... and then we're here under Section 18 of PACE. Happy now?"

Charlotte didn't immediately hear a response from Vernon, so she was content that would have shut him up... but just to make sure... "Do that NOW Vernon... Thank you."

The first bit was a definite order - Vernon was under no illusions about that. The second was merely added to make the first bit seem less order-y... but he knew Charlotte wasn't really thanking him.

The trail had gone on for a lot longer than they practised in mantrailing class, and Charlotte was getting worried about how long they had left.

"What time is it?"

"3:50, Ma'am." Ayesha replied.

This didn't fill Charlotte with confidence they would make it.

Suddenly, Bronte went off the path, into the undergrowth. "Oh, ok..." said Charlotte. After a while, he started rummaging in the undergrowth and digging slightly. Charlotte dropped to her knees to see if she could see what had caught Bronte's interest so much.

By now, Vernon had caught up from hanging back to make the phone call to the station, and once looking on sceptically. Ever the pessimist - especially if it meant putting the boot into Charlotte - he piped up "Great! I knew this was a bad idea. It's probably found a bone or something."

Charlotte was about to turn around to throw him the 'stare of doom', when Toni put her hand on Charlotte's shoulder and squeezed it slightly, as if to say 'I've got this one'. A turn and a stare from Toni, and the negative Detective Sergeant was firmly put in his place - dropping his head to the ground like a petulant schoolboy.

Charlotte bent down to where Bronte was, and

picked something up in her gloved hand.

"Actually no..." she said, holding a set of car keys up to Ayesha - and then folded the glove in on itself to hand them over. "Sarah's car keys, I presume..." she said, holding the bag up to share the reward with the group. All eyes turned to the Naysayer Vernon, who tried to avoid all their gazes with a sheepish look.

Bronte was back on the trail, and then reached a clear fork in the path. On the left was a narrow unmade muddy track, thick with vegetation; on the right, a clear open, wide path.

Bronte stopped and sniffed both directions. He is sure he knows the right way, but after the incident in the mantrailing class, he was unsure and looked up to Charlotte.

'Trust your dog...' Charlotte thought.

With a look of deep love at Bronte, she said "You can do it... Trail!"

The dog, now emboldened, sniffed again, and took the overgrown track with gusto

He pushed through on the track, until they reached an old single-story brick building, with windows almost closed up with wooden boards and a very solid-looking wooden door - complete with a very big padlock.

Bronte sat down in front of the door. Here's where the trail ends.

"Good boy! Well done!" Charlotte said, giving Bronte a huge fuss.

The Expectation in the air was palpable as Charlotte turned to the others and said, "The trail ends here."

Toni came across to take Bronte out of the way, as Dean tried the door. It wasn't going to budge - but this time he decided not to try to kick it.

Charlotte turned to the two PCs with the Big Red Key and said, "Lads..."

The two wasted no time in breaking the door down.

The building was some sort of old gardener's hut from the time the wood was part of the country estate, but it was well built - and perfect for the job of holding someone captive.

Inside - illuminated by a single shaft of daylight was Sarah Knight; tied up and bound.

They'd found her in time! A huge sense of elation engulfed the team..

"Get her out of there!" Charlotte shouted. The uniformed officers raced in and carried Sarah out on the chair she's tied to for safety.

Dean pushed past everyone to get to a shelf on the far wall. Resting on the shelf was a device, and he was clear about what it was. "Gov, it's an IED!" he shouted.

Charlotte pushed past what looked to be an old potting table for a closer look. She agreed, adding "...rigged to trigger when that phone receives a text."

She looked around the shelf, and pointing to the container said "And I think we can guess what is in there..."

Charlotte put her hands on both of Dean's shoulders

and talked directly into his eyes. “If my hunch is right, that phone doesn't have a screen lock on. Can you get the phone number of that SIM card?”

Dean was already in the process of putting on a pair of evidence gloves. “On it Gov.”

He tapped on the phone's screen, and in a matter of moments found the mobile phone’s number. “07700 900254”

Vernon dutifully wrote the number down in his notebook.

“Get some uniform and get down to Ms Remington's house. You're looking for a smartphone.” Charlotte said to both Dean and Vernon, full of urgency.

Vernon, ever the one for an easy life, instantly suspected this would be a lot like hard work and effort. “That's a needle in a haystack, Ma'am, in that house!” he blurted out, almost involuntarily.

“Ah, but it won't be, will it? It'll have to be somewhere in the rooms on the left upstairs.” Charlotte looked to Ayesha to tell the group why...

“Because....” she started out steadily, until the reason formed in her head, “that's the only place in the house with a mobile signal!”

Ayesha looked very pleased with herself, and she received a congratulatory wink from Charlotte, as Dean and Vernon left the building at a pace.

Charlotte took a moment to compose herself.

But there was something seriously bothering Ayesha. “Ma'am?” she said with a desperate tone.

“Yes?”

“It's three minutes to four!!”

“Bloody hell!!”

The was the small matter of the suspected bomb.

Charlotte pulled her Swiss Army Knife from trouser pocket and cut the wires on the IED to the battery and the mobile phone.

Just as she did, the phone buzzed into life with a text message.

“The bloody witch! She set it early!!!” Charlotte shouted.

She exchanged a look of terror with Ayesha.

Just how close did they come to death?

Chapter 29

The village of Norton had only just survived the last invasion, and now it seemed like another one was about to happen.

The three vehicles of Ayesha, Toni and a marked police car are parked on the main road outside the Knight house, causing not insignificant traffic disruption. The two uniformed officers helped Sarah Knight out of Toni's minibus, through the gates of the drive and up to the front door. One of them rang the doorbell, as the rest of the party - Charlotte with Bronte on his lead, Ayesha and Toni - stopped a respectful distance inside the gates.

The sound of small footsteps racing down the stairs in excitement could be heard from outside. There's a fumbling for the keys, and the front door opens to a beaming Jason. Before he could embrace his wife, Daniel pushes past him and runs to Sarah.

"MUMMY!! Mummy!" he yelled, clamping himself onto Sarah's legs with unbridled joy and relief.

"Daniel! Oh Daniel!" Sarah said, as she scooped him up and gave him the cuddle she wondered for days whether she'd ever be able to give him.

"I thought I'd never see you again!" he said with tears already rolling down his face.

"These police officers found me."

Sarah moved Daniel around so he could see the

others. Charlotte winked at Daniel and shouted from the end of the drive. "See?" she said with a slight nod of her head, "I told you we were from the 'Finding Mummies' part of the police."

Daniel smiled from his safe place; his Mum giving him another squeezy cuddle.

"I'll let you into a secret. Actually it was Bronte here who found your mummy - with his amazing nose!" Charlotte continued.

Daniel looked up at his Mum, and then ran over to give Bronte a cuddle. Bronte took the cuddle and after a while replied with a big dog kiss on the side of Daniel's face. The boy laughed - it was a sound that made Charlotte's heart soar.

Daniel looked up at Charlotte. "Thank you Lottie." he said, before running back up the drive to his Mum and Dad.

'He remembered my name!' she thought, as she watched the boy become safe around his Mum and Dad. Charlotte looked up a little higher to the height of the adults to see Sarah mouth "thank you" as she turned around with Jason and Daniel to walk into their house.

They were a family once more - thanks to Charlotte.

Toni patted Charlotte on the back. "Feeling pretty good right now?"

Charlotte was basking in the glow of the moment. "Yeah."

Toni walked in front of Charlotte. "Is giving this up such a good idea?" she asked, as she took Bronte off her to put him in the cages for her minibus and then around to the driver's seat.

That ripped Charlotte out of the glow. "I'll see you back at the station." Toni said, as she closed her door and started the minibus up. Within seconds, she was off.

* * *

It was quiet in the interview room.

A stony silence.

Amber was waiting for one of them to say something.

It had been two minutes since Ayesha had started the interview recording machine and told it those present were DCI Walker, DC Stoker, Amber and Amber's solicitor.

And since then... nothing.

Silence.

And it was killing her.

She looked across at Charlotte, then Ayesha, then back to Charlotte - but the two detectives were doing anything other than looking at her. Amber turned to look angrily at her solicitor, who shrugged his shoulders back.

Amber could see on the table in front of Charlotte the two mobile phones she had waved at her through the window of the Interview Room. They were still in the evidence bags, with the relevant codes and identity markings on them. She couldn't decide whether she should look at them or not.

'Why isn't anyone talking??' she thought, getting more cross by the second.

Then, eventually, Charlotte decided Amber had been on the back foot enough, and slid both mobile phones across the table towards her.

Amber looked down at the phones, and then up to meet Charlotte's hard stare just as she started to speak. "Because we were able to recover this phone from the place where Sarah was being held before it disintegrated, we could check the number of mobile phone that sent the activation text." She frowned for effect as she said "And who'd have thought it, that mobile phone was found in one of the few rooms in your house with a mobile signal."

Amber glanced over at her solicitor, and then back at Charlotte. "I've never seen that phone in my life." she shrugged.

Charlotte's eyebrows did their dance again. "Interesting. As it's coated with your fingerprints." replied Charlotte, leaning back in her seat.

Amber's solicitor turned to look at her, but Amber ignored him and continued to glare at the DCI.

Charlotte sat upright in her seat, placed both elbows on the desk and put her hands together. "Are you sitting comfortably? Good. Then I'll tell you a story..." she started, mimicking the voice a parent would use to read to a young child. Amber's look could have shot daggers at Charlotte.

"Once upon a time, there was a little girl called Amber who had to move from place to place..."

"Give it a rest!" Amber exclaimed, looking around at Ayesha and her solicitor. Charlotte stopped, looking a little put out that Amber didn't want to play along. She brushed it off and continued.

"You were well down on your luck before you met Carl; but then everything changed. In 2009 you were working as a waitress for a party company. Serving drinks to the posh people really suited you - and one of them was Carl Remington. What was it? Your eyes met across a crowded room?"

"Something like that."

"A year later, you'd worked your magic on Carl to such an extent it was you being served drinks by waitresses whilst you hung onto the arm of Carl in a tasty frock. Living the high life was very easy for you, and the fact you didn't really love him wasn't a problem.

"That was until his diagnosis with a heart condition made him think about his will, and when he told you Scott would inherit the company on his death, you planned another strategy.

"So the night Carl had his heart attack in 2012, instead of helping him, you watched him die, and then played the grieving lover to eventually end up with Scott.

"This time you decided you needed to be hitched to make sure you'd get everything, so a year later, you persuaded him to marry you.

"But then Scott discovered you were having a long-term affair with Oleg Petrov, and so you two separated. You weren't bothered as you were still married and still stood to inherit everything."

"And then came the fly in the ointment, in the form of Sarah Knight. With you two separated, and as Scott built up the company, he spent more and more time with Sarah, and he started to fall in love with her. So he decided to finally divorce you and ask Sarah to marry him.

"That would have cut you out of the company, so between you and Oleg, you concocted a plan. Having the form he had, Oleg had no problems finding the bits for a bomb and he made the IED."

"You had access to an early version of Sarah's text scheduling app - version v0.13 - and you saw its potential as a way to supply you with the perfect alibi for killing Scott and getting control of the company."

Amber blinked several times, and used the time to formulate her response. "An interesting story, Inspector.... but you've no proof."

Charlotte pointed to the mobile phone Dean and Vernon found at Amber's house. "When we checked that mobile phone just now, it was running a text scheduling app. The text scheduling app that Sarah wrote for Tempto Digital in 2017." Amber swallowed hard. Charlotte continued, "And what's interesting is that app is 'version 0.13' - the version Sarah sent to you - and you alone - for testing, before you blocked it for release.

"What you didn't realise is the app makes a log of the scheduled text messages, and the times they were scheduled for. And on the very day, of the very hour, of the very minute the fire started in Scott's shed, you scheduled a text to be sent."

"Well, anyone could have done that." retorted Amber.

"Yeah, but would anyone else have put in the message... *'Vale Scott, Amber xx'*

Amber's face was impassive.

"You see, all that was needed was a empty text message to trigger the bomb, but you couldn't resist your little extra touch..."

That caused a little wry smile to cross Amber's face.

Charlotte took a deep breath, as though to start a new chapter.

"So, fast-forward to now. You knew all about the blackmail scheme using the mapping apps - because you were running it; that's why you didn't want someone as intelligent as Sarah to be looking into the disappearing locations - you knew she'd find out the truth.

"So when Kelvin phoned you to say Sarah had evidence of who was behind it, you got Sarah to come to your house on the pretext of working together to sort it out - all the time wondering whether she knew you were behind it all.

"It turned out the documents Sarah had uncovered didn't show you were involved, but they did show a certain Frank Drashler was. You couldn't have Frank exposed because it would reveal his true identity - Oleg Petrov - and his involvement with you in the murder of your husband would more than likely come out.

"So you silenced Sarah temporarily, and called Oleg to come over to sort her out. He took Sarah to April Wood early Friday morning, knowing that was now fenced off and private - so she wouldn't be discovered by passers-by, and you took the detailed mapping of April Wood off Tempto's base map, so it wouldn't be shown on all the map apps, just for good measure. And you wiped Sarah's laptop, and put it in her car, which Oleg drove to the other side of town as a red herring, casually throwing the keys aside in April Wood when he went back to check on her.

"All you needed now was to secure the backup copies of the documents Kelvin told you Sarah said she had made on a USB stick. With Sarah refusing to say where it was, Oleg broke into the Knight's house to try to find it - and got the USB stick Sarah had left in the locked drawer as a decoy.

"When you both realised the encrypted files on the stick didn't have the documents you wanted on it, you had the Tempto Digital offices searched - which found nothing. Then you were fairly confident that if you couldn't find the USB stick with those incriminating documents, nobody else would, so another unfortunate building fire to get rid of Sarah would tie up the loose ends - with you far away again for your alibi.

"But you didn't bank on Sarah backing up the documents on an SD card, not a USB stick, or on me finding the SD card in the most logical place it could be - in a computer in Meeting Room 105, where Sarah had her meeting with Kelvin. I mean, it was a much safer place than putting it in a locked drawer in her house...

“So, when we came for you this afternoon, it was a bit of a shock - not expecting us to have any evidence that you were remotely involved - but we had that SD card; which gave us Frank Drashler; which gave us Oleg Petrov; who gave us…” Charlotte leaned across the desk to say the last word, “...you.”

Amber pulled in a huge breath and held it in anger..

“Even then, your mind was working overtime. You figured that if the jig was up for you on blackmail, then at least come 4pm today, you'd have the satisfaction of knowing the woman Scott loved all those years ago would be dying - and you'd have a pretty water-tight alibi being in a police station at the time...

“But, just like your scheduled text message to the phone that killed Scott, you just couldn't help yourself, could you?

"She'll be dead by I V"

“Giving me that "I V" line? You were pretty sure even if I did figure out you meant *four o’clock*, that I'd have no chance of finding where Sarah was, and then locating her in time.”

“Which we did thanks to Bronte!” chipped in Ayesha.

Amber shot Ayesha a condescending frown..

Charlotte smiled at Ayesha’s intervention. “So, Ms Amber Remington... as the Romans would have said... ‘Veni, vidi, vici’.”

Even Ayesha knew this one. “I came, I saw, I conquered!" she said with glee.

The rage which was building up inside Amber was palpable and her solicitor, who had done very little for his seemingly extravagant fee so far, placed a hand on her shoulder for her to calm down. She took this advice, folded her arms and glared at them both and they left the room.

* * *

Ayesha closed the Interview Room door behind her, and sprinted a little dodging the passing officers all seemingly heading the other way to catch up Charlotte, who was already some distance down the corridor. “Ma'am?” she opened.

Charlotte was deep in some thought somewhere. “Mmm?”

“I'm still not entirely sure how you knew Sarah was being held in April Wood...” she said, eager to understand more about DCI Walker’s methods.

Charlotte was happy to pass on her wisdom. “It was the only location that wasn't a business that had been removed from the base map. And seeing as though there wasn't an owner to blackmail, there had to be another reason - because there was something or someone there Amber and Oleg didn't want helped finding with an accurate map.”

This seemed to only partially answer Ayesha’s query. “But, Ma'am, there *was* an owner to blackmail? The new owner of the wood - Electrum Investments.”

Charlotte stopped walking suddenly, allowing Ayesha to catch up, standing level with Charlotte. The taller detective leaned down a little closer to Ayesha, as if to almost whisper in her ear. “Electrum is Latin for Amber.”

Ayesha turned slowly to look at Charlotte, and saw the knowing smile.

Suddenly, the penny dropped. “It was her company!” she exclaimed with a burst. And then Charlotte was ready with the killer blow.

“And guess what month Amber's birthday is in…”

Ayesha thought for a moment, and then it came to her. “April!”

Charlotte looked at Ayesha with her *‘you've got it’* look, and continued to walk off down the corridor - leaving Ayesha wondering in amazement.

Chapter 30

"So Remington was behind Electrum Investments?" Sharon asked with interest.

Charlotte was looking around Sharon's office as the question was asked. "Mmmm." she affirmed. "Buying up woods and closing them off so no-one else can enjoy them. Would make an excellent Psychology case study."

"And all the businesses that paid the blackmail?"

"Kelvin Thomas and the people at Tempto Digital that we haven't taken in as being part of it all, they've put everyone back on the base maps and will be paying back all the money too." Charlotte broke out in a wry smile. "Turned out Amber wasn't that clever as she never got her henchmen to put the money in a separate account. So paying it back will be easy."

Sharon nodded. "And Oleg Petrov..."

Charlotte paused for a moment, almost mourning the 'passing' of Frank Drashler, now they knew who he *really* was. "Yeap, and we're taken his courier buddies off the street too."

"And Sarah Knight?"

"Bearing up. Glad to be home, with her family."

With the mention of 'family', Sharon moved slightly one of the photo frames Charlotte could only see the back of.

Sharon considered everything. Despite the

challenges Charlotte had throughout this case, she'd pulled another rabbit out of the hat. After a deep breath of pride in her protege, she said, "Excellent result."

"Thank you." Charlotte tried to take the compliment well, but ended up slightly shifting in her seat and looking around the room with the awkward pause that followed.

The pause wasn't intended to make Charlotte uncomfortable, it was merely Sharon's attempt to make her next comment more humorous.

"Despite you being a technophobe!" she said with a wide grin.

Charlotte recognised this for being the banter that it was. "Hey! I just like to keep technology in its place, that's all!"

"All part of being a good DCI."

"*Was* all part of being a good DCI."

And then it suddenly hit Charlotte her time as a DCI was very close to being over. The old friends exchanged looks which were coated in so many emotions; sadness, regret, anxiety, trepidation, eagerness. It was the end of an era, and Sharon broke the look first, embarrassed it had come to this.

In the ensuing silence, it became clear to both, Charlotte desperately wanted deep down to find some way to be the police officer she was born to be, and yet enter a new chapter in her life.

And Sharon hoped she had the answer.

Without words, she opened the drawer, pulled

out the envelope and pushed it on the desk towards Charlotte.

It was dry now, of course, but the corners of the envelope showed the signs of intense paper to mouth compilation.

Charlotte considered the envelope.

“What's this?”

“I can't do this anymore.”

They realise they've been here before. Sharon’s gaze was fixed on Charlotte and they exchanged another look. Only this time Charlotte looked away first.

“I can't afford to lose a senior officer with your record.”

Charlotte shifted uncomfortably in her seat. It's a compliment that she didn’t necessarily want right now… “So what now?” she asked.

Sharon looked directly at Charlotte and said “Stay.”

A moment or two passed before Charlotte spoke. “I don't know, Sharon. I'd got it into my head this was it. I'd have a new start. No more abductions, no more robberies, no more death. No more future's ripped apart because of this bloody job.”

Sharon started to become a little tetchy. “So what are you going to do then, eh? Take up knitting whilst listening to The Archers?” she said, with a bite to the words.

“Maybe.” came the defensive, but not convincing reply.

Sharon decided that if she was going to lose Charlotte, she wasn't going to lose her without a fight. With fire in her eyes she looked again straight at Charlotte, as if addressing her soul. "This is who you are! You're a copper. And a bloody good one at that. Do you think you'll stop being a copper when you leave here tonight? Eh? You were off-duty when you stopped that ATM raid for god's sake. Can't stop being a copper just because you don't have DCI in front of your name."

Sharon paused. She knew what she'd said had pieced Charlotte's defences. Her head had dropped slightly and her eyebrows were squeezed together into a frown which told its own story. Charlotte knew all of this, but she'd rather not be hearing this inconvenient truth.

"It's who we are. It's who YOU are." Sharon continued, quieter.

Charlotte contemplated this for a second, then looked away with a deep sigh. Her frown was in danger of becoming engrained.

Sharon clenched her teeth together and walked over to the window. She looked out, as if to find inspiration. When she eventually spoke, she sounded different; more friendly, more personable. She'd left the police chief at the desk again.

"There is another option Lottie…" still looking out of the window.

The frown on Charlotte's face managed to change slightly, like an oil tanker trying to undertake a u-turn. She turned her head across her shoulders to look at Sharon.

“I'm listening.”

Sharon put her hands together, intertwined her fingers and rested her chin on them. How will she take it? Only one way to find out.

“I'm one of a few who has been tasked to start a new National Special Operations Unit...”

“Right...” came the slightly interested reply.

Sensing she might have some interest here, Sharon turned to face Charlotte, still with her chin resting on her hands, and continued, “who can be called upon as and when needed on cases around the country.”

Charlotte started to consider the possibility. “So, like freelance travelling police then?” she surmised.

“I guess you could say that.” It wasn't a description Sharon would have chosen, but under the circumstances it seemed prudent to her to agree. “You'd have some freedom to work whenever, but we'd have a certain number of cases we'd need you to have. And you could be called upon to lead investigations anywhere in the country.” Sharon saw that Charlotte was starting to look more favourably at the possibility. “Could be more opportunities for walking...” She knew how to sweeten the deal.

That did sound interesting. Especially in light of the item she was just about to purchase - although no-one else knew about that yet.

But Charlotte still had doubts. “And the day-to-day stuff?”

“Not your responsibility.“ And before Charlotte asked, she added “Neither is the paperwork - all done by the local force."

One of Charlotte's downfalls as a DCI was her inability to complete the required documentation, especially the inputting of the case details and developments into HOLMES 2, the UK-wide police IT system. So this was particularly welcome news from Charlotte's point of view.

"I'd still be a DCI?"

"Yes, everyone on the same rank."

"There'd be others too?"

"It's going to be a small team; brand new. You'd be in at the start."

Charlotte found herself very interested. "Can I think about it?"

"No." said Sharon, semi-playfully. The accompanying look actually said she probably could, but Sharon wanted an answer now - that was clear.

So Charlotte thought about it.

She thought about everything that had happened over the past five days and who she had touched; Alistair and his family, Sarah and her family; even the family of Carl and Scott Remington, who would have closure on the deaths of those two now. All the businesses around the country blackmailed on the mapping apps. And Amber and Oleg, and their associates.

She made a difference.

And she thought about Daniel. How he trusted *her* to find his mummy and bring her back to him. And the thanks afterward.

Charlotte closed her eyes, and said, “Ok. Count me in.”

Sharon’s demeanour changed in an instant to a mixture of excitement and relief. “Fantastic!” she shouted. That wonderful smile Charlotte saw often outside of work making a rare appearance in the office.

Charlotte got up to shake Sharon's hand, but received a massive hug from her instead. Again, hugging was rarely something Sharon did when in uniform; in fact never had Charlotte known it, so it came as a big surprise. Charlotte relaxed into the hug and hugged her friend back.

When it finished, there was a slight awkwardness as both didn't quite know what to do. Sharon reverted quickly to her desk to become Assistant Chief Constable Tate once again.

Charlotte too returned to her chair, just in time to see Sharon push the envelope closer towards her on the desk.

“There.” she said, with a smile.

Thinking it is her resignation letter, Charlotte replied, “I don't want it back. Just bin it.”

“Best not...it's your job offer and contract - already signed by the Home Secretary.” Sharon said with a flourish.

Charlotte sensed she’d been stitched up a bit here. “Right... assumed I'd say yes then?”

“Thought it would save time.”

"Yeah, right!"

"Welcome to the National Special Operations Unit, DCI Walker! The start of a whole new chapter."

"I guess it is. " Charlotte said. The enormity of what she'd agreed to still hadn't fully sunk in. But right now, her mind was on something else - the appointment she'd made for 6:30. "Oh bugger, I've got to get there for half past!"

Sharon looked up at the clock on the wall - 5:59 - and then quizzically back to Charlotte. Get to where?

There was an impatient air to Charlotte now. She needed to go. "You're off now, aren't you? Are you alright for an hour?"

"What for?"

"You need to look at this.." Charlotte had developed a very large grin. She'd just realised how fantastic what she was about to buy would be for the new role she had. And she wanted everyone who mattered to her to see.

"You need to look at this..." she said, as she raced out of Sharon's office, leaving Sharon to follow, none the wiser, but intrigued.

Chapter 31

Charlotte and Sharon pushed through the double doors from the corridor into the Incident Room. For a moment, Charlotte is confused. The room is in total darkness. 'What the hell?' she wondered, as she tried to remember where the light switch was. There must be one at the side of the door, you'd have thought.

Suddenly, the lights burst on and it looked like the whole station was present in the room. There were balloons of various colours pinned into the corners, and banners proclaiming 'Sorry to see you go' and 'Good Luck' were everywhere.

The room is in darkness. Charlotte and Sharon push through the double doors from the corridor. The light shafts into the dark.

Dean pushed his way to meet a very astonished Charlotte, and putting a friendly arm around her shoulder guided her to face the assembled mass.

"Hi Gov, err, we couldn't let you go without all saying goodbye..." he shouted cheerily over the party atmosphere that had swept in.

Without having Charlotte a chance to say anything, Dean started to lead the singalong...

"Foooor, she's a jolly good fellow.."

The room endured several verses of well-meaning, but ultimately out of time and tune, singing. Charlotte looked around sheepishly to Sharon, who seemed to be greatly enjoying her discomfort - as only special close friends do.

As the singing came to an end, it descended into cheers that could easily have been mistaken for one of the football matches uniform cover, along with shouts of “We're going to miss you Ma'am!” and “Way to go Ma’am!”

Constable Giles started “Speech!”, which, much to Charlotte’s irritation, gathered pace around the room. Eventually Dean quietened everyone with some over-exuberance hand gestures which wouldn’t look out of place if he was landing a plane.

The floor was all Charlotte’s.

“Thank you, well, this was a bit of a surprise! Who do I have to lynch for this then?” she asked with more than a little sarcasm. The assembled crowd laughed and pointed over to Dean. “DI Dean Sheldon, I might have known!” Dean held his hands up in surrender, amidst shouts of “It’s a fair cop, Gov!” Spirits were high, and Charlotte wondered whether liquid slightly more intoxicating than Tizer was secretly on offer.

“Well, as most of you know, I’m leaving.” The statement met with universal dismay. Well, almost universal. There was one notable exception at the back of the room… in a tweed jacket.

Charlotte paused, and looked a tad sheepish. She had the room in the palm of her hand.

“Well, wow, Errrr, well, about that... I've got some news and...it turns out I'm not leaving…”

There was widespread confusion, not least from

Vernon, who looked as though his world had crashed down.

"...well, I *am* leaving, but I'll still be around. Occasionally. Every so often. Here and there." Charlotte clarified without actually doing so.

The room was looking around at itself, trying to understand what was going on. Everyone was none the wiser.

"Well, what it is, is, I'm taking on a new role... " She struggled to explain what had just been agreed. Possibly because she wasn't that sure herself. She needed a lifeline....

"Assistant Chief Constable Tate will explain..."

The polite smile Sharon was wearing as she stood next to the floundering Charlotte disappeared in a flash, as the eyes of the room turned instantly and together on to her.

Charlotte leaned into Sharon's ear and said "Downstairs in 5, or we'll be late." Sharon turned to her with a face that said 'What for?' Then turned back to the crowd of officers she now unintentionally had the attention of. Sharon started to brief the team on the new unit she'd be co-leading, and about DCI Walker's new role within it.

Charlotte didn't need to hear from Sharon about what the new role DCI Walker was undertaking, and so pushed through the crowd, eventually bumping into Vernon towards the back of the room, who had a face of someone living through a nightmare.

"Ma'am." he said through gritted teeth.

"DS Price." Charlotte replied. "Turns out you need me around for a bit longer to get you up to speed..."

"Ma'am?"

"Yes - a refresher in car identification first I think..." His face drained of colour. Charlotte moved closer to Vernon to talk into his ear. "...so we can tell the difference between a petrol and an electric car in the future." she continued. He turned to look at her, and had half a mind to say something, and then wisely decided against it. Instead, he walked out of the Incident Room shaking his head to make his way to the canteen.

The briefing had apparently come to an end, and Ayesha pushed through the crowd to reach Charlotte.

Beaming from ear to ear, she offered "Congratulations Ma'am!"

"Thank you DC Stoker. And the good news is we'll still get to work together."

"Is that good news Ma'am?" Ayesha checked, hesitantly.

"Oh, I think so!" Charlotte leaned closer into her. "We make quite a team."

Ayesha's wide-eyed bright smile at hearing this was contagious; her puffed-out chest demonstrating the pride she felt. A welcome bit of praise.

"You're going to make one hell of a great detective." Charlotte continued.

"You think so Ma'am?"

"Of course! How could you not when you've got the best possible teacher...?"

Ayesha smiled. She had indeed moved her whole world to work with the mighty DCI Charlotte Walker, and against all hope, she'd still be able to do so.

Charlotte tapped Ayesha on the shoulder, as though saying goodbye, and then stopped. If she wanted all the people who mattered to come with her this evening, then DC Ayesha Stoker was now on that list.

"Hey, Ayesha?"

The young DC turned around, recognising Charlotte had used her first name only for the second time.

"You're finished here now, right?" Ayesha nodded with a worried frown. "You can come too then..."

"Come where?" Ayesha asked, but Charlotte was already out of the incident room and heading down the corridor. Eventually, curiosity got the back of her, and she followed Charlotte, just missing Sharon wrapping up her impromptu briefing.

Chapter 32

It looked like it was going to turn into a lovely evening. The sun was succeeding in its quest to push the light clouds away and elongate the day still further. Toni had parked her minibus in the car park directly outside the police station, signed 'Marked Police Vehicles Only. No Public Parking'. Well, after all she wasn't parking, only waiting… and she was on official police business with the forces' newest dog recruit Bronte!

The border collie had worked hard in the woods finding Sarah, and had been asleep in his cage since they left the Knight house. But now he was awake, fully recharged and ready to see his human mum – although the lamb rib Toni had given him was keeping him suitably occupied for now. The open back door allowed some evening fresh air to circulate around Bronte. Toni was standing near to the back of the minibus, watching the various people passing as they headed to their cars after work. Many stopped to chat and to fuss Bronte through the cage doors

Charlotte burst out of the doors of the police station and bounded down the steps as if she was hosting a 1990s Saturday night entertainment programme; her co-host Ayesha a little way behind.

"Hi Tones!" she shouted to Toni, and then a bigger "Hi boy!!" to Bronte, who was very happy to see his significant human.

Toni held her mobile phone aloft and waved it towards Charlotte and shouted “I'm back on the map!!”

Charlotte smiled back at her. Kelvin and Sarah promised they'd get Toni back on the map quickly, but the speed of that surprised Charlotte. The look of relief on her friend's face was palpable. Then the smile on Charlotte's face wasn't just because of Toni, but because just then she realised she'd still be able to make a positive difference in the world. Then, Toni snapped her back.

“So... No longer a copper, then?” she asked, in her typical bold fashion.

Charlotte leaned on the side of Toni's minibus and enigmatically replied “Errrr, not exactly!”

The look on Toni's face clearly said *'What do you mean?'*

“I'll tell you on the way.” she said, shaking her head slightly as though trying to come to terms with what she had just agreed to..

“Hi again!” Toni said to Ayesha.

“Hello!”

Sharon walked down the steps and headed towards the minibus, taking in the scene, and Toni looked across at her. Noticing Toni was looking at her, she nodded across to the blue sign. Toni pretended to protest. “I'm not parking...” she said, smiling. The smile was returned.

Ayesha turned around to see who Toni was talking to, and was a little shocked to see it was the gaffer. Charlotte looked around too, just in time to see

Ayesha visibly straighten up her posture and shake her shoulders ready for Sharon. That raised a little smile.

Charlotte shouted across to Sharon, "You know Amelia... " The question was rhetorical; of course she did. And she'd got her name wrong on purpose.

"It's Ayesha, Ma'am." she said still in awe across to Sharon, who by now was standing next to them at the minibus.

"I know!" she replied, with her pure plum-like tones. "And it's Sharon, please, we're off duty now."

Toni was still out of the loop as to their next destination, and the taxi driver inside her found not knowing a very difficult concept. "So, *where* are we going exactly?" she asked Charlotte, cupping her hands together praying for a definitive answer.

"Just follow what I say." came the reply, as Charlotte walked around to the passenger side.

Toni fussed Bronte and closed the boot door, then made her way around to the driver's door. "As per usual then..." she replied, her tongue firmly in her cheek, and catching the knowing smile from Charlotte across the bonnet.

"Just get in and drive." Charlotte said sarcastically. Sharon and Ayesha climbed in the back, and then, with all the doors closing in unison, they were off.

But only one of them knew where.

* * *

The party of ladies plus one dog had been travelling for around twenty five minutes. For most of that, they'd been heading northwards on the A1(M), but now they'd left the motorway, and open fields surrounded them.

The country lane they were on was just about wide enough for two vehicles - as had just been proved with a rather impatient BMW driver deciding he didn't want to go the speed the minibus was. Toni was driving at that speed you do when you aren't quite sure about where you are going. And that's because she didn't have a clue.

She looked across at Charlotte for inspiration. Charlotte waved a hand out in front of her, as if to say *'just carry on'*. Toni shook her head with mock disapprovement.

It took the rank of Sharon to voice what everyone other than Charlotte had been thinking. "We're lost, aren't we?" she said, gently pulling Charlotte's leg.

Charlotte took it in the manner it was meant and rolled her eyes. "After the case I've just solved? Please!" she retorted, elongating the last word beyond a sensible point.

A short while later, the vehicle came up to a T-junction on the road. Toni stopped, and made a bigger play of pulling on the handbrake as she needed to. "So, which way now, oh great navigator?"

"It's left here." Charlotte replied, with a tiny element of doubt.

"Are you sure?" questioned Toni, with more leg pulling, as she released the handbrake, indicated and pulled out left.

"Sod the lot of you!" shouted Charlotte.

The infectious sound of ladies laughing followed the minibus down the road.

* * *

Toni's minibus pulled up on a gravel farmyard in front of a farmhouse. It was a long building, not very tall, which had been restored to a high standard; the original stonework cleaned until it gleamed. The various outbuildings on either side, however, hadn't had that good fortune yet, and looked to be full of old farm machinery and vehicles.

"This is it!"

Charlotte got out of the minibus, and before she closed the door, said, "Wait here.".

The others duly obliged.

Charlotte walked over to a man who was waiting outside the open front door of the farmhouse. From the minibus, the trio could see at a distance the power of Charlotte. They were late, and the man looked as though punctuality was very important to him; his arms folded in an unhappy stance. A few seconds talking to the animated Charlotte, however, and the arms were unfolded; his attitude changed to open candour.

Then, in a complete turnaround, the man looked as though he was crying, and Charlotte put an arm around him as they walked together around the back of the farmhouse. The occupants of the minibus looked quizzically at each other and Toni's mind started to wander.

"You don't think she's bought this farm, do you?" she asked the others, slowly.

From the back, Sharon said emphatically, "No."

Toni caught her gaze through the rear-view mirror, and spotted her possibly re-assessing her original conviction. "No...." came a second, much less convincing reply. This might be so serious Toni had to turn around to look at Sharon...

"Or another dog?" Ayesha offered. "Want a brother or a sister, Bronte?"

Bronte had the look of an animal who was very happy being an only dog, thank you very much...

Suddenly, the dulcet tones of Errol Brown echoed around the minibus; 'You sexy thing, you...'. The display in the centre of the dashboard showed it was Charlotte calling. Toni pressed on the steering wheel button to answer.

Before Toni could say anything, Charlotte was in full flow...

"So, you remember that I needed to change my life?" her voice coming through the vehicle's speakers via Bluetooth.

"Yes - that's why you got rid of that lovely car and swapped it for a tiny thing with no roof..." replied Toni.

The teasing obviously passed down the phone

line, as Charlotte ignored it *"Well, I decided I deserve something I've always, always wanted..."*

"You've bought a farm, haven't you?"

"No! I'm changing things up, not going mad, you know."

The three in the minibus all looked at each other, not really knowing how to respond to that.

Once again, Charlotte ignored their response - or lack of. *"So, I did some digging, and I've found this... "* she broke off, clearly struggling with something. *"Bugger!"* she shouted at the top of her voice.

The others smiled - that's our Charlotte...

Suddenly, some sort of an engine started up over the phone and through the speakers. A few bangs, coughs and wheezes, but eventually the engine sounded rather sweet.

The others looked between themselves quizzically.

Over the speakers, the sound of crunching metal grates as Charlotte tried to find first gear. *"Get in!!"* she shouted, and then came a *"There!"* when she found it.

The engine is clearly moving - and after a while emerged around the corner of the farmhouse was a very happy Charlotte beaming at the wheel of a 1967 Split Screen VW Campervan!

Struggling a bit to connect with her new-to-her vehicle, she made another mistake with the gears, and her voice boomed over the speakers again... "Bugger!"

Finally, she parked it next to the minibus, and promptly stalled it by putting on the handbrake whilst it was in gear... It responded by jolting forward.

"Oh wow!!" said Sharon.

There's a collective opening of doors, as everyone got out of their respective vehicles and congregated around the Campervan. Toni opened the boot of the minibus so Bronte could see what was happening.

"Well? What do you think?" asked a beaming Charlotte.

The others walked around the van, the familiar shape of the VW camper raising smiles from them all.

Sharon was instantly in love. "Fantastic!"

Toni, ever the pragmatist, viewed the vehicle with a healthy suspicion. "Needs a bit of work..." she said, as she ran her hand over a bit of trim, which promptly fell off in her hand. She looked at Charlotte, and threw it through the open side window onto the seat.

"Yes, well," Charlotte said slowly and quietly, "you might do when you're this age..."

Charlotte got Bronte out of the minibus, and showed him the Campervan. He sniffed all around it. "What do you think, beautiful boy?" The wagging tail seemed to show his approval. Charlotte opened the side door to reveal a dog cage. "And this is for you!"

Without hesitation, Bronte wandered into the cage and laid down. As Charlotte closed the side door, Ayesha said "I've always wanted one of these!"

The new owner opened the driver's door and climbed into the drivers' seat.

Toni pushed the driver's door closed, and then pushed it harder, as it wouldn't close properly the first time. Charlotte wound the window down, exaggerating the fact that it was a manual, and not electronic, window. Toni looked at her as if to say *'What have you done?'*

"Just a few niggles to sort out..." she said to Toni, as the others congregated around the open window. Charlotte continued the conversation with Ayesha.

"Me too... so I thought, new start and all..."

Charlotte turned the ignition and half-closed her eyes in hope - but this time the campervan started first time. Things were better already! But she decided to rev the engine a few times, in case. When it was clear the engine wasn't going to just suddenly stop, she looked enthusiastically to the others.

Toni moved closer to the door, and raised her voice over the noise of the badly-maintained engine. "So, you'll be taking Bronte, going walking everywhere and solving mysteries in your Scooby Doo van?"

"Yeah." Charlotte said, with a massive smile on her face. "Sounds pretty perfect!"

ACKNOWLEDGEMENTS

A few thank yous:

To the Linear Leechers group on Twitter; Cameron Yarde Jnr, Tobias Forrest and Hassaan Mohammad for their support in the development of the original ideas around the TV version of The Walker Mysteries.

To Dave Mycroft, Mark & Helen Richards and Alan Hinkes for the nudging to push myself outside my comfort zone and attempt something different.

To my fellow mantrailers Paula Thorpe, Gillian Fotherby,
Jan Smith, Hannah Starr and Davina Roberts; and my fellow flyballers Lucy Jaques, Joanne & Martin Heavey, Ricky Bradley and Laura Evans for dog-related support.

To Sue & Chris Dennis for unflinching support.

To Amanda and Olivia, for putting up with the last, mad push to get this finished in time.

And most of all, thank you to Alannah, for all her help in developing the characters, the backstory and being so supportive that her old Dad could do something very different.

ABOUT THE AUTHOR

Andrew White

A lifelong walker with 6 border collies, Andrew is the presenter and producer of the TV series "Walks Around Britain", and created the mystery/crime series "The Walker Mysteries" in 2021 with the first book in the series (this one) released in February 2022.

He also writes regularly for magazines such as BBC Countryfile, RAIL, BRITAIN, Camping and Dogs Monthly, as well as appearing frequently on BBC Radio talking about walking.

Andrew is a passionate Yorkshireman, and has devised a two route long-distance trail around and through his home county - called the South Yorkshire Way.

THE WALKER MYSTERIES

Follow DCI Charlotte Walker - the sassy, smart, shrewd, sexy, sarcastic and strong redhead - and her dog Bronte throughout the next stories in the series.

The Walker Mysteries... on the trail of crime.

Home To Roost - Book 2

Settling into her new "travelling detective" role, Charlotte visits her parent's new bed and breakfast venture on their farm in the Yorkshire Dales, for a family reunion. But it's not quite the quiet family get-together when some of their farm machinery is stolen, leading Charlotte and her father to uncover a nasty criminal ring.

Reel For Murder - Book 3

Whilst walking in the Snowdonia mountains with her police friend Karen, Charlotte and Bronte discover the body of outdoor film-maker Trevor Dicks, killed whilst filming for his next project. Trevor had a way of rubbing people up the wrong way, so which one of Trevor's many enemies decided enough was enough?

BOOKS BY THIS AUTHOR

Aa Guide To Yorkshire (The Aa Guide To)

The largest county in England - 'God's Own County' to its inhabitants - Yorkshire offers the visitor everything from the beauty of its three national parks to some of the best shopping in the country. The AA Guide to Yorkshire gives you everything you need to know to get the most out of your visit to this wonderful county; each entry is packed with the very best sites to see, things to do, recommendations for eating and drinking, and places to explore nearby. With everything from local legends to must-see festivals and events, this authoritative and practical guide ensures you will never be lost for something to do.

50 Walks In Yorkshire Dales (Aa 50 Walks)

Walking is one of Britain's favourite leisure activities, and AA 50 Walks in the Yorkshire Dales features a variety of mapped walks of two to ten miles, to suit all abilities. The book features all the practical detail you need, accompanied by fascinating background reading on the history and wildlife of the Yorkshire Dales, and clear full colour mapping for ease of use. Every route has been colour coded according to difficulty. All walks are annotated with local points of interest and places to stop for refreshments. Every walk is given a summary of distance, time, gradient, level of difficulty, type of surface and access, landscape, dog friendliness, parking and public toilets.

FOLLOW THE WALKER MYSTERIES

You can follow The Walker Mysteries on our e-mail newsletter, on Twitter, on Facebook and on Instagram

Sign up for the The Walker Mysteries e-mail newsletter for behind the scenes news, cover reveals, free book promotions and discounted deals for a limited time.

Visit www.thewalkermysteries.com

Twitter - www.twitter.com/WalkerMysteries

Facebook - www.facebook.com/TheWalkerMysteries

Instagram - www.instagram.com/TheWalkerMysteries

Printed in Great Britain
by Amazon

82529905R00205